1

THE INCIDENT

Blood seeped from my gums. The metallic taste made me flinch, allowing my opponent to land a punch to my head. It didn't help that the air had a slight hint of smoke to it. The stench of ash further nauseated me. Unfortunately, I had to swallow the pain and keep fighting. Although he always won, I wouldn't let him off easy. If the instructors had seen blood, he would've been automatically disqualified. Good thing the bleeding was internal. I wanted to fight him.

Tae Kwon Do was usually closed on Sundays. This wasn't a normal class; it was a sparring seminar. I signed up to get extra practice for a tournament coming up next week. It was the first day of January, which was strange because it was hot. The sun cooked my skin as I fought my opponent. My whole body was sweating, making my uniform stick to me, heating me further. Nothing was worse than the feeling of the sun boiling you alive with fearsome rays.

The warm weather forced us to fight outside. The small workout room at Tae Kwon Do would have trapped in the heat. We begged to fight inside. The floor had soft blue carpeting, while the parking lot behind the academy had rough, unkempt blacktop. Our bare feet were getting cut up.

My opponent, David, was the best martial artist in my academy. We were both 1st-degree Black Belts and had trained for six years at Maplewell Martial Arts. The academy was hard-core. Our black belt test was four hours long. Before the

1

test, there were numerous prerequisites, including an essay and a written exam. It was important to know the South Korean history behind our forms.

David always did better than me at tournaments. He pulled off the most ridiculous, gravity-defying jump-spin-kicks. I wasn't the best, though I excelled at sparring. The difference was when fighting, one doesn't have to use proper technique. When doing forms, it's all about precision, deep stances, and fully prepared movements. David did well no matter what. He was great at forms, weapons, and sparring. The instructors told me I was decent. They claimed my moves lacked power and deep stances. I wasn't as good as David when it came to sparring. It wasn't a one-sided fight, though. I could take hits without getting hurt and read an opponent to predict their moves. We were a great match.

"Go, Mr. Corleone!" the main instructor at my academy, Mr. Michaelson, yelled. At Tae Kwon Do, last names were used to refer to Black Belts and above. That's why my instructor called me Mr. Corleone instead of Andrew. It was odd that he was cheering me on. If you were going to bet on someone to win, it would be David. I was average, and being average meant my chances of success were fifty-fifty. It was possible that Mr. Michaelson felt bad for me. His booming voice encouraged me to push myself.

It was a continuous sparring match, which meant we didn't stop fighting until Mr. Michaelson stopped us. I didn't know if the match was timed or if he stopped us once someone made it to five points. All I knew was that I had to fight and stop when told to do so.

David scooted back before leaping forward with a jump front kick. I could see the perfect technique in his moves. The ball of his foot stuck out flawlessly, unlike my sloppy, speedy attacks. I lowered my hand to block. He punched me in the stomach while my hand was lowered. I tightened my abdominal muscles to prevent the next hits from hurting. We had padded gear on our feet, hands, and head, not the stomach.

I was about average height, yet I had long legs which I used to fight at a further range than most. David was a few inches shorter than me, giving me a tiny advantage. I did a fake front kick that barely reached him, and just before he blocked it, I fully extended my leg and raised it to round-kick him in the

2

head! It worked perfectly. He lowered his hands to block the fake kick and was unprepared to block the real one. I scooted back again to gain more distance for my kicks. I stared into his eyes to try and predict his next move. His eyes were fixed on my stomach. I prepared my arms to move downward at the first sight of movement from David. His eyes glanced at my face before releasing a barrage of multiple punches. I quickly darted my hands downward to block. I was able to swipe away most of his hits. He still landed a few. His fists mostly hit my arm or hand, which wasn't a point. I don't think he scored more than one point from all those punches.

David slid in and pressed his hips against mine to jam any future kicks. He tried to do his rapid punch thing again, but he hit my arm as I spun toward my back leg, then lifted it into the air and hook-kicked him in the head! I didn't have to move forward or backward to land the kick. I was able to pull it off, thanks to my natural flexibility. It was a gift I used often to keep it in shape. My leg stretched up and slammed into the right side of his headgear. The loud smacking sound of plastic coating made it clear to Mr. Michaelson that I had made contact.

"Break! Time's up," Mr. Michaelson shouted. I spun around and placed my foot down as I caught my balance. Other students watched us closely. We were the last to fight that session. Most of them were cheering for David. I had to tune them out the whole time. Mr. Michaelson looked at us both with an emotionless stare. Only then did I realize Mr. Michaelson was wearing his favorite "Spar Wars" t-shirt underneath his uniform. That shirt always made me smile. "Mr. Kong wins!" he declared. David threw off his headgear and shook his sweaty, black hair. Beads of sweat flew as his long hair flopped around. He removed his mouthguard to tell me I was a great opponent.

"Alright, that's it for tonight! Class dismissed!" shouted Mr. Michaelson. He put his hand on my shoulder as I walked to find my gear bag. My bag was amongst the pile clumped against the outside wall of the small classroom. I took out my slimy mouthguard as I scanned the black bags to spot which one was mine. "Try to change up your moves a bit. You depend on your right side too much. Don't become predictable," Mr. Michaelson advised.

3

"Yes, sir," I replied out of breath.

Monday rolled around in the blink of an eye. My high school was huge. Visitors often remarked that it could pass for a community college. It was a fortress of red bricks and giant glass windowpanes. Inside, each hallway was painted a different color. Some were yellow, while others were green or white. The classes were ninety minutes long, the subjects were challenging, and the teachers were either brutally strict or tremendously nice with no in-between. It drove new students crazy, though most people were fine with the school.

The fresh scrapes on the bottom of my feet made it even more painful when someone stepped on my foot. Looking up, I spotted a string of bruises around a big, bulky neck, Zach. His bruises were most likely hickies from the searing look he shot me once he caught me staring at them. What a weirdo. It was unsurprising to see that Zach was the culprit. The hallway was crowded, though that was no excuse. He did that sort of thing often. "Watch where you're going, dumbass!" Zach spat as he passed me. He stepped on *me,* but sure, it was my fault.

"Amazing game yesterday, congratulations!" a nearby teacher complimented. Zach swore at me within earshot, and he got praised? Several kids could do anything they wanted and never get in trouble because of their athletic abilities. God forbid a star athlete gets suspended and can't make it to a game.

The teacher stared at me. I waited for them to comment on Zach's behavior. Instead, I was met with a confused stare. Was I invisible?

It was strange, I know, yet I couldn't shake this need to be more than just a face in a crowd. Unfortunately, I wasn't the type of person who could walk up to people and make new friends. I had to wait for some miracle where I could prove myself. One big reason why I cared about being seen in the first place was girls. To be honest, it was *a* girl rather than girls. I'd never had a girlfriend before. I was what one might have called a loser. Although I loved my family and friends, a tiny void was opening up inside. Day by day, it ate away at me. There had to be some way I could get Avery to notice me. If I tried my best to be a good person, maybe it'll come back to me. The void will be filled.

4

A small smile was plastered on my face throughout Biology class. It was barely noticeable, though I couldn't shake it. Science was my favorite subject for two reasons. One was that I always got an A+ on everything because almost all the topics were interesting. The second was that Avery was in that class. She was in a few of my classes over the years, and I kind of developed a little crush on her. It might have been more like a major crush. Considering I never really talked to her, it was a little pathetic. At least from what I'd overheard when she spoke to her friends and from class presentations, she seemed quite brilliant.

My eyes drifted off my Biology notebook to glance up at Avery. Her blue eyes shot right through me. They were so bright compared to my dark brown eyes. My face felt hot. I looked back down and waited for her to look away. I pretended to write something in my notebook, then peered up at the whiteboard. My eyes gradually ventured away from the board and onto Avery. My short brown hair was the opposite of her long, flowing blonde hair. We were very different in appearance. She was so pretty. Somehow, she had a slight tan in the middle of Winter. My skin was almost always a plain white color, only it got a little olive-colored at times during the Summer. We looked different, yet I was positive we matched on the inside. She was still staring at me. Maybe this was my chance? After class, I could ask her why she was staring me down? What if she wasn't staring at me? If that's the case, it would be creepy to ask about it. It was best to stay silent.

Our teacher, Mr. Poundz, could tell I was daydreaming in the middle of his lesson. He asked, "This is a chemical reaction much like burning, which means, Andrew?"

"It's nonreversible," I answered without looking up from my notebook. We were learning about natural selection; I didn't know what his question had to do with our lesson. People laughed at my nerdiness. I ignored them. It was an answer on our test from the previous unit. It wasn't weird that I knew that. Of course, most had already forgotten about that, so I looked kind of strange.

"Correct now, blah blah blah," I tuned Mr. Poundz out as I turned my attention to the classwork. The board had more facts than my notebook. I was far behind. My hand scribbled nearly illegible words from the board in a mad rush to catch up.

Although it was mostly rudimentary science, the notes would still be useful to study from later. His tests were closely based on the class notes. There was almost an entire page of notes to copy. It took me a few minutes to finish jotting everything down. I peered up from my notebook to listen to Mr. Poundz ramble away.

The bell rang as soon as I gazed up from my work. Everyone bolted out the door as if their lives depended on it. I spent the whole class daydreaming and trying to catch up. I often found myself lost in thought. How did I manage to waste so much time thinking about Avery? My stomach hurt as I realized I was way too obsessive. I shoved my torn, yellow notebook into my backpack and swung it around one shoulder. Someone followed me as I headed out the door. When I turned around, Mr. Poundz's dark eyes stared back at me.

"Did you pay attention today?" he asked.

"Yes. I- uh." I didn't have an excuse.

"You have an excellent grade in my class, Andrew, though it won't last long if you lose focus. You can't do the homework if you don't pay attention," Mr. Poundz smiled warmly. He crammed his big hands into his oversized, white lab coat pockets. It was clean, as if he never conducted any experiments. Maybe he was neat and never spilled anything.

"I'm sorry," I apologized. "I know everything you reviewed today. I'll be able to do the homework."

"Good man!" Mr. Poundz stated with a nod. He pulled out his hand and pointed at me as if he were scolding me. "Can you come here during lunch? I wanna talk to you about dreaming during my entire lesson." He paused and examined my blank expression. "It's not such a bad thing, really. I think the world needs more dreamers," He added, trying to cheer me up.

"Ok," I replied, annoyed. Mr. Poundz nodded again and walked away. As he entered his classroom, he tapped the door frame with his hand for no reason. I was never punished in school because I never did anything wrong. Today's class wasn't even important. It was a review of the material from before winter break. Why did he give me lunch detention? Was it even a lunch detention?

My next class after science was math, Pre-Calculus, to be exact. I didn't have any friends in that class. This

6

encouraged me to sit in the far back of the room. My grades in Pre-Calc were decent, not above average. There were a lot of smart kids in that class. They were able to answer everything the teacher dished out. I paid more attention in Pre-Calc, though it was difficult. I kept thinking about Mr. Poundz and how I had to visit his class during lunch. There were two classes before all four grades had lunch at the same time. This meant I had to see Mr. Poundz immediately after math class. When the bell rang, I slowly grabbed my backpack and trudged down the packed hallway.

"Why is only one door open?" asked a towering senior. "It's making the hallway even more crowded!" he complained, talking to no one in particular. I was squished as I walked through the herd of people heading to the cafeteria. Lunch tables were scattered throughout our school, yet everyone raced for a spot in the main cafeteria. Finally, I broke free from the crowd as I turned the corner to go down the science wing.

To my surprise, Mr. Poundz's classroom was empty. The lights were off, and all the tables were clear of equipment. I walked over to wait for Mr. Poundz at one of the lab benches. An odd buzzing noise rang throughout the room. It was coming from inside the side room where equipment and chemicals for experiments were stored. Students were not allowed inside. Therefore, it had to be a teacher in there. A frustrated growl roared from inside. It sounded like Mr. Poundz's voice, only a bit louder.

I knocked on the door. "Mr. Poundz?" I called anxiously. I waited a few seconds before knocking again. He turned around and saw me through the window.

"Andrew! Come in here! Help me!" Mr. Poundz yelled urgently. Something was wrong. I rushed inside and flicked on the lights. There was a long, plastic collapsible table covered in various glass beakers and rubber tubes. Several different colored liquids and powders decorated the table as well. I inspected some of the tools he had in the room and didn't recognize any of them. Some had a logo that said Argone on them, while others read Armageddon.

"Argone? How did you get these? What are they?" I asked suspiciously. A long time ago, I had heard about a company by the same name that went bankrupt. Armageddon was the company that bought them out. They didn't sell lab equipment. I was astounded that Mr. Poundz had a whole collection of their tools.

"I used to work there before it went under, and that- that, psychopath, blew up the place. Principal Perfetto wanted- shit!" Mr. Poundz cursed in a hurry. He panted as he moved back and forth to different pieces of equipment. "I need you to read that computer screen while I stand over here," he ordered. Mr. Poundz ran to a metal gas tank with a long, clear tube connected to what looked like a gas mask. The reflective metal tank had an Argone logo on it. He put the mask on around his mouth and nose and pointed to the computer. Before I could question him, he slammed a remote button that triggered the gas tank to pump a blue gas through the tube and into the mask. He breathed deeply to get as much gas in his lungs as possible. I checked the computer screen to find a loading bar filled only five percent of the way. Suddenly, the computer froze. Nothing I clicked on responded. The computer beeped loudly before shutting down without my input. It wouldn't restart.

"Um," I blurted out nervously. I turned to see Mr. Poundz rubbing his sweaty forehead with his hand. He was stumbling in place, having a hard time standing. "Stop breathing that stuff!" I commanded. I had no idea what was going on. The gas appeared to be hurting him. Obviously, this was not what he intended for me when he asked me to come back during lunch. No, this was some bizarre project I was never supposed to see.

He tore off the mask in frustration. "It's the serum!" he coughed. The dark blue gas quickly began to fill the room. "No!" Mr. Poundz yelled, stumbling to find his balance. He toppled over onto the table, sending everything crashing to the ground. The table itself gave out. Mr. Poundz grabbed the gas tank and stood up. He fumbled with the mask but was too dizzy to put it on. His face was turning blue. Streaks of dark blue veins ran across his cheeks. Mr. Poundz frantically pointed at something. My eyes followed his finger to the mess on the ground. A puddle of chemicals had been splattered onto a sparking outlet.

"Guh-guh-guh," Mr. Poundz choked out. The colorful liquids bubbled violently. They were reacting with the electricity. Flames shot out from the drenched outlet. Suddenly, he yelled, "Get out!"

8

I ran outside the small room and into the classroom. Mr. Poundz stumbled behind me as a loud explosion lit up the equipment room! The blast sent us soaring across the classroom. Our bodies crashed onto the unforgiving floor as the mysterious gas filled the room. My ears rang painfully. I found it hard to keep my eyes open. The gas leaked into the hallway. It had already filled my lungs. Mr. Poundz pulled the fire alarm next to the doorway. The blaring sound did little to motivate me. My body refused to move. Knives sliced at my throat with every breath. The room spun around me. Mr. Poundz's frantic yelling felt distant despite him being a foot away. Suddenly, everything went black.

2

AFTERMATH

A small crowd of classmates circled around me. Something was off. They were all talking about Bianca, yet they were staring at me. My head hurt. It was difficult to breathe at first. Each breath scorched my throat. The pain slowly faded as I caught my breath. Sitting up proved to be another challenge. My chest ached when I tried to move. It took a few attempts to get my muscles to listen.

"Bianca likes Andrew!" I heard a girl's voice tease.

"Shut up! She has a boyfriend!" yelled another.

"She saved his life," a tall boy whispered. My sight slowly cleared up. I felt like I was wiping a camera lens, cleaner and cleaner with every blink.

"Yeah, but it was gross. She didn't have to kiss him," the first girl replied.

"What the hell was she supposed to do?" questioned my friend Seamus.

"What happened?" I asked. My voice was rough. It sounded as if I were sick. A popping noise shot out of my bones as I cautiously sat up.

Seamus pushed his way through the crowd to see me. His face was beet-red and sweating. A lot must have happened while I was out. "Mr. Poundz saw everything," Seamus answered, pointing behind him. Mr. Poundz followed Seamus through the crowd, coughing as he reached the center. "I dragged you out here. Seamus spotted you and rushed over. We realized you had stopped breathing and screamed for help. That's when Bianca ran over and gave you mouth-to-mouth. She saved you. That's when everyone crowded around you. Bianca ran away once you were breathing on your own," Mr. Poundz explained.

Bianca, champion of the swim team, saved my life? She was a popular girl in my grade. I had always assumed she was obnoxious since she was dating the dreaded Zach Ratulie. Bianca was quite beautiful too. She had long brown hair and brown eyes. As a matter of fact, she had some of the longest hair out of any girl at my school. It was always well-kept and cascaded elegantly down to just above her waist.

As more classmates whispered gossip, it became clear why there was such a huge commotion. Some idiots believed Bianca kissed me and were mad at her since she had a boyfriend. It was mostly the immature freshmen whispering such things. She saved my life! Why do they think she likes me? I screamed in my head. How does one confuse CPR for a romantic kiss? I racked my brain and could not figure out how they could put such a negative spin on this. Some classmates purposely made everything dramatic.

"Where's Bianca?" I asked as soon as I stood up. Drums pounded in my head. To save myself from embarrassment, I usually avoided conversations. This was different. If I didn't thank Bianca, I'd be the biggest jerk in the world. Avoiding her would've been ruder than the people creating rumors about her.

"Over there!" Seamus shouted. He pointed to a bare maple tree. The crowd of classmates had thinned out and moved on. They were busy talking amongst themselves, gossiping about what caused the evacuation. When they cleared out of the way, I spotted the small tree standing alone in the grassy field outside school. Bianca sat beneath it with her hands wrapped around her knees. Her fingers absent-mindedly played with the tears in her blue jeans. She looked lost in thought. Her sleeveless blue shirt looked agonizingly cold.

My muscles felt cramped as I walked. A slight tingling sensation ran through my legs. The thin, little tree was only a little further. As I got closer to Bianca, I could see her face was red with embarrassment. She had saved my life. If it weren't for all those kids making it into something it wasn't, she would've been real proud of what she did.

My heart skipped a beat. I wasn't a pathetic loser, though it still freaked me out to stroll up to such a stunning girl and initiate a conversation. My breath snagged in my throat for a moment as I tried to get out the words I needed to say. Bianca continued to stare at the ground. She didn't acknowledge me. Even after saving my life, I remained invisible. I couldn't let that happen. Finally, the words broke free.

"Th-thank you," I blurted out nervously. "That was an amazing thing you did back there," I whispered. The more I spoke, the more confident I grew. "I'm sorry everyone is treating you like this. You saved my life. You didn't do anything wrong."

"I don't care. They don't understand," Bianca huffed. She let go of her legs and unbent her knees.

"What do you mean?"

"It was sad. Seamus screamed that you weren't breathing. People came running over, but none of them did anything. I was the only one who could help you, so I did. When they teach you CPR for swim team and my lifeguard training, they make you swear that you won't hesitate to use it in an emergency. I didn't hesitate. I did exactly as I was told, and they hate me for it." Bianca peered down at the ground again.

"You did the right thing, Bianca. Who cares what they think?" I whispered. "I can give you my number if you want to talk about this later?" I offered. My vision blurred for a moment.

"No, I have a boyfriend. He's the jealous type. He would get mad," Bianca answered solemnly. Her reaction proved that people were really getting to her. I turned my back to her as I headed over to the crowd. "Wait, are you leaving?" Bianca called after me.

I turned to face her. "I'm sorry, I don't feel well. I think I'll ask if I can leave school early." I rubbed my forehead. My skin was like a running faucet. The freezing weather should've kept me cool, yet I was drenched in sweat.

"Are you kidding?" Bianca laughed. "School is canceled for today. You can't go back in there. Look, people are getting on buses already." She pointed towards the line of

12

yellow school buses. Behind them, I spotted the aftermath of the incident in school. Blue gas filled every window. Nobody could go inside. Everyone was loading onto the buses except the seniors who drove themselves.

"Are you ok? They called an ambulance for you. You should wait for it. Your skin is really white!" Bianca asked in a concerned tone. She stared deep into my eyes.

"I know, I don't tan, I burn!" I joked. Bianca frowned and stood up. She dusted grass off her pants as she spoke. "No, I mean your skin, it's see-through. It's turning blue."

I inspected my hands to see that all my veins were visible through my skin and tinted a dark blue, like the gas. They were popping through my arms like I'd been lifting heavy weights. My heart felt like it might implode. Being hauled away in an ambulance in front of everyone would make things worse. I could die of embarrassment. No good excuses came to mind. I had to run and hide before she only remembered me as the boy who turned blue. "No, I'm fine, just a bit tired. I think I'll go home and rest," I replied as I headed towards the buses. I turned slightly to wave goodbye.

"Wait!" Bianca yelled. The chilly grass crunched as she ran up to me. A big smile lit up her face when I turned around. She handed me a yellow sticky note with a phone number hastily scribbled in red ink. "Text me when you're not blue. I want to make sure you're ok."

It didn't take long for me to get home. The familiar red bricks of my small, squat house were relieving to see in the distance. On the inside, the walls were mostly painted white, creamy yellow, or beige. Everything looked blue to me at the moment. Something was wrong with me. I raced around the house in a panic. My parents were both at work. I was all alone. My Dad worked at TCNJ while my Mom taught at Princeton. It was the middle of a school day, so they both wouldn't be home for a while. The room started to spin.

I dropped my backpack off on one of the three swivel seats surrounding the kitchen island counter. I always put it there so I wouldn't forget it in the morning. A loud noise grabbed my attention. It was coming from the basement. My body begged me to ignore it and sit down. The noise repeated. It sounded urgent. My cat Oliver is in the basement! I had to check on him! He was locked in his massive cage since he got into trouble when left alone. My backpack almost fell over as I rushed out of the kitchen.

My Dad found Oliver on the side of a road about eleven years ago. I don't know why I named him Oliver. It ended up fitting him well. He was an uncommon type of cat because he was pure orange and no other color. Even his eyes were a golden orange. He was such a young kitten that we had to bottle-feed him milk. We kind of grew up together since I was so little myself when we got him. He was very special to me.

As I walked down the stairs to the basement, I felt myself getting weaker with each step. My hands sprung out and clung to the rail. The stairs creaked as I stumbled down the last few steps. The cold, concrete floor numbed my feet. It was suddenly difficult to move. I turned the corner and hobbled a little further until my legs gave up. I collapsed onto my hands and knees. The hard basement floor scraped up my knee.

Bizarre noises emitted from Oliver. His enclosure was just out of reach. He saw me fall. His little paws banged on the wire cage. I crawled on the ground as I tried to reach him, but I didn't have the energy to keep going.

My skin was bluer than earlier. It was as if I were blushing blue instead of red. My muscles squeezed, and my skin shriveled close together. I cried out in pain. My head felt as if it were being split open. Watery tears filled my eyes. I could barely see Oliver through them. There was no more energy left in my body. I tried to move. It was no use. Although I couldn't lift my head, I could see Oliver come bounding over to me. *How did he get out,* I thought as he scampered over. He ran up beside my outstretched arm and stared into my eyes. His eyes glowed in the dim light of the basement. An unbearable pain surged throughout my body. Oliver never broke eye contact. He stood there and stared at me inches from my face as every cell in my body felt like it was being electrocuted.

My pupils became thin slivers like a cat. I couldn't see them, but I felt them tightening and shrinking. What was happening? Images of DNA, viruses, and cells flashed inside my head. A war was going on inside me. Colors rushed back and forth. Chemicals fought each other while flowing through my veins. Was I seeing what was going on inside me? It was all too much to take in. DNA broke apart. Pain erupted throughout my body each time this happened. It really was happening to me! Orange-colored strands of DNA replaced the broken segments. A strange blue glow took over the segments. It was tainting the cells and destroying my DNA! The blue was taking over. The orange segments couldn't keep up. The pain was overwhelming. I was being torn apart!

3

RISE

My body was cold and covered in goosebumps. It was bright, too bright. The only light came from a small window at the top of the basement wall. I had to shield my eyes. Not much light could stream through a window level with the ground, yet it was enough to irritate my tired eyes.

"Are you ok?" whispered an unfamiliar voice. It sounded close.

"What? Yeah, uh, who's there?" I answered, searching the basement. There was nobody there except Oliver. My vision focused the more I blinked. Still, there was nobody there. My eyes were wet with tears from the searing pain. My head felt like it had melted. Every inch of my body ached.

"It's me, Oliver," greeted the voice. I peered down to see him purring at my feet. His tail waved back and forth as he sat.

"Oh no. I don't wanna be a crazy cat person. No, you're not talking!" I told myself while rubbing sweat off my face. I paced back and forth. I didn't want to believe it, but Oliver was the only one there. How did he get out of his cage?

"I'm talking to you telepathically. Nobody can hear me except you," Oliver walked closer and sat on my feet. I could feel him breathe as he purred. *"The same gas they tested on me was killing you. I repaired your DNA manually, piece by piece. It kept destroying yours, so I had to replace the damaged parts with mine."*

16

The more I breathed, the emptier my lungs felt. It was as if I held my breath throughout that experience. "What?" I choked out. Speaking was even harder than breathing. I scanned Oliver up and down, waiting for an answer. He looked up at me and meowed. Great, I was imagining things. Five seconds ago, I swore my cat had talked.

Ding-Dong Ding! Ding! Ding!

Someone rang the doorbell frantically. Sweat loosened my grip on the railing as I stumbled upstairs. It felt like climbing a mountain just to reach the door upstairs. To my surprise, it was Bianca pounding on the front door. She seemed to be in such a hurry that she didn't notice me through the doorway window. Bianca practically fell inside once I opened the door. She turned around quickly and hugged me tight. She sniffled as she clung to me. I grabbed onto her shoulders to break free from her embrace. Tears rolled down her face. Her eyes were red from crying.

"What's wrong?" It was obvious that something terrible had happened. Her face was pale as a ghost.

"I- I," Bianca could barely speak as she continued to cry. She wiped her eyes and nose with her hand. "I thought you were dead!" she finally blurted out.

It was hard to hide my confusion. My lips twisted as I looked at her cautiously. "What? Why would you think that?" I asked.

Bianca sniffled and wiped her eyes again. "Didn't you see the news?" Her voice trembled as she spoke. She was a mess.

"No, I was, um, busy," I answered carefully.

"Fine, I'll look it up," Bianca paused before adding, "Here!" She shoved her phone in my face. It was impossible to read it with her hands shaking. I took her phone in my hands. She stopped wiping her face and put her hands to her sides. Her breathing slowed to a normal rate. She was so beautiful. Even while crying, her eyes glistened remarkably.

"Mr. Poundz died from the gas. I came over to see if you were ok, but I guess the gas never touched you," Bianca explained. She held her arms across her chest. It looked like she was cold.

I couldn't speak. I didn't know what was going on. The article she pulled up on her phone confirmed that Mr. Poundz

17

died shortly after the students were sent home. An investigation was going to be launched to discover the cause of the incident and identify the mysterious gas. School was going to be closed for a while. That part I understood, but Mr. Poundz I didn't get. I didn't understand how he could die from the gas while I was fine. He was exposed to the gas for only a few breaths more than me. Was that enough of a head start to kill him and not me?

"It did touch you, didn't it," Bianca whispered. She had analyzed my horrified expression. She knew I was questioning how I survived. It made no sense. The gas should've killed us both.

"Yes, but I feel fine," I admitted. The truth was my head felt like it had been hit by a brick. I wasn't sure if I was going to be ok. All I knew was that I didn't want Bianca to worry about me. She had already forced her mom to drive her over here just to check on me. I'm willing to bet she found my address in those old kindergarten friend finder pamphlets. "But I don't know why I'm ok," I whispered.

"It's because I saved you!" Oliver interrupted angrily. I looked down to see Oliver rubbing the scent glands on his face and body all over Bianca in a typical cat greeting.

"Oh, you have a cat! How cute! What's her name?" Bianca cooed as she picked Oliver up. She held him in the way he hated, limbs dangling downward like a ragdoll.

"HER! HER? I'm a male!" Oliver complained.

"Ahh! Did he talk?" Bianca screamed, dropping Oliver to the floor. His little paws made a soft thud as he landed on the hardwood floor of the entrance.

"Oliver!" I scolded. Not only had he blown his cover, but he was also being annoying about it. How did he go his entire life keeping his telepathic powers a secret only to accidentally speak to Bianca as soon as he met her? He meowed in response as if nothing had happened. A knock at the door transferred our attention off of Oliver. My heart stopped. Bianca gasped. There was a police officer at the doorway. Red and blue lights flashed in the distance.

"You must be Andrew Corleone; can I ask you a few questions?" the officer boomed. He was a large man who didn't appear in the best shape.

"I should go," Bianca announced. She stared at her phone. It must have been her mom texting her. She was waiting outside the whole time. Bianca slid her phone back into her pocket before slipping past the policeman.

"I'm Officer Hanson," the man introduced himself while rolling his eyes. It had only taken a brief moment to say goodbye to Bianca, yet he seemed pissed off that I ignored him. "From what we gathered so far, only you and Ken Poundz came into contact with the substance before the evacuation. The gas remains in high concentration within the school, and we're supposed to investigate, which is hindering our progress. Can you tell me anything about the events that transpired beforehand?" There was a strange element in his voice. It was as if he didn't really want to be here.

"Something smells off about him. Tread carefully," Oliver warned.

The moment I opened my mouth to speak, I was silenced. Mr. Poundz was dead, yet he didn't mention it. He didn't ask if I was ok or how I was feeling. Officer Hanson didn't care about me. Maybe I was being paranoid, and he was simply too focused on his work to realize he should probably check to make sure the deadly gas didn't hurt me too. Either way, I thought it was odd. Perhaps it was best to ensure he was on my side before I brought up talking cats and crazy experiments gone wrong.

"Mr. Poundz asked me to meet him during lunch. I got in trouble during his class, so he wanted to talk to me. When I arrived in his classroom, there was a big explosion. Before I knew what was happening, Mr. Poundz was carrying me outside while the school was filled with blue gas." I lied. There was enough truth in the statement that it should be undetectable.

Officer Hanson narrowed his brow. He acted like I had given him extremely intricate details that took time to absorb. His head nodded slightly as though he agreed with my story. The smell of his flop sweat made me gag. I closed the door partially to try and block it. "So, the gas explosion originated from the laboratory storage room connected to Mr. Poundz's classroom. Did he tell you anything about the gas previously? Did he tell you what he was trying to do?" Officer Hanson slipped up. My skin turned cold. He couldn't be trusted.

"I told you all that I know and everything that happened beforehand. I don't know anything about that gas. I'm sorry." I apologized. My acting was not good. He could tell I couldn't care less about giving him information. Something was up with him. He knew where the gas originated from despite claiming it was hazardous to enter the building. Each question he asked felt like he was testing how much I knew about that secret gas project rather than seeking answers.

"Disturbance at Armageddon facility. Man with mechanized suit seen exi-" Officer Hanson silenced his radio. He sighed and bid me farewell. The door clicked softly behind him. I was glad to be rid of him. It made me nervous talking to him. The hair on the back of my neck was practically standing up.

"It's probably your keen cat-like senses," Oliver informed. *"You can smell his fear, sense his uneasiness in his voice. Your heightened smell and hearing can be useful if you learn how to master them."* He peered up at me with big, round eyes. His tail was perked up all happy-like.

"Cat-like what?" I echoed.

"You have cat-like abilities from me and psychic powers from that gas," Oliver explained. He rolled onto his stomach. His tail flickered, then stopped by his side. *"The gas and I rewrote your DNA, Andrew. You're not completely human anymore."*

4

SILENCE OF THE CAT

Oliver's statement that night shocked me. My jaw didn't drop to the floor. Instead, I was frozen. It was terrifying to think of myself as less human. I covered my surprise with a blank expression. I continued to wear it when my parents came home. It was there the entire night. I didn't tell them what happened at school. They knew about the explosion and that school would be closed for a while; nothing else. Bianca, Oliver, scrambled DNA; it all remained a secret.

Even though school was closed, my body was used to waking up early. No alarm needed. My vision felt a bit off. Everything in my room looked brighter. The brown wood dresser, nightstand and desk all looked lighter. The silver-colored knobs of my dresser shone like they were radiating sunlight. As I raced out of my room, my navy blue covers plopped to the floor. It was unusually bright outside. I gazed out the hallway window to discover that the sun was low in the sky, yet I saw everything as bright as it would be at noon. *"What's going on?"* I asked Oliver in my mind. He did not respond.

Oliver stood up and circled me. He purred as he rubbed his cheek against my shin. No matter how hard I tried, he would not speak to me. Maybe the gas made me insane? No, Bianca was here yesterday. She heard him speak telepathically. I had to text her to make sure it wasn't all a dream.

21

I remembered reading that cats could see better in the dark because their eyes could reflect small amounts of light. However, their eyes required light to reflect; they couldn't see perfectly in the dark. This was different. My eyes reflected so much light that there was no darkness. There wasn't anything on the ground or in the sky that I couldn't see. Even if something was hiding in a shadow, I could spot it. In fact, there were no shadows, only light.

Seeing in the dark sounded cool until I thought about what it would be like when I tried to fall asleep. The thought of never experiencing night made me uneasy. Oliver seemed to sense my disappointment because he meowed loudly. It dawned on me. I was thinking like a person, not a cat. Cat's eyes change shape according to the light in their environment. There was a way to control it! As I anxiously waited for Bianca to text me about Oliver's silence, I opened the camera app on my phone. My pupils looked larger than life!

The muscles around my eyes tightened as I squinted at myself in the camera. My eyes were getting tense. The tenser my eyes became, the darker everything looked. The sky shifted into a dark blue like early morning. Objects in the distance slowly regained their shadows. It was a sensation I could not describe, like flexing a muscle I never knew existed. When I peered back down at my phone, my pupils looked like thin, cat-like slits.

Oliver started to strut away.

"Everything is clearer and focused now!" I exclaimed, admiring my new ability. *"It looks normal, well, still brighter, but a lot darker than before,"* I proclaimed telepathically as I walked down the stairs. Oliver meowed in response.

My parents had already left for work. That meant I had to make myself breakfast. Blueberry pancakes were waiting for me in the fridge. Oliver meowed when I placed them in the microwave. I guess, technically, I didn't make myself breakfast. I reheated it. The pancakes took about a minute to warm up. After adding a generous dollop of whipped cream, I grabbed a fork and plopped down at the island counter. I dug into my blueberry pancakes to discover that they tasted like I was eating raw wheat. They didn't go bad; I had watched my Mom make them the day before. I continued eating them slowly and found that it was mainly the whipped cream and blueberries that tasted disgusting.

"Um, Oliver?" I started to ask him something, though I stopped when I realized he hadn't answered me all morning. My heart felt unsteady as I looked up my question online. Something told me I wasn't going to like what I would find. Sure enough, the first result stated plainly: cats can't taste sweet. Utterly horrifying.

Oliver made a chirp-like noise as he left the room, tail high. I watched him skip away as I finished my unpleasant breakfast. With my sweet tooth, this was a major blow to my mood. Candy, cookies, and dessert would be dearly missed. At least, it would force me to be healthier. *Maybe I'll finally get muscles,* I thought, *that would be cool. Then people might think I'm hot shit. No, that's a stretch,* I concluded.

Ooooom! Oooom! Oooom!

A bizarre sound echoed in my ears. The house should be shaking from such a booming noise; however, nothing was out of place. The only clue that it wasn't in my head was Oliver. His fur was standing on end. Come to think of it, so was the hair on the back of my neck.

Wub, wub wub, ooommm!

The sound repeated. It was far away. Whatever it was, it hurt. The sound was too distant to be obnoxious. There was something about the frequency that gave me an instant headache. I peeked outside to see what was going on. Nothing. The sound was coming from too far away. My neighbor strolled by walking their dog. When the noise repeated, the dog turned their head toward the sound, but my neighbor didn't react.

A brilliant idea came to mind. If I had cat-like abilities, I could test them out by locating this annoying sound. First, I went back up to my room to get dressed. Finding an unassuming, blank, black shirt in my unorganized closet was hard. A clean pair of black and grey shorts from my dresser would match my lazy look. I dashed downstairs and slid the glass door in the kitchen to go out into the backyard. It was early in the morning. The outside air was freezing. My winter clothes were in the washer machine. Shorts were all I had. I regretted my decision immediately.

My fingers already felt numb. With my powers, I couldn't tell if it had gotten any brighter out. I walked across the splintery wooden floorboards of the deck to open the gate my Dad and I had made from scraps of wood from another project.

My feet slipped on the wet, dewy grass. I removed my black and red sneakers and shoved my socks inside. They uncrumpled in my shoes as I tossed the pair aside. I didn't trust my shoes for what I was about to do. Cats could jump several times their height. I needed all the balance and traction I could get if I didn't want to land on my face.

The dirt and grass stuck to my toes. The ground was frigid. There was no point in hesitating because of the cold. It wasn't going to get warmer anytime soon. I bent real low to the grass. With one quick motion, I heaved all the force I could produce into the ground and launched myself into the air! The wind blew against my face as I rocketed into the sky. It was hard to breathe. I forced my eyes open. I was roughly forty feet in the air based on my relative position to my house. The powerful wind made me shut my eyes as I began to fall back down. The air whistled in my ears. I landed on my feet without damaging the ground or my legs. A gust of wind blew the surrounding grass away from me before another chilled breeze returned them upright.

That was a bust. The point of leaping up high was to scout out the source of that infernal racket. I clutched my ears in pain as the low, baritone-like sound drummed away at my skull. If there was no wind resistance, I would be able to see while jumping. That wasn't exactly a solvable problem. At least I knew the general direction it was emanating from.

House cats were faster than the fastest human sprinters. If I had all these cat-like enhancements, I should be able to track down the sound on foot quite quickly. I went several times higher than any human or cat when I jumped. I assumed I would be able to run faster than a human, too.

My heart beat out of my chest. I couldn't tell if it was from falling forty feet or from how pumped I was to learn all I could do. I was beginning to enjoy my transformation. It was scary at first; before I gradually learned how awesome I had become. It felt nice to finally have some self-confidence.

I crouched low to the ground. I focused on the small playground across the street. The sound was in that direction, maybe a mile or two away. A countdown began in my head. *Three, two, one!* I bolted across the lawn and over the paved street! The intense wind kept me from opening my eyes. My foot crashed into the side of the road where the stone partition separated the black top from the grass. My body launched into the air! I hit the ground hard and continued to tumble forward. The wet grass helped me slide along until my body lost momentum and came to a complete stop. Dirt and grass fell from my clothes as I stood. A green stain had already formed on my right knee. A slight pain brewed within my kneecaps before rapidly subsiding.

"I can run faster," I claimed triumphantly. The wind blew fiercely in my eyes. I couldn't breathe either. If I had something to protect my face, I could've run much faster. It took me a few seconds to catch my breath. The sound of my heartbeat faded away as I recovered. I tried to feel my pulse by placing two fingers on my throat. It didn't work. I measured my pulse again by putting my hand over my heart in a very unathletic fashion. My heartbeat had returned to a resting rate.

It would not win me any fashion awards, but I had an idea. Once again, I emerged from my house hellbent on finding that disturbing sound. This time, I was prepared with high-tech equipment. I donned a pair of swim goggles to keep the wind from blasting in my eyes. In addition, a black scarf was wrapped around my mouth, nose, and neck. This would help me breathe and hopefully keep me a little warmer.

Ooom! Ooom! I bolted the second the noise started. Each time, the sound was different. There were no patterns that I could detect. The world blurred around me as I ran. I was much faster than I anticipated. Cars honked their horns at me as I weaved in and out of traffic. Due to the speed limit in the area, I was faster than the cars! My scarf hid my giant, goofy smile. Bianca was going to think I was the coolest man alive!

Bam! I swerved to dodge a car and ended up faceplanting off the side of the road. When I recovered, I noticed that the sound had ceased. My heart sank for a moment. I was in the middle of a super-powered investigation. It was going to be so cool! I was about to call it quits when I recognized where I was. This intersection was a block away from my school. Maybe I could investigate what happened yesterday instead.

There was something off about the school already. No cops, no forensics, nobody anywhere. Officer Hanson made it seem like there was a big ruckus at my school, yet the day after a massive incident, nothing was going on. Besides the cautionary yellow tape, nothing indicated anything out of the ordinary had occurred. I looked both ways before slicing the tape. If the scarf wasn't covering most of my face, I would've been bright red. Sneaking into school like this was not something a goody-two-shoes like me would ever normally do. However, my cat talked to me yesterday. I needed answers.

Obviously, the door was locked. I sighed in defeat. Another investigation prematurely busted. Except I had powers now. There had to be something I could do to open the door. As I took time to think, my heart rate settled. Oliver said I had psychic powers, too. If I could figure out how to use them, I could unlock the door with only my mind. After staring at the lock for longer than I'd like to admit, I gave up.

There was no way to figure out how to use powers I wasn't sure I had. Maybe I had to start with something simpler. The grass was littered with sticks from nearby pine trees. My eyes locked on a small stick four feet in front of me. I imagined the stick floating upward. Nothing happened. I tried again and again to no avail. Before giving up, I tried one last time while also moving my hand. I gestured toward the stick with my arm outstretched, then raised it upward. The stick shot up and floated in line with where my arm was pointing! It was floating because of me! The feeling was almost as if I were holding it in my hands, only the hands were imaginary. The stick fell to the ground. I needed to concentrate for it to work.

My attention was now laser-focused on the lock. I thought all about the door and how the locking mechanism functioned. I imagined the bolt moving backward and mimicked that motion with my hand. The door unlocked with an ultra-satisfying click! I practically raced inside! Where to start? Up and down the halls, I zoomed from classroom to classroom. Nothing had changed. Everything was where I would expect it to be after a sudden evacuation.

Mr. Poundz's room was the only one of interest, and that was the same. There was no investigation there. Although

26

they might have wanted to ensure the building was clear of the mysterious gas before entering, I had my doubts. Officer Hanson was too sketchy for this to be a coincidence. I took pictures of all the strange equipment. Everything was as it was previously. It felt like I had hit a dead end, but there was one place left to look.

Principal Perfetto's office was quite pristine. There was no way that Mr. Poundz could conduct such an expansive experiment without others knowing. In the very least, the principal should know what he was up to. That equipment probably cost the school a lot of money, and it sure wasn't going towards anything to help the students. Principal Perfetto had to be in on it.

Papers flew across the room as I ransacked the principal's desk. Some documents looked important, though they lacked any jargon related to equipment, experiments, gas, Mr. Poundz, anything I was interested in. He had a few textbooks on his bookshelf, which I found odd. The principal did not need any textbooks. There were barely enough for the students. Among his bookshelf were AP English, Chemistry; Matter and Reactions, U.S. History I, Calculus I, and the rest were all regular books. Maybe he used the textbooks as weights to work out? I laughed to myself. It was the only thing I could do to keep from being upset. I'd only had my powers for a day and was already using them irresponsibly. That was unless I found something. Which I might have.

One of the pens on Principal Perfetto's desk stood out to me. All his pens were from school events, pizza places, and dealerships, except for one. The pen in question was from Armageddon. When I checked my photos of Mr. Poundz's equipment, I noticed he had some Argone tools. Armageddon was a real company that was thriving to this day. Argone was long gone. I took a picture of the pen and its slogan, "Be prepared for anything, -Armageddon". Despite not knowing much about Armageddon, I knew enough that it was suspicious. They were not the company an average Joe would ever interact with. It was more like scientific instruments developed for industries or military use.

After taking pictures of everything I deemed important, I ran into one last problem. The police tape I had broken to enter the school. If I left it there, it would be painfully obvious that someone had broken into the school. With my psychic powers, I was easily able to lock the door again. Maybe I could use them to fix the tape? It was worth a shot. I concentrated on the bright yellow tape. Without touching them, they moved in sync with my hands. The broken ends of the tape lined up where they were split. My head hurt. My vision zoomed in. The chemical structure of the tape was visible. I could see exactly where the tape was ripped. Using my telekinesis, I realigned the tape to continue the pattern of compounds that I saw. The broken bonds were close enough that they bonded back together! My vision instantly returned to normal. The police tape was repaired as if it were never broken! I was more powerful than I had ever imagined!

A chime noise caught my attention. It was Bianca. She finally texted me back! A dumb smile spread across my face. Not only did her response confirm that she heard Oliver yesterday, but she also claimed she'd never forget something like that. I wasn't crazy.

5

THE TALK

To my surprise, Bianca didn't just text me, she called me! Who calls anymore? It was so cool to hear her voice. I wished it was at a better time since a scarf covered my mouth. My paranoia of being caught prevented me from removing the scarf in case the cameras still functioned outside school. She invited me over to talk at her place. It felt surreal. Bianca De La Cruz, star of the swim team, wanted to hang out with me.

It took some time to look up where Bianca lived. Luckily, she didn't live too far away. It was only a twenty-minute walk from school. Of course, I had to return home to grab a pair of shoes. Her house wasn't as big as mine. Her backyard was tiny and surrounded by trees. My house had a long backyard with no trees until the back edge, where there was a small hill. Bianca's house was white with a lengthy driveway that stretched down a gigantic front yard. The yard must've been huge to make up for her backyard, which got interrupted by trees less than twenty feet in.

I walked up the driveway and followed the stone path to her porch. They had a dog-shaped doorbell where the nose of the dog was the button. The cute doorbell made me smile. As I waited for someone to answer, I scanned the porch, taking in every detail. There was a padded, metal bench suspended from the roof that people could swing on and a blue wooden chair that appeared to be covering a small crack in the concrete base of the porch.

The sound of footsteps steadily grew louder. They were followed by the click of someone turning a lock. Bianca opened the main red door; she had two doors attached to her front entrance. Next, she opened the screen door to let me in. She wore blue jeans and a sleeveless, olive-colored shirt. I bent down to take off my shoes. "Leave them on. We'll talk outside," Bianca whispered. The sound of running water came from somewhere inside the house. That was probably why she wanted to talk outside. She was afraid that her mom or dad or whoever was washing their hands would overhear us. If that happened, there'd be no telling how they'd react. Something told me Bianca's parents didn't want her hanging out with a cat-like freak. It was a good idea to talk outside.

Bianca rushed upstairs to put on socks. Then she came outside and took a seat on the swinging bench. I closed the door behind her and sat on the blue wooden chair. The paint on the armrests was chipping, making them uncomfortable to use. There was room next to Bianca on the bench, but I was a little nervous around her. I didn't want to make her or myself feel awkward by sitting next to her.

"Are you ok? You don't look blue anymore," Bianca asked. I could see the fear in her eyes. She was genuinely concerned for me.

"Yes, I'm different but fine," I answered. The sides of my lips curved upward in the smallest of smiles. There was an unusual reason for why we were hanging out. Bianca knew about my talking cat and strange powers. That's why I was at her house. To figure out what was going on. That's why I was there, though. It wasn't why I was happy to be there. I was hanging out with a popular kid. Not just a popular kid but a marvelous person. Bianca really cared about me. She barely knew me, yet she saved my life. This was my chance to befriend her.

"Yeah, how exactly are you different?" Bianca raised one eyebrow. She cocked her head to the side as if she caught me in a lie.

"Watch," I ordered confidently. My fingers fidgeted nervously in my lap. I raised my left hand and pointed at my eyes with two fingers. Bianca nodded and leaned forward, staring into my eyes. My reflection shimmered in her brown eyes. I stared into my reflection until I felt my pupils and irises become thin slits like a cat.

"Wow, that's so cool!" Bianca beamed. She backed away from my face once she saw my eyes shift. Her laugh was soft and quiet. It had a cheerful, bubbly quality that matched her personality perfectly. We talked for a long time, several hours at least. At one point, Bianca said it was getting dark, I had to take her word for it. When she started shivering, I gave her my scarf to stay outside and continue talking. We discussed school, music, movies, and everything that led up to her saving me. I sat in the same blue chair while she rocked back and forth on the bench. She placed my wide scarf across her lap like a blanket to keep her warm.

Bianca's smile weakened. "What are you going to do with your," she stopped to think of the right word, "powers?" She looked at me, her eyes beckoning me to answer. "You can get anything you want!"

"That's not right," I responded carefully. I always followed the rules. Breaking a rule made me nervous. Breaking the law was out of the question. "I wouldn't do that. I'm not like that. It wasn't right for me to break into school today. That alone has been eating me up inside. I felt I had no choice. It's like I have to find out what Mr. Poundz was up to. I'm not sure how to explain the feeling. The gas he created is connected to my cat somehow. Oliver knew what it was and has similar psychic abilities from it like his telepathy. Not only that, but it's not possible for Mr. Poundz to do all that without our school knowing. I'm going to use these powers to get answers." The rest of the world faded away as I spoke with her. It felt as though I was the only one who mattered to her. A serene warmth filled my chest. We were starting to become friends.

"That's what I hoped you'd say," Bianca smiled. She leaned back and sighed in relief. She was testing me to try and see if I could be persuaded into doing the wrong thing. I knew some kids she hung out with didn't have the best morals. She was used to spending time with people who would've seen nothing wrong with committing a crime if it was impossible to be caught. It seemed like she needed to know if I was like her close friends or the troublesome ones.

31

"You could use your powers to help people, too!" Bianca exclaimed. Her turquoise socks rubbed against the cement floor as she spoke. "You could save people just like the heroes in those action movies!" Bianca paused, "Sci-fi action movies, in your case," she added with a smile. "You've got powers and years of martial arts training; you won't get hurt!" Bianca proclaimed, practically begging.

I sighed. A sinking feeling seeped in. I regretted telling her about Tae Kwon Do. My black belt test was beyond brutal, though it didn't mean I could survive anything. I was not brave enough to risk my life and imitate those strong movie hero characters. "I just got my powers," I replied quietly. "I don't know everything I can do." Suddenly, I felt lost. Her words reminded me that I wasn't completely human anymore. I had no clue what I was going to do. In only a day or so, I became a different person, capable of things most people could never dream of, attempt, or believe.

Bianca stopped swinging on the bench. Her brown eyes sparkled with stars so bright they could shine in daylight. "Lots of people don't know what they can do," Bianca whispered. "You'll never know what you're capable of unless you try," she added. Bianca reached forward to touch my hand. Her nails were painted pink with little yellow flowers on them. It was the first time I noticed them. I brushed her hand off me. Not only was her hand cold, but her touch made me nervous. I wasn't used to people touching me. Tae Kwon Do made me quite defensive.

"If you're taking the law into your own hands by investigating the gas at school, then you might as well do some real good while you're at it. I don't want all this sneaking around for clues leading you down a dark path. Helping people might help keep your mind straight. Promise me you'll think about it?" Bianca asked politely. There was almost a sadness in her voice. She sounded innocent and pure. It made me freeze. My eyes locked on her radiant smile. She stared back at me while waiting for an answer.

"Ok," I agreed, leaning back as far as I could in the old chair. Bianca wanted me to be a hero. Heroes were supposed to risk their lives and receive nothing in return. However, there was something I desperately wanted in return. Being a hero could grant me fame. I wanted to be popular like Bianca and

32

her friends. I saw myself as a good person who cared for others, but it felt like nobody noticed. If I acted like a hero, saved lives, and fought crime, I had to become famous. There was no way a real-life hero could go unnoticed.

If I used my strange powers to save people and stop thieves, that would certainly attract the eyes of millions. With my powers, my shy, quiet self finally had a chance to be seen! I had been under the radar my whole life, unheard of, silent. Being a hero would change all of that. It was unclear if being famous would fill the emptiness I felt inside. It was possible fame could lead to me finding love, too. I wasn't sure why my heart ached so badly. The people already in my life loved me dearly, yet the void remained.

My decision was almost made. Some doubt remained as I worried about getting hurt. A cool breeze froze my hands. My powers could fulfill my dreams. I could be famous. That might give me more self-esteem and a confidence boost, which would aid in getting a girlfriend. Maybe all I needed was the confidence to ask out Avery. I shivered. I was fully aware my plan was a stretch. I didn't care. It was all for the right person. My fingers were red from rubbing them to warm up.

Bianca must've sensed my nervousness and changed the subject. "In the meantime, let's talk about something else," she suggested. "I'm getting to know you very well, but I could know you better. You're sixteen, right?"

"Yes, but my birthday is on Sunday," I answered quickly. "That's basic, though. I already know all the basics about you from being in the same math class last year. It seems you don't pay much attention," I smirked.

"You never talk!" Bianca exclaimed. "You know about me because I constantly talked to my friends. You only whispered jokes to your friend Mark!" she yelled. That was true. My friend Mark was in that class. We got to sit next to each other.

"You're right, I'm sorry," I apologized. Bianca sat back in her seat and pulled the scarf up to cover her chest.

"Thank you," Bianca replied. The devious smile returned to her face. "Now for the main question," she paused to lean in again. "Who do you like?"

"What? You mean like a crush? Nobody right now," I answered calmly. My relaxed response was sure to fool her. It

33

didn't work. She saw right through my lie. I might have been blushing at the time. This seemed to be the question she was anxiously waiting to ask me. It was the most interesting and common question asked throughout high school. Friends and enemies alike were interested in that sort of information. Bianca and I had talked about everything else; I should've seen it coming.

"Come on! Everyone likes someone!" Bianca laughed. She rocked the bench back and forth. "I have a boyfriend, so you already know who I like. Tell me who you like!" Somehow, that seemed fair to her.

"Nobody," I replied, "I just don't have a crush right now," I responded calmly once again. This time, I couldn't help but squirm in my chair. "What do you like about Zach?" I asked. He was one of the most obnoxious, popular athletes in our grade. I was itching to know why Bianca would date someone like him.

"Fine, if I tell you why I like Zach, will you tell me who you like?" Bianca pleaded persuasively. She shifted my scarf around to protect her arms from the cold. I didn't acknowledge her question. "You'll feel better after," Bianca begged, "It hurts if you keep a secret for too long." Once again, I didn't reply. "Fine, I'll tell you why I like Zach first, and maybe you'll tell me who you like after," she huffed. I continued to stare at her with a vacant expression. I had to do something to hide how fascinated I was with our conversation.

"It was the beginning of the 2nd marking period in November," Bianca began. "I met Zach in gym class when he was playing basketball with his friends. From being in the same class as him in previous years, I knew he was good at almost all sports. His friends noticed I was watching him and dared him to ask me out. When he turned to see me, he claims, his jaw dropped," she giggled. "We got to talking, and he said I was the coolest person he'd ever met. I told him we were in the same gym class before, but Zach smiled and said, 'Yeah, but that doesn't mean I lied.' After a while, he asked me out. I was surprised and said, 'I hardly even know you.' That's when he leaned in and whispered, 'We can fix that.'"

"That's it?" I demand. "That's so cheesy!" I laughed.

"Well, I admired his courage to walk over and ask me out," Bianca replied as if she had read my mind. "He's also handsome. He's tall, with dark brown hair, brown eyes, and big muscles. He's so athletic. Did you know he plays basketball, football, and baseball?"

"Oh wow!" I rolled my eyes.

Bianca laughed despite being annoyed with me. "You know he's not the big meanie people make him out to be. His parents got divorced a few years back, and he hasn't seen his mom since. He's going through a lot right now. There's more to him than you think."

"Oh, I'm so sorry. I never knew that," I apologized. Although that sounded like a terrible situation, his treatment of others prevented me from feeling too bad for him.

"Ok, then, tell me who you like! You're too scared to tell me one little name, and I told you Zach's big secret!" Bianca complained.

"Fine!" I scoffed. It was hard to tell her since I hadn't told anyone I liked Avery. What made it worse was Bianca had been friends with her forever. I felt like she would end up telling her eventually. It was one of the first times I had a true conversation with Bianca. It made me feel uneasy trusting her with my secret. Of course, it dawned on me that she was already keeping a much larger secret for me. "I kinda have a crush on Avery," I admitted. My words trickled out slowly. I avoided eye contact by staring at my hands. "Don't tell her," I quickly added.

Her warm smile transformed into a devious grin. "Wait, the Avery that I'm friends with?"

"Yes, the Avery you're friends with, so please don't tell her!" I begged. My hands anxiously clenched into fists on my lap. I stared at Bianca, awaiting her response.

"I won't, I won't tell her," Bianca replied as her expression grew serious. "So," Bianca paused and smiled, "why do you like her?" she asked curiously. I sighed and gave her an annoyed look. She was suddenly acting very nosey, and I wasn't a fan of it.

Bianca appeared to have realized I wasn't going to say anything, so she came up with a plan. "Tell me, or I'll tell her!" Bianca yelled, holding up her phone.

"Alright!" I huffed. Bianca had me cornered. "Well," I paused nervously. It was hard for me to reveal so many secrets to a person who I only recently started to become friends with.

35

"Of course, I like her because she's beyond beautiful and all that stuff, but that's not all," I said as my voice mellowed into a whisper.

"I've been in many classes with her throughout the years, and I've learned that she has an amazing sense of humor. When her friends make a good joke or do something funny, she has the most amazing laugh. I also know that she has a heart of gold. Avery always helps her friends in Biology whenever they get stuck on a question. If she can't figure out the answer, she makes the cutest little face," I stopped talking, looked up from the ground, and stared into Bianca's eyes. They were shimmering, begging me to continue.

I continued speaking as if I had never stopped. "Avery also talks to her friends about going to movies, and it seems like she's gone to the same ones as me. Her friends in Bio, Jeremy and Gian, I think, don't listen to music. Avery couldn't believe it. Turns out she has a similar taste in music as me. She's never mentioned my favorite artist, but I'd like to think she'd love his songs. Sometimes she sneaks snacks into class and takes small bites when the teacher isn't looking, it's so freakin' adorable. I know that she's insanely smart because she's gotten an A plus on almost every test so far. She even whispers the answers to all the teacher's questions to herself as if she can't help herself." I could say more, though I decided to keep it to myself. I felt like I had said too much. My secrets were spilling out of me. It was hard to stop the constant flow.

Bianca sat back on her bench and thought for a moment. She was leaning in the whole time I spoke, absorbing every word I uttered. Her expression barely changed; I had no idea what she was thinking. There was a good chance I sounded like an infatuated maniac. She tilted her head up as though she were lost in thought. It was as if she was replaying everything I had said in her mind. She sat up straight and adjusted my scarf to shield her legs. Every inch of my scarf was stretched thin at this point. "I think you should tell her," Bianca whispered.

"What? You said you wouldn't do this!"

"I never promised you anything!" Bianca reminded. "Besides, I thought you were just gonna say she's hot, but this is deeper! Andrew, you gotta tell her!" she pleaded.

"No," I snapped sharply.

"I'm her friend. I know for a fact that if you tell her what you told me, she'll go out with you! Consider you two sealed and shipped. I'll make it happen," Bianca continued. I looked back at her in shock. It was strange that she cared so much. Whenever I meet new people, the conversations have never gotten this personal and had never gone on for this long. *Bianca is quite a special person,* I thought, *she's already looking out for me and wants to help me.* A sly smile crept across her face. "Show her your powers! Any girl in the world would be captivated by your talents!" Bianca grinned.

"You think I'm talented? I mean, no!" I yelled. "I won't use my powers to get anything or anyone! I don't want to use them to get a girlfriend. If I did, I know something bad would happen. If people discover my powers, who knows what will happen to me? Scientists will take me away and experiment on me for all I know. I want whoever I end up with to like me for me, not the spectacle of my powers. Bianca, this has to be a secret," I complained.

"Alright, I'll keep your powers a secret, but not your love. You're telling her!" Bianca insisted. Her face was bright red from arguing back and forth. The word love stopped me cold. I paused and thought for a while. Could this be love? I had never had a girlfriend before, so I couldn't tell. Was I in love? Was Bianca in love with Zach? In every T.V. show, parents always told their teenage children that they don't know what love is. I concluded that I, too, didn't know, which meant I didn't love Avery. Though, wasn't love supposed to be a mysterious thing?

"I have a plan," Bianca announced. Her voice broke me from my trance. "I'll invite you, Zach, and Avery to my house sometime. Regardless of what goes down, you'll feel better after you tell her. You won't be holding in any secrets, and you'll find out if she likes you! You may also leave with a girlfriend!" Bianca proclaimed as she held my hand again.

I moved my hand away. "Woah! Girlfriend? That's coming on way too strong! Keep in mind, I've barely talked to her before! I'd come off as desperate," I complained.

The night was silent. The cold weather drove away any crickets. We kept our voices down from time to time to keep the peaceful night quiet. "Let's get together beforehand to plan," Bianca proposed happily. "We could go to Princeton to hang out and talk again. I could at least give you some tips, like her likes and dislikes, so it won't feel as if you're talking to a stranger," Bianca suggested with a smile.

"What time should I come over?" I sighed. Verbal fights weren't my thing.

"Yes! Alright! I'll text you later then!" Bianca shrieked with excitement. I didn't know why, though. Did she really care? I didn't think I'd become friends with a popular person that easily. It wasn't easy. I almost died from that gas. Besides that moment, I barely did anything. I only acted myself. Hopefully, Avery would like me as I was too.

A booming voice echoed from inside the house. "Are you still outside? Do you know what time it is? Get inside before you catch a cold!" Mrs. De La Cruz hollered. Bianca's scream must have woken her mom. She moved my scarf off her lap and pulled out her tiny pink phone to check the time. It was already midnight. She stared at the screen of her phone a while before sliding it into her pocket. My powers made me see as if it were as bright as day. It could have been noon, and I wouldn't have known the difference. I looked up at the sky. There were no stars, only a plain blue sky with a dash of clouds. The moon caught my eye. It was incredibly bright. *My eyes reflect light,* I remembered. *I must be reflecting light from the moon and stars to see clearly at night.*

"I better go," I told Bianca. It was late; I didn't want to make her mother upset. I had texted my parents saying I was going to be at a friend's house. I didn't tell them what time I'd be home. My Mom was going to be angry with me if I didn't leave soon. I hoped they'd understand that I lost track of time. It rarely happens, so I didn't think I'd get in trouble.

"Yeah, that's a good idea," Bianca agreed. She glanced at the window to her right. It had dark green shutters that stood out against her plain white house. She was probably nervous her mom was going to yell again. "Bye, Andrew!" Bianca cheered as she handed me my scarf. I waved goodbye in return. The night dew almost caused me to slip down the steps of her porch. Luckily, cat-like balance triggered, and I stabilized myself. How odd. "Hey!" Bianca called as she reopened her front door an inch. "Remember what you promised me!"

It wasn't possible to forget my promise. Bianca's words echoed in my head as I trudged home. The cold night froze my joints. There was no way I was going to be able to walk home. I had to run. Jack Frost numbed my limbs. It was going to be hard to run. Thoughts of my warm bed filled my head. In an instant, I was gone. Did I teleport? I teleported! That's not something cats can do. It had to be one of my psychic abilities! Only I had no clue where I was. The room I appeared in was unfamiliar. The strong desire to be elsewhere, combined with my thoughts of home, allowed me to teleport. Except it should've sent me to my bedroom. I held my hand up to my face. I couldn't see it. The walls and floor were made of solid stone. Wherever I was, there was no way out.

THE LONGEST CHAPTER

The surrounding stone walls were engraved. With no light, it was impossible to see what the markings were. My phone wouldn't turn on. I screamed aloud and telepathically. There was no response. My heartbeat raced. The panicked state I was in prevented me from using my psychic powers. Without them, I was trapped. I kicked the wall. It was impenetrable. Whatever it was made of, it didn't crack an inch. All my strength did nothing against the wall. I couldn't break out.

I didn't dare step further into the room. The pure abyss of darkness scared me. There was no telling what was in front of me. One wrong step could have spelled doom for me. I touched the rough wall. With one hand on the wall, I walked around the far edges of the room. My hand never left the wall as I walked.

It wasn't a large room from what I could tell. Sharp corners with a ninety-degree angle indicated the room was in the shape of a square or rectangle. I groped up and down the walls, searching for an exit. There were no doors or windows.

My only option was to calm down and try to teleport again. I sat down with my back against the wall. The room was much warmer than outside. Sweat accumulated on my forehead. I closed my eyes and imagined my bedroom. Memories of home flashed through my mind. Nothing happened. I wracked my brain to no avail. A thunderstorm brewed in my head. The constant worrying exhausted me. I was trying to think so hard that I forgot to breathe. It made me dizzy.

Each time I attempted to concentrate, my panic set in and steered my thoughts in another direction. Psychic energy buzzed within me. It coursed through me like electric blood. With my eyes shut, I breathed deeply. The energy pooled in my mind. *Calm down, think about home, and teleport there,* I instructed myself. *Don't think about this place and how you're trapped.* In an instant, the energy dissipated. Psychic energy was fickle. One doubt, one small thought alone was all it took for my connection to this wonderous energy to be severed. A dam formed within my mind. It blocked any access to the river of strange energy that fueled my psychic powers. Without it, I felt empty.

As time went on, I started to lose hope. Eventually, I was too tired to think. All thoughts vacated my head. The room and I were an empty void. A strange feeling washed over me. It cleansed and rejuvenated my body. There was no need to be afraid. It felt as though I were meant to be in this strange room. The room and I were connected. After all, teleporting was the only way in or out.

The odd, soothing feeling took over. With my mind cleared, it was easier to focus. I breathed in and exhaled as slowly as I could. My bedroom appeared in front of me. It was only in my mind. I imagined teleporting home. The smell of fresh bedsheets streamed into my nose. When I opened my eyes, there was red dust around me. The dust disappeared in an instant. I had done it! I had teleported home! A wave of relief rolled and crashed inside of me. I could teleport! What couldn't I do? What else could I do?

The thought of that peculiar room sent a shiver down my spine. I forced it out of my mind. All the fear and panic poured out of me. Teleportation was fascinating, though I wasn't good at it. I needed to practice. That could not happen again. I could not allow myself to get trapped in some random location. Oliver meowed at me. He rubbed his cheek against the leg of my bed. I didn't tell him what happened. It was too creepy to think about. The darkness of that room was etched in my memory. There was a soul-sucking dreadful quality to it.

7

RETURN OF THE OOOM OOOMS

A dab of blue, minty toothpaste squirted onto my toothbrush. The rubbery handle dripped with saliva. Bianca wanted to hang out with me in Princeton! I rushed to get ready. My powers made my hand move back and forth in a blur. "Ah!" I blurted out. The swift speed and pressure of my toothbrush hurt my gums. I raised my toothbrush once again to finish brushing my teeth. That time, I moved slowly to stop my strength from hurting me. There was something odd about my teeth. They felt different. My canine teeth were bigger and sharper, like the fangs of a cat. I carefully rubbed them with my fingertip, and they retracted to a normal length. It was like how a cat's claws could retract, except with fangs.

"That's really weird," I said to myself. I had retractable cat-fangs. I was glad I could retract them because it would've been weird to always walk around with vampire teeth. I observed my fangs one last time in the mirror. They had retracted back to the same height as the rest of my teeth. They remained sharper than the others, though. "Huh," I commented, admiring my bizarre powers. It was convenient, yet strange.

I checked myself out in the mirror. I was still wearing my long red winter pajamas, and my short brown hair was all messed up from sleeping. My bangs were a little too long. A quick fix I loved was to apply hair gel to make my bangs stand up and brush them out of my face. In seconds, my incredible speed allowed me to dash out of the bathroom and throw on a pair of grey sweatpants and a black long-sleeved shirt. A black jacket was hastily scooped up to combat the cold later.

My phone buzzed in my pocket. It was a text from Bianca saying, "Meet me outside Nassau Hall at 12!" I dashed downstairs as fast as I could. My hand had barely touched the doorknob when my Dad stopped me.

"Where are you going?" he questioned.

I turned around slowly to see my Dad wearing an old blue hoodie with multiple paint splatter spots. That was his go-to indoor look, regardless of what the temperature was.

"What are you doing home?" I asked, frowning.

"Mom wanted me to take care of you while you're home from school," he answered. He tried to look casual by leaning on the bathroom door frame. It looked too much like he was trying to be a hip youngster.

"You're going to take off from work for the whole week?" I asked.

"No, I can work from home," He replied, pointing towards his laptop on the island counter. "Mom wanted to stay home with you, but she has to teach class."

My Dad worked in advertising. As far as I knew, all his work could be done on a computer, making it possible for him to work from home at times.

Ooom! Ooom! Ooom!

No way, that sound is back! It couldn't have come at a worse time. Bianca was already in Princeton waiting for me, and my Dad was trying to strike up a conversation. I had to get out of there! "Oh. I'm going to Princeton with a friend. Is that okay?" I asked. It was hard to hide my concern with that strange noise ringing in my ears.

"Yeah, sure, just text me what time you'll be coming home, or else, *I'll* text you the time that you *have* to be home!" he threatened as he walked back to his laptop. "You need a ride?"

"No, I have a ride," I paused, "in fact, I think they're here now!" I lied as I walked out the front door.

"Ok, bye! Don't be too late!"

I waved goodbye and shut the door behind me. I imagined Nassau Hall, the grand, ivy-covered building in Princeton. The front entrance had lion statues on each side with a stone path leading up to it. A cold sensation ran through my body. Something felt wrong. It broke my concentration.

I focused back on Nassau Hall, taking in every detail I could remember. That time, I saw spots of red across the ground, some by the street and a few by the windows of the building. *Those spots must mean I shouldn't teleport there,* I assumed. It was like there were red stains on the building inside my memory. I pictured the front steps of Nassau Hall, and in the blink of an eye, I was there. I ended up teleporting right behind Bianca.

"Hey!" I greeted.

"Whoa!" Bianca yelped. She jumped in surprise and turned around, displaying a bright, red, embarrassed smile.

"Sorry, I didn't mean to scare you," I apologized, holding back a grin.

"Did, did you just?"

"Teleport? Yeah," I replied as if it were a casual thing to do.

"That's so cool! You might wanna be careful. There are a lot of people around here," Bianca whispered.

"Don't worry about it." I glanced over my shoulder. A few people walked around, talked, shopped, or took pictures. I was right. The places they were facing were all the spots that appeared red when I imagined Nassau Hall. That cold chill must have been part of my cat-like instincts. My powers, though different, were working together!

"Come on! Let's get something to eat!" Bianca declared. She waved at me to follow her. Bianca turned to check a stoplight before crossing the street. I followed as she speed-walked to make it across in time. Her brown boots scampered along without making a sound. "We usually go to this hoagie place when I'm here with Zach. I forget the name of it, but it's life-changing. I think you'll like it," Bianca suggested.

I followed Bianca through Princeton, taking a few turns here and there until we ended up at the hoagie place. She dragged me in so fast that I didn't get to read the restaurant's name. It was a ridiculously small place. There were only three tables and the counter where they take your order. The kitchen was located directly behind the counter.

"Do you like fat sandwiches?" Bianca questioned. I looked up and down her slender frame. The champion of the swim team guzzles down fat sandwiches? Her lips curled into a sly smile. "Mild or spicy? We're splitting a Kaiju!" she declared. The Kaiju was the largest fat sandwich on the menu. It contained hot cherry peppers, homemade hot sauce, buffalo chicken strips, French fries, fried mac and cheese bites, and secret sauce.

"Spicy!" I answered without hesitation. I loved spicy food, especially when my Mom cooked hot Calabrian meals.

Bianca ordered for us while I stood awkwardly by her side. *Ooom! Ooom!* The sound rang out louder than ever before! I had never been this close to it! My head instinctively swiveled toward the sound. I looked like a wierdo, snapping my neck since nobody else heard it. Blood rushed to my face. The embarrassment clouded my mind as we sat down at one of the small, circular tables. The walls were splattered with peeling white paint. Rock music played from an old sound system connected to visible wires running across the ceiling.

"I hope I don't get sauce on my shirt," Bianca prayed while examining her white short-sleeved shirt. "They really drench the heroes in sauce here."

Wearing a white shirt while eating messy food was never a good idea. Bianca's shirt didn't cover her arms, making her more likely to get sauce on herself. Short sleeves in the dead of winter also wasn't the best choice. Goosebumps covered her bare arms. It was almost freezing out, with snow forecasted for next weekend. I had long sleeves and a jacket that Bianca eyed enviously.

"You wanna borrow my jacket?" I asked.

"No, I'm fine," Bianca replied. She rubbed her arms to heat them up. Her response was instantaneous. There was no thought put into it. Bianca shivered and closed her mouth to hide her chattering teeth. I held up my jacket in one hand. "Fine," Bianca mumbled. She grumpily admitted defeat and took my jacket.

"Here you go!" muttered a cook. She wore a yellow shirt with a black silhouette of a buffalo in the middle. Her sauce-stained, white apron covered up the name of the restaurant on her shirt. The lady placed a massive hoagie with two empty paper plates on the table. "You can pay after," reminded the lady as she wiped her sauce-covered gloves on her apron. She turned and walked back behind the counter.

Bianca quickly snagged the larger half. The massive, greasy sandwich tasted better than anything I had eaten since I got my powers. *Of course,* I thought, *I can't taste sweet so spicy food must taste even better now!* It was one of the few meals where the flavor didn't change. Everything tasted exactly as it should.

"Andrew!" Bianca scolded. "Now isn't the time for that," she whispered nervously. It seemed like she was scanning the room for witnesses. Although I was only eating, Bianca was afraid of something I was doing.

"What're you talking about?"

She pointed to her eyes with two fingers and mouthed, "Your eyes."

It was the chicken. The delicious taste made my pupils turn into tiny slits. The meat had triggered some type of cat-like response to the tasty stimulus. I concentrated on my eyes and felt them returning to normal. As a test, I ate another bite of my sandwich. My eyes didn't turn into slits. These strange powers were going to take some getting used to.

"Better?" I asked to double-check.

"Yeah, you're fine now." Bianca's voice was a normal pitch again. "Now, let's talk about what we came here for," she announced with yet another suspicious smile.

"You have sauce on your face."

"Like you don't!" Bianca shot back. She grabbed a couple more napkins from a silver dispenser in the center of the table. There was nothing on her face anymore, yet she wiped it again just to be safe. We had accumulated quite a nice pile of used napkins in a short amount of time.

"So, you, Avery, and Zach will come to my house at one o'clock, ok?" Bianca asked. The way she spoke made it sound more like a command than a question.

"Alright," I agreed.

"I think you should ask her out later, towards the end of the day, after dark. Maybe right before you guys go home." Bianca picked up her sandwich again. She definitely ate more than me. It puzzled me initially, though she was more active and had lean muscles from swimming. All my strength came from my powers. I was only slightly more toned than a stick.

OooooooooOOooommmmmm! That was the most devastating sound yet. My ears were twitching! Bianca's lips twisted in confusion. She could tell something was wrong. My eyes turned into cat-like slits. It was growing obvious when my eyes shifted, and shadows sprang out of nowhere. The source of that sound was close. I had to find it, yet I didn't want to blow it with Bianca. I squirmed in my seat, trying to think of a way out.

"Andrew, are yo-" Bianca's phone cut her off. She glanced down at the screen. "Oop, it's Zach. Give me a minute," Bianca held up her index finger and excused herself from the table. "Hi baby," Bianca greeted in a sweet, high-pitched voice. She had her back turned as she walked away from the table. This was my chance!

The restaurant was on the corner of a four-way intersection. Something odd was happening. The second I stepped outside the ground shook! *Oommmm!* The sound was no longer a low frequency vibrating deep within my eardrums. The sound was real. It was close! Everyone on the street turned in the direction of the sound. It wasn't in my head. I was the only one who could hear it at a distance, but now I was right by it.

My frigid hands fumbled around in my pockets. They were already red by the time I got out my swim goggles. I left my scarf at home. If I ran in short bursts, I could probably bolt a block or two without needing it to aid my breathing. Man, I felt like a dork with goggles on in the middle of the street. *Here goes nothing,* I thought to myself as I took off toward the sound.

The world blurred by me as I ran. *Wub, wub, wub!* The sound was right around the corner. Suddenly, an explosion rocked the building to my left. I turned the corner to finally discover the source of the strange sound. It was a man standing in front of a building with a circular hole in the middle.

How did some random guy make that sound? I inched closer. What was I supposed to do? I had powers. I was supposed to be some hero for Bianca, so does that mean I fight him? Do I just run up and start punching this guy? It felt weird. My face grew hot. I'm wearing goggles in the middle of the street, staring at some strange man in a hockey mask.

The man did not acknowledge my presence. He grabbed a black duffle bag and headed toward a wall. Before I could question his actions, he raised his arm and pointed his palm at the brick wall. An invisible blast shot out from his palm. *Oooom!* It was sound! He was wearing some strange suit that let him attack using sound waves. All those weird repeating frequencies were individual blasts fired by that suit this whole time!

My legs shook as I snuck closer. There wasn't a single thought behind my eyes. All I really wanted was a closer look at that weird suit he had on. It was made of a combination of black armor-like plates and flexible leather or fibrous material of some sort. The most glaring details were the speakers embedded throughout the suit. A massive speaker was in the center of his body, mid-chest, mid-stomach area. Another massive speaker was on his upper back in a higher position than the one on the front. What looked like two smaller speakers were on each elbow and one on each calf.

A woman shrieked as the masked man blasted a small red car out of the way. I ran up and caught it before it could crash into the nearest building! The tiny car was easy to catch yet too heavy to keep holding. I dropped it almost instantly. The windows shattered, and the alarm went off. "Oops," I blurted out. The strange man was now aware of my existence. I guess I fight him now?

"Yo, you gonna play some rock and roll with that suit or-" he didn't let me finish my joke. He aimed his palm at me and fired a sonic blast. My ears hurt before the rest of my nerves could catch up. The concentrated sound felt like an explosion went off in front of my feet. I was flung backward into a parked truck. Glass crumbled into my hair. Dust coated my shoulders. My body felt embedded into the metal frame of the truck.

"Ow, I knew I should've said punk or metal," I choked out. It was hard to keep from coughing. His attacks whipped up too much debris into the air. My vision was off. With great difficulty, I sat up to remove my goggles. The lenses had shattered. That's why my vision was suddenly obscured. Without my goggles, I had no way of running. The man aimed his palm-speaker to my face for a point-blank attack.

OOOM OOMS BAD

These whimsical powers of mine couldn't save me. There was nothing I could do. My rapid heartbeat led me to believe that I was too panicked to use my psychic powers. The well of psychic energy within me was sealed off. It was strange how tangible the blockade felt within my mind. Even on a good day, it took immense concentration to get that aspect of my powers to work. All I could do was clench my hands into fists and brace for impact. I involuntarily flinched, raising my hands to protect my face.

Thunk!

Out of nowhere, a golden glow radiated from my palms! The glow elongated. It stretched out from between my closed fists and then extended past them. As quickly as the shimmering light appeared, it vanished. Only the light left something in its place. It was a black, metal Bo Staff! They were part of our curriculum at Tae Kwon Do. I knew how to use it!

This odd feature took place within seconds. The glow started when my hands moved up to my face and faded by the time they got there. When the Bo Staff appeared out of thin air, it struck the strange man in the chin. It dazed him enough that he didn't fire a point-blank shot. He had to take a moment to adjust his crummy hockey mask. While he stood and struggled to figure out what had happened, I accepted it and moved on. If I was making it out of this alive, I had to act quickly.

My hands gripped the Bo Staff with one palm facing up, the other in. As the man aimed his palm at me, I raised the staff above my head and crossed my arms in a downward strike. The hit was directed into the back of his right leg behind his knee. This caused him to partially lose his balance and fire at the sky. The loud noise hurt up close. There was no time to worry about my ears. I couldn't ease up on him, or he'd obliterate me with that sonic cannon. I uncrossed my arms, pulling my right hand back to me and pushing my left hand up, performing an upward strike.

Thwack!

A piece of his armor flew off his chest plate. It was working. I could beat him. The man must have recognized this at the same time as me. He used the speaker-like apparatus on the back of his elbow to emit small, controlled blasts to amplify the speed of his armored punches. After enduring a hit or two, I dropped the Bo Staff. To my horror, the golden glow consumed it instantly. The staff vanished.

Oooom!

My body was hurled across the street like a ragdoll. The close-range blast didn't kill me; however, it didn't feel too great either. It felt like the sound was vibrating my chest even afterward. The man pressed a button on his sleek, black gauntlet. He didn't look at me. The large speaker in the center of his chest appeared to be vibrating. No sound was produced. He paid me no mind as he picked up the duffle bag he was holding before I had intervened.

"Hey!" I shouted. Nothing came out. There was no sound. No matter how much I yelled, it didn't make a noise. My throat was strained and sore from yelling. At that point, police cars arrived on the scene. Their sirens were silent. My footsteps were silent. An unsettling feeling washed over me. Everything felt cold.

How did I make the Bo Staff appear? I tried to summon the weapon once more. My mind was racing. There was no way I could use my psychic powers at a time like this, yet I must have done something to trigger it earlier. The man was already walking away. "Wait!" I called out. Silence. Nothing made a sound, no cars, no birds, not even me. What did I do to conjure up that staff? Was I magic? Drums pounded in my brain. It wasn't working. What did I do before that I wasn't doing now?

It dawned on me. My hands! I raised my hands from my waist up to guard my face. The glow appeared and vanished, leaving a Bo Staff in its place! It was the action of going from ready position to fighting stance! That was the key. It was hardwired into me from years of martial arts training. That sound-guy was in for it now. I chased after him, weapon in hand. The man pointed a palm at the ground and blasted up a cloud of dust and rubble. I lost sight of him!

Cat-like super hearing didn't help me track him. There was no noise. I spun around in a circle, frantically looking in each direction. The total lack of sound was disorienting. As time passed, I was able to catch my breath. The Bo Staff vanished when I let my guard down. It was too late. The return of the sound of birds and tires confirmed it. He was gone.

9

SO THAT HAPPENED

The thumping in my head grew louder. My face turned bright red. To my left, I spotted the building that the strange man broke into. It was a jewelry store. This powerful sound-guy was a low-level crook, and I couldn't stop him. Nobody got hurt except my ego. The goggles I had brought stared up at me from the rubble. Their shattered lenses reminded me of my failure. I collected them and the scrap of armor I chipped off the weird guy. From there, I retraced my steps back to Bianca.

It was an easy jog back to the hoagie place. The streets had been cleared due to all the commotion of that sonic sound man. I thought of giving him a name, though I honestly hoped I would never see him again. At least there was no one around to see me get my butt kicked. All of that just for gemstones. I couldn't believe it. The sound of arguing pulled me out of my thoughts.

"No, it's- I don't have to tell you, you're not- ok, ok I understand, but I gotta go. I love yo-" Bianca hung up in a huff. It was awkward pretending not to hear any of that. I wouldn't have heard it if I didn't have weirdo cat powers.

"Is everything ok?" I asked carefully. This was new to me. I didn't want to overstep any boundaries.

"Yeah, it's all good. Zach was checking in on me. He noticed I was in Princeton and wanted to make sure I was ok," Bianca smiled. I wanted to ask how he knew where she was, but she changed the topic. Her attitude returned to bubbly quite

52

fast. I wished I could be half as outgoing as her. She wrapped up her half of the hoagie. "I'm not really hungry anymore."

"Really? You were shoveling it down a second ago like you haven't eaten in days and-" I cut myself off. Bianca's face turned redder than mine had in a decade. It was the most self-conscious I had ever seen her.

Police sirens broke the awkward silence. An alarm rang in my head. "You wanna get out of here?" I asked. The commotion outside made me nervous. Totally forgot I should lay low after fighting that guy in the street. There weren't any witnesses to my knowledge. Out of paranoia, I didn't want to stick around to find out if that was true.

Bianca nodded. She gave me a strange look. I must have looked like the cat that swallowed the canary. Her sly expression had the mischievous air of 'I know what you did'. "Here, grab my hands. I can teleport us to-"

As soon as Bianca touched me, the world went dark. My skin grew hot. She squeezed my hand so tight. Unfortunately, my stupid powers teleported me to that horrible prison-like room again. We were cut off from the rest of the world. Hopelessness spread within me. The feeling of unending dread consumed me. It only vanished once I heard an odd noise.

"Shit!" Bianca shrieked.

"What is it?" I gasped.

"I dropped my sandwich," Bianca replied calmly. "Can you let go now? Is it safe? Are we teleporting?" She sounded nervous. I hastily let go of her hand to hide my fear. After she yelped, I'd been squeezing her hand too tight. My heart sank. How could I confess that I had no clue where we were or how to get out? Before I could attempt a lousy explanation, Bianca stepped forward and gasped. The grinding of stone against stone could be heard. It was a pressure plate. The room flooded with light immediately. She triggered it with her footstep.

The dramatic shift in light stung my eyes. Bianca shrieked. In a few seconds, our eyes adjusted to the light. The walls, floor, and ceiling were made from the same yellow-colored stone. It had a luminous quality to it, which bathed the room in light. The bricks that made up the walls were all perfect squares with different engravings on each one. The end of the room had two silver statues of lions. They reminded me of the ones commonly displayed outside of entrances. These statues were not guarding an entrance but an object. The statue on the left was of a tall, male lion with a bulky mane and thick, powerful muscles. The statue on the right was a female lion with smaller yet powerful-looking muscles. Both statues had their mouths wide open, revealing sharp fanged teeth and a large tongue.

A mask was securely locked in each lion's mouth, guarded by their metal teeth. Both masks looked Venetian. It appeared the masks would cover the area around the eyes and the bridge of the nose. The one in the male lion's mouth was white with purple, green, and black patches around the eyes. The mask had a fancy gold trim around the entirety of its border. Another flat, gold border was painted around the edge of the eye holes. The middle part, above the nose, displayed a symbol of a golden olive branch or ivy of some kind.

The mask in the mouth of the lioness was a lot larger. It was similar to the male one, except it continued to cover the entire forehead. The female mask also had a gold border, but the main part was only one color, a glossy dark purple that appeared black from some angles. It was much darker than the other mask, giving it a more mysterious look. There weren't any symbols on it, though it did have gold lines resembling ivy that tangled across the mask, shooting in all directions.

"Whoa! Where are we?" Bianca whispered, looking around in awe.

"Legendary Lionheart, let this be your sanctuary," an unfamiliar voice proclaimed. We collectively gasped and scanned the room. Nobody else was there. The lion statue had gleaming eyes. They weren't illuminated earlier.

"Hey Andrew, isn't this our school?" Bianca called out. Her hands ran over an engraving on the wall. Upon further inspection, I could confirm it was a small drawing that heavily resembled our school. What made it worse was the depiction of an explosion and a gas cloud on the brick adjacent to it. My fingertips traced the engravings backward. There were depictions of a cat, people practicing martial arts, a birthday party, a kid skinning his knee from falling off a bike, a kitten gifted to a small child, and endless scenes before and after. It made me uneasy. These hieroglyph-like etchings were events in my life!

54

The golden room spun. "Is this a prank? What is this?" I blurted out. A knot formed in my stomach. An unpleasant combination of fear and rage brewed within me. Bianca didn't believe me when I explained that the walls showed my life events. That was until we found one of a man and a woman standing in front of a lion and lioness statue, us in the present. When we looked at the depictions of the future, they were hard to make out. The drawings were easier to recognize when we knew what the events were. I noticed a man with waves coming out of his palms. The man I fought earlier. We were going to meet again.

Bianca's eyes went wide. Her flesh was covered in goosebumps. "This room is a big gift box for you?" she exclaimed. I walked over to the wall she was pointing at. The scene was unfamiliar. It looked like she skipped right to the end of the depictions. There was an image of a gift box with the statues inside it next to a clock. This room was a gift sent through time for me to find. Teleportation was the only way in or out. It had to be for me.

What helped me figure it out was an engraving of the Bo Staff I summoned previously. It was one of the gifts sent through time. Bianca was confused. It came to me; I didn't use my powers. That explained how something was teleported to me when I was too freaked out to use my psychic abilities. Although it appeared to be a normal Bo Staff, it was made from technology from the future. It was programmed to teleport to me when my motions summoned it.

To demonstrate it for Bianca, I reached down to my hips and then up to my face. The action mimicked someone pulling something from their belt. A golden light appeared again, only to be replaced with a pair of nunchucks. That was a new one. It was also one of the weapons we used at Tae Kwon Do. It seemed like I had no control over what weapon I received when I summoned them. The nunchucks disappeared when I reversed the motion that summoned them. One of the bricks on the wall glowed for a moment. That brick only had one engraving, a pair of nunchucks. This room was where these weapons were stored. Everything about this place was connected to me in some way. It wasn't easy to keep from throwing up.

"What does that mean? Is the mask for me, too?" I asked in Bianca's direction. She shrugged.

"Careful, Andrew," Bianca warned.

I reached out and grabbed the mask with my fingertips. It was made from a sturdy yet soft material that didn't bend. I tried to remove it from the lion's mouth. It wouldn't budge. The eyes of the lion statue unexpectedly changed to a scarlet red. My last name was Corleone, so I felt I had a good chance of being this Lionheart guy the statue mentioned. Despite this, the statue wouldn't let me take the mask. I decided to demonstrate my powers by responding telepathically. I touched the mask and telepathically replied, *"I am Lionheart!"*

The teeth of the statue retracted slightly. *Click!* The mask released into my hands. The same voice spoke again, this time in a lighter tone, *"Indeed! May these gifts help you on your journey and prevent the worst from happening. Save our timeline. In times of hardship, peer into our eyes."* The statue spoke for the last time. Its voice was a whisper as if to signify it was fading away.

Bianca and I were speechless. I stared into the eyes of the mask, amazed by everything that had happened. I listened to what the statue said and lifted the mask to my face. Instead of wearing it, I held the mask facing me, staring into its eyes as if it were a person. Nothing happened at first. I brought the mask up against my face and peered through its eyeholes. An image flashed in my view. It was the two of us teleporting home, and then I saw Bianca waving goodbye, a glass shattering then rebuilding itself, the sun, me walking into school, trudging through the hallway. I quickly brought the mask away from my face before I could see more visions.

"It showed me the future," I whispered, eyes wide in shock.

"If it's all the same to you, can we go home now?" Bianca begged. She trembled in place. This was a bit too much for both of us. At least I had experienced enough unbelievable occurrences recently that it was a little easier for me not to get overwhelmed. Bianca appeared sick. I nodded and positioned myself next to her. Instead of grabbing my hand, she clutched my shoulder. Her painted nails dug into me.

In an instant, we were in the hallway of my house. Oliver trotted to the front of the door and sat between Bianca and me. His eyes glowed white. Bianca tried to brush off the red dust, but it vanished before she could touch it. *"Sorry, I was trying to teleport Andrew. I didn't realize you were wearing his jacket,"* Oliver apologized. He hadn't used his telepathy in a while. Bianca rolled her eyes. We had enough weird for one day.

"You teleported us to that creepy room?" I asked.

"Huh? No, I was trying to teleport you home since you were trying to do that, but were too stressed to use your psychic powers. You can barely teleport yourself; you don't have the skill to teleport others yet. Try to be more careful next time. Don't put yourself in a dangerous position where you're too freaked out to teleport home," Oliver warned.

Rats, I really thought it was me who teleported Bianca and me around. Oliver slumped over. We raced to his side. He was sleeping. His tiny body didn't have the energy to use psychic abilities to communicate and teleport others here and there. We accidentally took a lot out of him.

A buzzing noise rattled the front pocket of Bianca's jeans. She reached down to pull out her phone. "Shoot! My mom texted me twenty minutes ago," Bianca gasped. "Damn, ten missed calls from Zach too! He's gonna be pissed!" With all the interesting and impossible events, it was no surprise we didn't hear her phone go off. "My mom is out front. I gotta go," she reported sadly. "Bye, Andrew! I'll text you the details about our meet-up with Avery and Zach! Today was, um, interesting. Sounds like you're meant to be a real hero! I can't wait!"

"Bye, Bianca! Remind me to tell you about the weird sound man I fought today!" I called as she walked out the front door.

"Wha- I don't think I want to know," Bianca shook her head as she left. The door clicked shut behind her. She waved goodbye exactly like in my vision. Creepy.

The venetian-looking mask was still in my hands. Without any strings, there was no way for me to keep it on my face. I tried it on anyway. When the mask was within an inch from my face, it leapt from my grasp and suctioned onto me. I stumbled back in shock. No matter how much I moved my head, the mask didn't budge. It was sealed in place.

I wasn't sure how it would protect my identity. The mask didn't cover much. Perhaps it served a different purpose. It did allow me to see the future. Maybe it was linked to my psychic powers. Only I had no intention of using that future sight again. It would ruin me if I spoiled something wonderful or saw something devastating.

My eyes widened with fear. I was not ready for this. I got my powers from an accident, yet that sanctuary acted like it was written. People in the future knew that accidents would happen. It was inscribed on those walls. They sent me resources so I could be a hero to save the future. There was no world-ending danger in my life. The sonic sound man? Was he the danger? The conspiracy at school with Mr. Poundz making that gas? What was I supposed to do? This was all a big mistake. I tried to remove the mask from my face. It wasn't meant for me; I was a random teenager. The mask didn't come off. No matter how hard I tried, it remained planted firmly on my face.

10

LOOK CLOSER

Pain shot through my skin as I tugged at the mask. It was cemented on my face. I started to panic. My Dad was home. I did not want him to see me with a stupid mask glued on me. In time, my hands grew sweaty from my many attempts, preventing me from getting a good grip on the mask. It was no use. The mask remained in place.

I took a deep breath. The mask was supposedly linked to my psychic powers. Those weapons I summoned were able to teleport to me on their own. This mask had to be able to teleport on and off me in a similar fashion. I relaxed my fingers and imagined the mask in my hands. In half a second, the mask was in my right hand. Tiny particles of red dust floated around it. The dumb mask almost gave me a heart attack.

Another sharp pain jabbed into my thigh. *"What now?"* I complained inside my head. Luckily, it was something stupid. Inside my pocket was the broken swim goggles and the piece of that sound-guy's armor. The jagged ends of the armor fragment were poking at me through my pocket. I couldn't help but breathe a sigh of relief. It had been a crazy day; I was not ready for another major issue.

The piece of armor was dead black without light. The material reflected brilliantly when the sunlight hit its smooth, glossy finish. What I found odd was how flexible it was. The torn edges were razor sharp, yet the tiny fragment could bend. Instead of leaving it alone, I tried to use my psychic powers to zoom in and see the material more closely like I had done when I repaired that caution tape.

Tiny dots vibrated in place. Most of these dots were connected. They were arranged in a specific, repeating pattern. Their close arrangement made it difficult to tell where one molecule started and the next began. I needed a piece of scrap paper. My backpack was still on the chair by the island counter. I sat down and got to work.

A rough sketch proved incorrect. There were too many bonds on one carbon atom. I zoomed in with my psychic atomic sight once more. It was impossible to draw while my vision was consumed entirely by tiny particles. I had to look, draw, look, draw until I created a feasible structure. After a few attempts, I had finally created a structure that, at least to my high school knowledge, was realistic.

Chemistry was not one of my classes in high school anymore. That was a course for the sophomore students below me. When I took that class, we were required to download software for drawing stick and ball representations of organic compounds. That program ate up a lot of space on my computer, yet there was a chance I hadn't deleted it yet. I crossed my fingers as I booted up my laptop. There it was! No wonder my computer was so slow. It took up a quarter of my storage.

Within the software, I began to recreate the structure I had drawn. It wasn't easy since I had to double-check which elements were in what compound. My Dad entered the room before I could finish. He removed his laptop from the counter to help give me space for mine.

"What am I looking at?" he questioned.

"Uh, homework," I lied. "It will be due when school reopens, so I might as well get it out of the way now."

Luckily, the suspicious response went over his head. He believed me since I always completed chores first so I could enjoy time off. Most of the time, he did not take any interest in my homework. The complex doodles of chemical structures somehow caught his eye. "I have not been able to help with your homework for years," he chuckled. His face crumpled in confusion. I laughed as he made weirder and weirder faces at my diagrams.

"If you need any help," he paused, "ask your mother." I smiled as he carried his laptop off to his office. When he was out of sight, I turned back to my work.

At last, I had completed the structure. The software could also label the structures you made. I highlighted my structure and clicked the label tab. To my surprise, the IUPAC name displayed prominently underneath it. I did it! I discovered what the material was! A smile wedged its way onto my face. My investigation wasn't over yet. I copied the chemical name into a search engine to try and find the common name.

"Well, that was easy," I stated in my head. The search results turned up the exact name of the material: Onarm. It was a failed creation by Armageddon. There were countless articles about this stuff. Apparently, it was responsible for the biggest stock market drop in Armageddon's history. The material was described as more flexible and protective than the leading bullet-proof materials on the market. Onarm was cheaper, lightweight, and protected against stabbing, unlike other bullet-resistant materials. It was a massive failure that cost Armageddon millions when it was discovered that Onarm was carcinogenic.

I stared at the piece of Onarm I had touched several times that day. Using my psychic powers, I levitated the material and shot it as far away as possible. The fragment broke the kitchen window as I cast it out like lightning. My powers were able to repair the window afterward. That was an overreaction on my part. If I had read a little further, I would have seen that the most dangerous part was the fumes created when manufacturing the material. However, it clearly stated that a bulletproof vest made from this material would be hazardous to wear. Prolonged exposure, including skin contact, could be deadly.

This was the second time that Armageddon popped up. The first was the pen in Principal Perfetto's office. Before that, there were the instruments in Mr. Poundz's room. No, some of the instruments were made by Argone, not Armageddon. I had to start writing all this down. It was starting to get overwhelming. There was too much going on with the gas, the sonic man, the principal, the sanctuary, Oliver's powers, and none of it was connected. I was an octopus, with each tentacle pulled in a different direction.

One thing was clear. Armageddon was worth looking into. That man had access to a material that was banned from being sold or produced. The suit he wore must be the only one in existence. If I could trace his steps to find where he got that mechanized armor, I would have a solid starting point. By looking into Armageddon, I would be killing two birds with one stone: Principal Perfetto's involvement with the company, and the sound man.

A quick search revealed all the Armageddon facilities in New Jersey. There were warehouses, labs, factories, offices, everything you could imagine throughout the state. Articles boasted about the Armageddon Greenhouse location's great success in developing potently medicinal plants, the Optics Division revealed a new high-tech helmet, the Sustainability Center made a minor breakthrough in desalinating seawater. What didn't they do?

Nothing mentioned sound-based technology. The company started in New Jersey. It would not be easy to pick the right location to investigate. As I narrowed the search to a radius within my immediate area, a sound brought my attention away from my research. *Oooommm! Wub, wub, wub!*

11

TIME TO BEGIN

The mask reappeared on my face with just a thought. Before I could process what was happening, I was surrounded by a shimmer of yellow light. After a second, the glow was gone. When it cleared, I was wearing a martial arts uniform. It wasn't mine, but it was extremely similar to the uniform I wore at Tae Kwon Do. There were some key differences. My real first-degree black belt had my name on it in English and Korean. This new black belt read "Lionheart" stitched in proud gold letters. Assumedly, the Korean on the other side said "Lionheart" as well.

I tugged at the uniform top to read the back. Where the uniform would normally have my name, this one spelled out "Lionheart" in black capital letters. The martial arts academy logo was replaced with a new one in the center of my back. The emblem appeared to be a silhouette of a lion from the side, stalking forward on quiet paws. The uniform's lapel had a red, white, and blue ribbon sewn into it. It was a standard white martial arts uniform other than those simple changes.

I tried to calm down and focus. My heart was already beating fast, and I hadn't done anything. This had to be another gift from that weird room. That place drove me crazy. I couldn't wrap my head around it. There were enough mysteries in my life. I couldn't begin to understand those statues, inscriptions, and gifts. Each time I tried to move on and forget about that place, something like this would happen to remind me.

I had promised Bianca that I'd use my powers to help people. It was too much. I was nothing. I was nobody. There were people better suited to handle the sound man. Although no one else had my powers. I wasn't a detective, and I wasn't a hero. It felt all too fake. Another thought crossed my mind. If it worked, if I could save people daily, I would be seen. My heart swelled. A smile formed across my face. Love and fame never felt so obtainable to me before. It was worth a try. If I can't figure out why Mr. Poundz made the gas at school, or who allowed him to, or if the sonic sound man proves too challenging, I could always call it quits. Before that happened, I promised Bianca I'd try this hero stuff.

Smoke billowed in the distance. The sonic guy should be more discreet next time. Footsteps echoed down the hall. I had to get going before my Dad saw me dressed like a weirdo. Red dust disappeared as I teleported to the middle of a nearby street. Luckily, I could see smoke dispersing in the sky. I bolted towards it.

The mask activated a light greenish-blue shield over the eyeholes to keep the wind out of my eyes. I was able to run with my eyes open! It was time to test how fast I could run. My feet pounded against the blacktop. The street provided a clear path without any obstacles except cars. I ran on the wrong side of the road for a moment before leaping over a car. I changed lanes and continued running alongside the cars on the correct side of the street. The soles of my already-worn shoes shredded away against the rocky asphalt.

I dashed past car after car, weaving in and out of traffic. Eventually, I realized I could run on the shoulder where the cars couldn't drive. Now that I truly had no obstacles, I ran a tad faster. My speed increased to a degree nobody had thought possible on foot. After a few minutes of running, leaping and dodging, I spotted a house on fire. A huge black cloud of smoke rose from the house. Flames poured out of the windows.

"Ah! Oh, my ugh," a voice gasped behind me. I turned to see a few people standing around the yard. There was a lady who I assumed was the one who jumped when I appeared and two men who must've been concerned neighbors. They were scared by my strange appearance. The woman took several careful steps away from me. I turned back to face the burning building. Two children were screaming from the second floor. Those weird sounds of the sound guy's sonic blasters had stopped. He was long gone. The flames glowed in my eyes. They danced around, mocking me, daring me to enter. I swallowed hard and headed in.

The heat of the floor immediately baked my feet. My shoes were completely worn out from running. Now, they were starting to melt from the fire, too. "I guess I don't need these anymore," I commented as I took them off and tossed them into the fire. The burned floor was painfully hot, yet not enough to burn my feet. It was cooler without the shoes on. As long as I didn't get too close to the flames, it should be ok. I examined the hallway. The house was dark with smoke and ash. My ears twitched. There was a faint sound of someone sniffling. I dashed up the burning, dilapidated stairs and into the first room on the left.

A bed was on fire, along with a dresser and closet. There were no signs of anyone in the room. The next room was similar except for blue wallpaper, and the bed was on the left side. Two small children, one boy and one girl, sat on the bed. The girl looked about seven or eight, and the boy had to be a few years younger. They both tried to scream when they saw me but started coughing instead. My mask activated what felt like a triangular-shaped psychic barrier over my mouth. The barrier extended out from the bottom of the mask to the tip of my chin. Fresh air was being teleported inside the covering. It really did have advanced, psychic-linked technology.

The floor gave way beneath me! Although the sudden fall surprised me, I wasted no time jumping back to the bedroom. "Don't be afraid," I comforted. My softspoken demeanor did not aid me in reassuring the children. There was no time to convince them to trust me. We had to evacuate immediately. They huddled together and watched as I crept closer across creaky floorboards. I reached out with one hand as if I wanted one of them to hold it. "We got this," I assured. To my surprise, the little girl took my hand and pulled me toward the window.

"Fireman?" the girl asked.

It wasn't clear if she was asking if I was a fireman or if one was on its way. I replied, "Yes," in an unsure, shaky voice.

65

Conversations had to wait. I grabbed both children, one under each arm. My super-strength allowed me to carry them with ease. I crouched down on the open windowsill, ensuring they would both make it through before leaping out. Soot flaked off their little faces as we glided through the air. We landed back on the street next to the small crowd of people. The kids, still in their pajamas, ran to one woman. They looked sick. The lady had tears running down her face. She ran up to the children and held them tight.

"I'm so sorry!" The woman cried. More tears trickled down her face as she wiped the ash off the kid's faces. "I was only at the neighbor's for a second. I didn't think that-" The woman stopped talking and sobbed. The young girl hugged the lady while the boy stared at me. It was as if he were in a trance.

"Who are you?" he asked in his little voice.

"Mrs. Poundz, are you okay?" one neighbor asked the woman. I was so stunned I could only reply to the little boy with a forced smile. That woman was Mr. Poundz's wife! She lost her husband and now her house. Unless that sound man was Mr. Poundz.

"I'm sorry to interrupt, but are you married to Ken Poundz, the teacher?" I asked. The words blurted out without thinking about her emotional state. It was not a good time to talk to this grieving woman, though I did need answers.

"Ye- yeah," Mrs. Poundz stated solemnly.

"Do you know who could've done this or someone who would want to?" I asked. Mrs. Poundz rubbed her daughter's back. The little girl was glued tight to her mother's hip.

"Maybe someone my husband knew? I don't know. I thought he was just a teacher until two days ago. Now it sounds like he was involved with a bad crowd all this time," Mrs. Poundz explained.

"What do you mean by that?" I asked quickly. There was palpable excitement in my voice.

"They say he acted alone, but he couldn't have! There's no way. The school had to be paying him. Someone had to be! He couldn't have done all that without the school knowing. He just couldn't have!" Mrs. Poundz wailed. I'd struck a nerve.

Unfortunately, Mrs. Poundz was acting on a hunch like me. There was no evidence that someone had been controlling him. The house fire was suspicious, though I couldn't pin it on anyone. The only connection was the sound of the sonic guy's blaster firing over a mile away before I left home. It was only a coincidence that I found this fire while running after that noise. I got distracted again. Next time I hear that sound, I'll chase after it no matter what.

In the meantime, I'd like to keep up with the investigation into this fire. If it were arson, that sound man would be a prime suspect based on the noises I heard beforehand. Until then, it's too perfect to be connected. When the firefighters arrived, I asked one when we'd know the cause of the fire. He looked me up and down. My weird attire did not reassure him that I was someone he could trust. He told me to get lost.

Instead, Mrs. Poundz was the main event. An EMT brushed past me and strolled up to her. The EMT's voice sounded rough. "This has something to do with your husband?" the man accused. He gestured toward the fire. Mrs. Poundz was startled at the bold statement. There were no introductions or gratuities. The EMT had a strict line of questions for her. Another, more helpful EMT lead the kids away from Mrs. Poundz to check on them. "We were here the other day for your husband, and now this? Do you need psychiatric attention? Are you-"

"You're blaming me for this? I am grieving, yes, but I didn't set my house on fire!" Mrs. Poundz spat.

"That's not what I meant to imply. I mean, you're rightfully distracted and distraught. It is possible that in your condition, you may-"

Mrs. Poundz was done talking. A policewoman interrupted the conversation and ushered Mrs. Poundz away. I had taken one step to follow them when another officer blocked my path. "What are you supposed to be?" he asked. Instead of replying, I attempted to step around him. The man stepped in front of me again and threw up a brow. It looked like the policewoman was comforting Mrs. Poundz and leading her to her children. I wished I could listen to their conversation to obtain more clues. The police officer in front of me glared at me as if I owed him answers.

I glanced back at the burning house. Water rained down on it from above. The front windows were completely blown apart into tiny fragments of glass. The left side of the roof was burned to nothing. The little boy continuously rubbed his ears, eyes, and nose. All that smoke and ash was not good for these little ones. An ambulance took the kids in for treatment. I was not needed here. Everything was under control now.

The mask deactivated the mouth shield. With the children safe and sound, I was able to relax. Something stirred within me. A dreadful sound echoed nearby. It was unclear what I was supposed to do as this Lionheart person. All I knew was I had made a promise to Bianca to, at the very least, try to make a difference. Those kids may not have made it if I hadn't been there to save them. The void within me shrunk. It was going to work; I was going to be a hero. I was going to be loved. The eerie sound grew louder.

12

SPEED LIMIT

A gentle hum buzzed in my ears. That sonic-sound-man was out there, yet I couldn't shake the desire to call Bianca. I had saved two kids from a fire! I was a kick-ass hero! She would be so excited to hear from me. At least, I thought she would love this new development. I started to doubt myself. We were only beginning to get to know each other. Would it be weird to call her? I didn't want to scare her away by constantly texting and calling her.

"She's just a friend, and she knows you like Avery, so there's nothing wrong with calling a friend," I instructed myself. "However, you do need her help in winning over Avery's affection, so you do have a good reason to be cautious about bothering her too much."

Screw it, just do it! I reached toward my pocket only to feel my leg. My Lionheart getup is a martial arts uniform, no pockets. That meant my phone was at home with the rest of my normal attire. It's not too late. I could teleport my phone to me, can't I? Picturing my phone in my hand did nothing. A pair of nunchucks appeared in my hand when I attempted to summon my phone the same way I summoned a weapon. Teleporting objects had to be possible. Oliver was able to teleport others. All I had to do was clear my mind. Last time, I had to think calmly to use my psychic powers. Nothing happened.

"Come on," I groaned. A car honked at me. There I was, standing on the side of the road in a martial arts uniform

69

with a venetian mask on, cursing at my hand for not having a phone appear in it. I paced back and forth underneath a speed limit sign. *Maybe I should start out smaller, something I can already do.* Houses lined each side of the road. I would have more privacy on one of those rooftops than out on the street. My eyes locked in on a roof three houses down and across the street. A few deep breaths later, and I felt electricity arc within my chest. Psychic energy rose within. Red dust scattered as I reappeared on the rooftop of my choice.

That was progress, though what I really wanted was to summon my phone. My fingers gripped the fridged, torn edges of black roofing. The material felt like sandpaper on my hands. I peeked over the edge of the roof. Nobody could see me up here, nor would anyone think to look at a random rooftop. Without the distraction of speeding cars, I was positive I'd be able to focus and teleport my phone. I scrambled to the top of the house and leaned against the chimney. When I held out my hand and concentrated real hard… nothing happened.

There was no mental block on my psychic powers. The energy was there, though faintly. It was as if I were capable of doing it, yet lacked the strength. *Ooooom!* I was distracting myself. There would always be time to talk to Bianca later. I had to stop that sound-guy before he disappeared again. If I could teleport, why was I running all the way there? I tried to picture that man. His face was covered with a hockey mask, his suit was all black with silver speakers everywhere. No, that wasn't right. The speakers were in specific locations. The thunderous energy flowing within simmered into a trickle. Teleporting to him was not going to work.

If I couldn't teleport to the source of the sound, perhaps I could teleport near it? I tilted my head until I found the correct direction. The reverberating sound in my ears made me wince. It gave me such an uneasy feeling. It was hard for me to comprehend that only I could hear it. The energy swelled within me when I thought of home. The sound was coming from the opposite direction. What town was that? The energy dissipated. *No!* I'm not sure if I've ever been down that direction. As far as I knew, the road off the main highway only led to trees.

Teleporting only worked if I could perfectly picture the person or place I was teleporting to. That's why I was able to teleport up here so easily. I could see it. The shift in psychic energy allowed me to judge the limits of what I can and can't do. A grey area remained where I felt a whisper of energy tapping me on the shoulder, though not enough to be useful. It would have been great if a cat that slept all day wasn't my only resource on how these powers worked.

Red dust appeared and ceased in a split second. I teleported as far as I could see into the distance. I tried this a few more times before I felt the energy within slow to a crawl. A thunderstorm brewed inside my head. The energy stuttered and sparked. It felt like I was working out a new muscle that had been dormant for too long. I was back to running towards the sound. It was a bad idea to drain myself of all that energy, but I had no clue what the limitations were beforehand.

13

GROWING PAINS

This house fire was a mile away. When I turned a corner, my ears twitched. *Oooom!* The sound man's sonic blasters resounded in my eardrums. There was something else too. It was a new sound. This new sound was consistent. Once I arrived, it was clear this new sound was the alarm of a security system.

It had to be the sonic sound man! The building to my right was under attack! Using my psychic sight, I zoomed in on the building. There was a man inside with a gun drawn. A smirk spread across my face. I had recharged enough energy to teleport right next to the guy to surprise him. *Boom!* I punched the man square in the face as I landed on a grey, concrete floor. I stopped to quietly take in my surroundings before anyone else noticed me.

"Wait, you're not the sound man," I blurted out. The thief took a disk out of his pocket and hurled it at me. A deafening screech emitted from the disk. They were using sound-based weapons. It wasn't the sound guy, but they were most definitely connected.

"Run!" The man commanded. Two men dashed out the closest exit, holding what appeared to be a duffle bag. The terrible, high-pitched sound incapacitated me. It ruined my chances of using my psychic powers again. Alarms within the building didn't help my situation. Cat-like super-hearing was what made everything worse. It felt like I couldn't move. The sound didn't stop until I stomped on the disk, crushing it into pieces.

There were numerous rows of the same type of machines. Whatever the machines made, it didn't look like it was for a single product. From what I could tell, the machines developed different metal parts. The parts looked unfamiliar to me. Cobwebs coated each machine.

I inspected the strange contraption on my left. A hefty vest lay on a conveyor belt. The vest appeared only half finished. It looked like some type of body armor. Only the front half of the chest plate was completed. The fabric of the armor felt strange. The chest plate wasn't made from metal like I had thought; it was bizarre, fuzzy material. I bent the armor slightly in my hands to test the durability of the unusual substance. It was Onarm. The armor dropped from my hands immediately. There must have been no fumes in the building since my mask didn't activate the mouth shield like in the fire.

"Armageddon" was printed in white letters to stand out against the black background of the armor. Behind the word Armageddon was a red lightning bolt. It was familiar. The logo was so close to the Argone logo. There were only subtle differences in the font.

A man dressed in all black, along with a black ski mask, shouted at me. I hopped over the row of machines in front of me. A certain weightlessness filled me whenever I jumped. I landed a few feet in front of the man. He was a bit stunned either by my speed or my outfit.

"Really, a ski mask?" I laughed. The man ignored me and reached inside his jacket pocket. I sprang forward and uppercut him in the chin with my right hand before he could pull something out from his coat. A gun fell to the ground as he collapsed to the floor. This gun had a speaker at the end of it. It looked like a prototype of what the sound man used. The exposed wires and motherboard made me think it was an earlier version of the sonic cannon. Either that or a hastily made one to quickly arm his cronies.

"Two down, four to go," I whispered to myself.

"Get him. He's a witness!" screamed one of the men. They scrambled around to get their weapons. Two men came rushing at me with knives. The other two took out their sonic guns and aimed. My mask activated the eye shield. I dashed to the side of the men carrying long, sharp knives and ran up the front wall of the building. I wasn't fast enough to run on walls as I felt my feet grow lighter. Gravity gave me a speed boost as I bolted down from the wall to attack the armed men.

Their blasters were small, but considering the damage they could do; I was still scared. *Oom! Ooom!* Two men fired at the same time. As soon as I heard the hum of their weapons charging for the shot, I reached to my belt and pulled out a weapon in each hand. Escrima sticks appeared. It felt random, though I could make it work. I had at least a year or two of training with escrima sticks.

The men didn't have time to react as I ran up and slammed their guns with my escrima sticks. Pieces of metal flew off their blasters as they crashed to the floor. I struck the first man with my right escrima stick, swinging it from my right shoulder across to my left hip. I hit the second man by bringing the same escrima on my hip back to my shoulder. The man bent over and held his temple in pain. He didn't fall to the ground like the other three men. I hit him one more time by lightly jabbing the handle of the escrima into his back. It was only enough force to bring him down. It didn't cause much more pain.

At that point, the two men with knives were only a few feet away from me. They wore the same clothes as the rest of the men: black leather jackets with a black shirt underneath. Black pants and a ski mask completed their classic robber outfit. The blades of the knives shimmered with reflected light from the vast factory ceiling.

The man on my right came at me, holding his knife in a reverse grip, slashing downward while the other man tried to stab me. I used my right escrima stick to block the slash and my left to stop the stab, forming a square block with my weapons. The man on the left dropped his knife. A loud echoing clang emitted when it hit the ground. The now defenseless man started to run away. The other man, however, pushed back on my escrima stick to try and stab me. His eyes watered as he tried to force my arm back. He placed both hands on the knife handle and pushed with all his might.

I kept my arm up, pushing back with my escrima stick, and kicked him in the stomach with my right foot. He flew backward and landed on the hard cement floor. He moaned as he sat up and grabbed his stomach. I took a deep breath. There wasn't a single scratch on me. My heartbeat relaxed.

"It's over," I announced. My escrima sticks teleported away. All the thieves were down except for one. The man I disarmed was trying to run away. My nerves were calmer now. Psychic energy flowed within me. "No, you don't," I taunted.

I teleported directly in front of the man, preventing him from exiting the building. I immediately punched him in the chest. He fell to the ground with a resounding thud.

"Wow! This would've been a ton easier if I could use my psychic powers the whole time," I laughed. The man had no time to react when I punched him. It was a major stepping stone. My first time beating a group of thieves.

"We did it! They got away!" the man I had kicked to the ground cheered. The man I had just hit chucked. Soon, all the men were laughing as they licked their wounds. My mind raced. I stopped them all. Why were they happy?

"What do you mean?"

"We stayed to fight, while the others got away with the loot. With what we're about to get paid for this job, it won't matter if we do a brief stint in jail. You, however, you may need a lawyer," the man spat.

Red and blue lights flashed against the blurred glass of the front doors. Car doors slammed shut outside. The silhouette of policemen cast against the red and blue light. Whatever they had set out to accomplish had been taken care of. A memory flashed in front of me. Two men left in the beginning while I was incapacitated. Tae Kwon Do practice was any minute. There was no time to track those thieves down. My parents would kill me if I wasn't home in time. I had won the fight but didn't see the bigger picture. Therefore, I had lost. Lionheart was a fraud.

14

AVERY IS HERE. DON'T BLOW IT

A vibrant red car sat in Bianca's driveway. It was no ordinary car. That car was easily recognizable as it was the most expensive car in the school parking lot each day. Zach was the nasty kid that drove it. He was so proud of it. His uncle gave it to him for his birthday. Zach teased my friend Mark once because he didn't get a car for his birthday. Seeing his car made me hesitate. I felt bad. Bianca was a great person, yet Zach's presence made the walk up her driveway difficult. Today was the day she had arranged for me to hang out with Avery. I could stomach Zach for that.

Mrs. De La Cruz answered the door. She was a bit shorter and slightly more tanned than Bianca. Bianca's mom had the same brown hair and brown eyes as her.

"Hello Mrs. De La Cruz, is Bianca there?" I greeted.

"Oh, I'm sorry, you must be Andrew. Come on in!" Mrs. De La Cruz smiled warmly. "Bianca, your friend is here!" she called out behind her. "They're out back." Mrs. De La Cruz pointed to a sliding glass door down the hall.

Not everyone was out back. I stumbled upon Zach in the kitchen. He stood behind a green marble countertop with a bright-colored oak base that matched the cabinets. The counter formed a square U-shape connected to the back wall. The cabinets followed the same pattern, curving to the right and ending at the fridge. The king-sized, silver refrigerator dispensed water into Zach's glass. He didn't notice me. My cat-like abilities let me tread silently.

Finally, Zach saw my reflection on the glossy doors of the fridge. He spun around frantically. The refrigerator accidentally dispensed some water onto the floor. He sported a painful-looking black eye as well as new bruises on his cheek. There was a scrape or two on his arms as well. Leave it to Zach to find a way to get into trouble while school was closed. There were no games recently. He likely got into a fight.

"You're here?" Zach groaned. He turned towards the back door, "Bianca!" he shouted. His face turned red as he waited for her to come. In seconds, Bianca rushed up to the glass door. She grabbed the handle and slid the door across in a hurry. "What?" she asked.

"Why is he here?" Zach demanded, pointing at me.

"I told you he was coming," Bianca responded in a mocking tone.

"What? When?" Zach whined and clenched his hands tight. The pressure caused the glass cup in his right hand to slip out of his grasp. It fell to the floor and shattered into minuscule shards. I was speechless. It was the same glass cup from the vision I had a while back. The glass broke into the same pattern of pieces. My vision had come true. This simple act caused me to be in awe of the cup. The ongoing bickering was not as interesting anymore.

"Let's talk about this outside where you can't break anything." Bianca led Zach out the back door. She quickly poked her head back inside. Her head jerked toward the backyard.

They walked outside and down a small set of concrete steps. Once I made sure no one was looking, I crouched down next to the mess of broken glass. I concentrated on the jagged shards. They gradually floated in the air. I moved them towards where the cup had hit the ground. The pieces slowly joined together, recreating the shape of the cup. I vibrated the molecular orbitals closer together until the cup was repaired.

The cup felt as if it were solid. It was like nothing had happened. A sense of pride flowed through me as I admired my work for a moment. It didn't last long. I didn't want to keep Bianca waiting. I scooted past the table and slid the back door open. Zach and Bianca were still going at it.

"Everyone's been saying you kissed him! Now you're hanging out with him. You said you were alone in Princeton. Be honest, were you with him?" Zach boomed. Beads of sweat formed in his spikey black hair. He cut it so short you could see the skin on his head. His hands flailed in his jacket pockets. Despite the freezing weather, his prized varsity jacket remained unzipped. At least he could still gesture wildly while keeping his hands warm this way.

"Hey!" I interrupted. "She didn't kiss me. She saved my life!"

Zach turned to face me. His teeth ground together. "Look, I wasn't there. I don't know what happened, but I don't want you talking to her," he warned. Bianca shot him an insulted look. Zach shrugged and took a deep breath. He placed an awkward hand on my shoulder as if we were pals. "I apologize. I got too heated too quickly. I'm going through a lot right now, and these rumors about my girlfriend cheating on me with someone like-" He interrupted himself to choose his words more carefully.

My eyebrows were raised in surprise. This guy was the bane of my existence, and here he was, trying to act all calm and cool. Bianca stood silently with her arms crossed. She let Zach finish his thought.

"My friends have been pretty ruthless teasing me about it is all. I think you two need to spend some time apart until these rumors die down, you know?" Zach suggested.

"You weren't there!" Bianca began to cry. "He was passed out on the ground. A crowd of people swarmed around him. They said he wasn't breathing. Nobody helped him. I knew what to do. I had the training and certification from swim team. I saved him! Mouth-to-mouth resuscitation. I did what I had to; I did what was right! I don't care about rumors. We know the truth. That's good enough. I can be friends with whoever I want, and you can't take this out on Andrew. He didn't do anything wrong!" Tears trickled down her face. She sniffled and rubbed her nose on her long, white sleeves. "You weren't there," she repeated.

Zach rushed to her side. He held her close and rubbed her back up and down. I'd never seen him console anyone before. There may be more to him than I thought. "Shhhh, shhhh, shhhh," Zach cooed. He massaged her shoulders as he broke their embrace to speak. Bianca looked down. Her hair cascaded in front of her, obscuring her face. Zach tried his best to look her in the eye as he spoke.

"Shhh, you're overreacting, baby," Zach comforted. "I never said you can't be friends with him. You can be friends with anyone you want. You're great at making friends. We just need those horrific rumors to go away, is all." Zach let go and patted her back. Bianca remained silent. Her face was hiding behind her hair. The slight movements of her head made it clear she was crying. It was so soft my enhanced hearing could hardly register it.

The strangest thing happened. Zach smiled at me as if nothing were wrong. He calmly held her hand in his. In a way, I understood Zach. Rumors were going around that she kissed me instead of saving my life with CPR. It must have made him insecure to see that I was friends with her now. I'd feel the same way if I were in his shoes. Even seeing her with him now made me burn with jealousy. Not that I was jealous that he was with Bianca, but jealous that someone like him had a girlfriend that loved him dearly.

This drama was entertaining, but it wasn't mine to participate in. My main worry was Avery. I had promised Bianca that I would talk to her. Hopefully I could at least become friends with her if she doesn't seem into me. *I can do this,* I thought nervously. Well, I'd need Avery to be here first. "Um, is Avery here?" I asked. My voice sounded more concerned than I intended.

"Yeah, follow the pathway to the pond," Bianca replied. She hadn't returned to her normal, excited self yet. A slender finger pointed to a forest of trees lining her backyard. There was a small gap in between two pine trees and what looked like a thin dirt trail buried in the shadows. "I need to talk to Zach. I'll meet you two down there!" Bianca called as she stepped back inside. Zach scoffed and followed her in.

A small dirt path cut through the forest. The ground was a sea of dead pine needles. A few wildflowers broke through the pine needle ocean, looking like ships at sea. My steps were silent. The path gently curved to the left, preventing me from seeing what was ahead. There were fewer trees further down the path. Spots of sunlight broke through the leaves. Eventually, I made it to a sharp left turn and arrived at a gargantuan pond. The forest was so dense that the pond seemed to have been bursting with light! My powers made it appear too bright. I adjusted my eyes to see like a normal person. The pond remained magnificent.

Although the pond of sunlight was amazing, it wasn't what left me breathless. There, sitting at the edge of a small dock, was Avery. It was the only dock in the pond. This was no surprise since the pond was not for swimming, only fishing. A moldy sign stated so. The dock was chock full of loose and broken planks. The boards were green with age.

A few steps closer Avery came into focus. The blinding light of the pond subsided; Avery was no longer a silhouette. My heart pounded louder than a drum. It felt like my chest was hollow except for my reverberating heartbeat. She wasn't doing anything, yet I was awestruck. She sat with her legs stretched out before her, staring at the glistening water.

Birds and crickets sang louder as if to announce my arrival. The planks where the dock met the dirt were covered in mud. Dried pine needles sprinkled the top of the dock. Caution was required to step onto the platform without slipping in mud. The next challenge was avoiding the splintered planks waiting to give in. Avery didn't move. Part of me wasn't sure if she knew I was there. I'd run headfirst into danger before, yet this was more nerve-wracking. Each plank creaked as I carefully made my way to the end of the dock.

Avery crossed one leg over the other and adjusted her hair. A white wool jacket kept her warm as her red shirt wasn't thick enough for the winter weather. Fluffy brown boots and black pants completed her outfit. Unlike me, it was clear she had fashion sense. The wind blew her long, golden-blonde hair to the side. It glowed a marvelous light yellow in the sun. She raised one hand to brush her hair behind her. When settled, her hair almost touched the dock. She tilted to the right a little, allowing the sun to shine upon the shadowy area behind her, creating a path of light from my feet to the space beside her.

My legs carried me forward as if in a trance. Avery finally turned toward me. "Hey," she greeted warmly. There was a soft warmth in her voice that melted away all my worries. It felt impossible to talk to someone so flawless, though all it took was for her to speak first, and the butterflies settled.

"Hey," I smiled.

She scooted to the right, inviting me to sit next to her. I crouched beside her, sitting with my legs slightly bent to keep from hanging over the edge of the dock. Out of all the insane experiences the past few days, hanging out with Avery was the most unbelievable thing that had happened to me. She was still, silent, like a powerful god.

Avery appeared deep in thought. It was unnatural how perfect she looked. Her face was stolen from an angel. Her bright blue eyes and white smile contrasted against her olive skin. No movie star could compare to her slender face and radiant smile. She was beauty incarnate.

"You're one of Zach's friends?" Avery asked. Her tone sounded disappointed.

I felt my heart skip a beat. "No, I'm friends with Bianca," I replied. On the outside, I was calm. On the inside, I was freaking out.

"Really?" Avery asked. She was oddly enthusiastic about my answer. Her deep blue eyes were a lot darker than I remembered. They lit up as if I had answered her question correctly and passed a test. "It's been hard for her to make friends lately as you know."

"I don't know. What's wrong?" I asked, confused.

Avery didn't like that response. The light dimmed within her. "Zach hates everyone," she stated plainly. Her tone was expressionless.

"That's good news. I thought Zach only hated me."

Avery shot me a look. "What do you mean good news? It's terrible!" She tried to frown, yet she still managed to smile at my joke.

"No, of course, that's horrible. I'm sorry," I apologized.

"Zach gets jealous pretty easily," Avery paused as if the story brought back bad memories. "His parents are the same way, very paranoid about everything. Hopefully, you never have to go to his place," she laughed. Her eyes looked distant. It felt like she was dancing around something she wanted to tell me.

"Is something wrong? I can leave you alone if you want me to?" I offered. Usually, I was the silent one. Her long pauses between thoughts made me wonder if my company was welcome.

81

A gentle smile replaced her poker face. She sighed to herself. A frozen breeze blew her hair aside. "Nothing is wrong, just overthinking. I'm always a ball of stress studying at school, and now I'm worrying over other people's relationships that aren't my business. We should change the subject," she decided quietly. "I don't want them catching us trash-talking Zach. Do you listen to music?"

The sudden burst of energy in Avery's demeanor surprised me. It was as if the random change in subject also changed her personality. "Yeah, I love listening to music," I replied, taken aback.

"Really? Sweet! I have to listen to my playlist at least once a day, or I'll go insane!" Avery laughed. "What type of music are you into? What's your favorite song?"

"Would you like me to show you?" I asked. My smile was impossible to hide. I pulled out my phone to reveal that my earbuds were already plugged in. A giddy excitement flooded through me. It felt so young and childish.

"Duh," Avery giggled. I scrolled through my collection of songs by my favorite artist. Avery took an earbud in each hand and carefully placed them in her ears. Her face lit up with joy.

When the song ended, Avery giggled and gave me my earbuds back. "You're such a goody-two-shoes! I think my music would kill you!" she teased.

"Try me!"

Avery pulled her phone out from her boot. This whole time, I never spotted it wedged in there. I plugged my earbuds in with a sharp click. The song she played for me was the opposite vibe. Mine was sweet, while hers was out for blood. Nevertheless, it was still a badass song.

"I've heard this before. I have it in my playlist, too," I commented as the song neared the end. Avery smirked.

"Sure,"

"No, really! Do you want me to show you?" I challenged. It took a bit of scrolling, but I pulled it up on my phone. Avery's eyes illuminated at the sight of it.

"What! Really? No!" Avery shouted as though she were experiencing a flood of emotions. "This song really makes me want to get a tattoo of either one of the lyrics, or like, the album cover. What do you think? Would you ever get a tattoo, good boy?" Avery mocked. She was not holding back on making fun of me. I was not sure if that was a good sign or not. My face turned pink regardless.

"I'm not sure about me, but you totally should! Right on your face, maybe your forehead or cheek," I countered. It wasn't my best effort, though it was something.

"Inking outside the box! Tat's the way I like it!" Avery beamed. She was beyond proud of herself for that response. If it were socially acceptable to applaud oneself, she would've done so.

"Ew."

"I know you did not just say 'ew' to my jokes!" Avery scolded in a fake-angry tone. Her smile bled through her pretend angry expression.

Oooooom! Ooooom! This was the worst possible time to hear that dreaded noise. I told myself I'd hunt it down to the ends of the earth next time I heard it. Nothing could make me leave Avery's side at that moment. Bianca pulled the strings to get everyone together. I wasn't going to run off on some fruitless adventure. The idea that some dangerous man was out there while I ignored the sound didn't sit right with me. A knot formed in my stomach as I tried to ignore the sound and live in the moment.

My ears twitched. Someone was coming! The sound man? My heart dropped. It was Zach and Bianca. They rounded the corner and spotted us on the dock. I turned to see what Avery was doing. She had her eyes closed, facing the pond.

Zach broke the silence. "Time for dinner!" he shouted.

Without saying another word to me, Avery stood and bolted to Bianca. Her boots pounded across the rickety dock. Suddenly, Zach and Bianca broke out laughing at something Avery had said. I panicked. It seemed like she was talking about me. Avery turned away from Bianca and Zach to wink at me playfully.

15

STARRY NIGHT

Cheerful music emanated from the kitchen. Sunflower was the only word I could make out since the lyrics were in Spanish. We sat around the wooden table by the back door of Bianca's house. The tall chairs were wooden with a backrest made up of long pillars. Bianca and Zach sat on one side of the table while I sat with Avery on the other. The table was set with blank, white plates and clear glass cups. The glass cups must have jogged Bianca's memory because she apologized to her mom about breaking the cup earlier.

"What cup?" Mrs. De La Cruz asked.

"The cup that shattered on the floor where you're standing!" Bianca laughed at her mom.

"I didn't clean up any broken glass," Mrs. De La Cruz argued.

I motioned with a finger over my mouth for Bianca to be quiet. "Oh, I think Andrew threw it out," she lied.

"Ok, I hope you were careful; broken glass can be dangerous. You should've told me. I have a dustpan in the pantry back here," Mrs. De La Cruz advised. She pointed to the door beside the refrigerator. "Oh, Zach, you left your cup on the counter here, honey." She picked it up and placed it in front of him. Zach laughed, thinking it was a new cup. However, Bianca stared at me in disbelief. A knowing grin spread across her face.

Brrr brrrt! Someone's phone vibrated. "Sorry," Avery blushed as she took hers out. Her eyes shot wide open. "No way!" she gasped.

"What is it?" Bianca asked curiously.

"It's breaking news from my dad's channel," Avery answered. "There was a break-in at a factory, and one guy stopped all the robbers!"

"Really? That's awesome!" Zach commented sarcastically.

"That's not the interesting part!" Avery scolded. "Look at this video. He's got like some type of ninja powers!" She handed her phone to Zach. No sound played, though his expression changed straightaway. Light flashed across his face as he watched a video. A red stain formed toward the center of his chest. He had picked at a scabbed wound until it was bleeding again in the middle of dinner. Disgusting as it was, nobody acknowledged it. The video was far more interesting. I got the impression that Zach not taking care of himself was quite common.

We crowded around Zach to watch the video. Sure enough, it was me fighting the thugs at the factory. It puzzled me how that fight could have been recorded. There were no camera crews at the crime scene. A series of numbers ticked at the bottom of the screen. The footage was from security cameras! I forgot to check for those! Most of the machines were coated in dust. It was surprising that their alarms worked. I didn't expect their cameras to be functional too!

"Is this real?" I asked. It occurred to me that I had to sound skeptical.

"Yup, and I know that it's not edited because my dad showed me how they process the clips for the news. They trim or brighten them, but they don't have any software to add special effects. This is a real person!" Avery declared.

Although I wanted to be famous, I never thought it would happen so quickly. All it took was a little clumsiness, being caught on video. When I saw Avery's reaction, I knew it was a good thing I was. She was amazed. She wasn't scared of my powers; she was curious about them. *I'm gonna be famous,* I thought. All I had to do was be this Lionheart guy. I cheered in my head. Maybe I should do more than chase after that sound man. Fighting more thugs would lead to more videos, fame, and adoration from Avery. I still wanted her to like me for me, though. It was tempting. I wasn't sure what I wanted to do anymore.

Everyone had their eyes glued on the video. "Whoa!" they gasped as I ran up the side of a wall. When I landed, I summoned the escrima sticks. "Where did those come from?" Zach shouted. "Did you see that? Where did he get those?" He pointed to me, striking the gunmen with the escrimas.

"Shhh!" Avery hushed. They watched in awe as I used my psychic powers to teleport. The video cut to a different camera to show me reappear and punch the man trying to escape. "Did he just teleport?" Avery gasped.

"Not sure if any of these dudes are real or not, but isn't this the dumbass that tried to fight Gravemaker?" Zach laughed. His demeanor shifted.

"Who?" I interrupted.

"You mean the murderer?" Avery interrogated. "My dad's channel calls him Gravemaker because of all the bodies he's put into the ground over the last few days."

"Yeah, he needs to be stopped," Zach replied solemnly. He turned bright red. His fingers tapped on the table mindlessly. "He's got cool explosion powers. If he were a good guy, he'd be the greatest. Did you see the video of the jewelry store?"

"You mean the one we aired? Yeah, I saw it." Avery rolled her eyes.

"Can you play it for me? I don't know who you're talking about," I whined.

"Sure," Avery skipped through a few videos in her camera roll to get to one from the other day. It was security camera footage from the jewelry store. Gravemaker was indeed the sound guy. Vomit rose in my throat before falling back down. I fought a murderer? He was a killer, and I tried to fight him head-on. There's no way that's the same guy. He backed out of the fight when I clearly didn't know what I was doing. The sound man wasn't a killer. Though there he was fighting me in 1080p.

"Boom!" Zach shouted when Gravemaker blew up a wall using the sound cannon on his palms. "Man, that suit is sick!" His compliments sounded painful. It was as if it brought him agony to compliment anyone other than himself.

"Grow two feet taller, and you might be able to fit in it," Avery teased. Zach folded his arms. That insult bruised his ego big time.

"Anyway, Lionheart is cooler! They're calling him Lionheart because of the writing on his martial arts uniform," Avery laughed out of nervous excitement. "They should call him something else, though. He seems more like a ninja than a cat."

"Settle down everyone. It's time for dinner," Mrs. De La Cruz ordered. She motioned for us to get seated again. My mouth watered. Mrs. De La Cruz placed monumental rice, black beans, and chicken dishes on the table. We thanked her and helped ourselves. The steaming hot food nearly burned the roof of my mouth. *Oooom! Oooom! Wub, wub, wub, wub!* The sickening sound made it hard to swallow. The thought of that Gravemaker guy currently being out there while I stuffed my face made it harder to ignore. If I weren't starving, I would've lost my appetite.

Throughout the meal, Avery and Zach argued over the validity of the video. He was able to concede that Lionheart was cooler, though he'd never admit that either video was real. It was almost as if he could never agree with someone. If he was wrong, he had to find some other angle where he was correct. Avery provided facts and supporting details to prove she was right, while Zach insisted teleportation and instant explosions were impossible. I didn't know what to say. It was hard to help without giving away my secret.

Eventually, I realized that only Zach and Avery had been talking for the past ten minutes. Bianca and I stared at each other. She fiddled with her sparkly earrings. "Say something," Bianca mouthed silently. I shrugged my shoulders in defeat. The quiet kid was not one for debates. Finally, Avery had enough and stormed off. She proceeded down the hall, muttering to herself. A thin, paper-white phone remained on the table. Bianca nodded at me. Despite often being oblivious, I knew what she was hinting at. I picked up the phone and chased after Avery. She had already put her coat back on, getting ready to leave.

"Wait," I called.

"What?" she growled back.

"You forgot your phone," I replied quietly. My voice was too soft. It sounded weak and shy. Part of me felt embarrassed. What did I think was going to happen. She'd fall madly in love with me because I remembered her phone? Her eyes watered. She reached out slowly. It was hard to tell what was wrong. I think she felt bad for snapping at me.

"I'm sorry," Avery apologized. Her voice was calmer.

"Are you leaving already?"

"No, I'm not leaving," Avery sighed softly. "I want to be alone for a while."

"Oh, alright." I started to return to the kitchen. My frown was a bit obvious. Avery was too upset to talk to anybody. Her boots clunked as she walked outside. The front door was almost closed when she called back inside. "I could use someone to talk to," she smiled.

"But then you wouldn't be alone," I commented stupidly. Luckily, she didn't hear me. I followed Avery outside. For a moment, it seemed like we wouldn't talk for the rest of the night. A rush of joy flowed over me. Bianca's plan may not have failed after all.

Avery ignored the chairs and sat on the steps of the porch. She stared up at the night sky. There must have been a lot of stars. I couldn't see them without focusing my eyes into cat-like slits. Instead, I pretended to admire the stars, mirroring her actions. The sky appeared to be the same clear blue as daytime. Endless days made me miss starry nights.

"Maybe we should do something about Zach," Avery blurted out. Her eyes were locked on the stars. I was surprised and reacted without thinking. "What?"

"He's so controlling," Avery complained. She realized she should keep her voice down and spoke more softly. "Bianca's such a good person. She deserves better than him." Her gaze fell from the stars. Her distant eyes stared through her lap, into another dimension.

Avery turned her head to face me. Her dark blue eyes pulled me in like the ocean tide. "I know it's not our place to meddle with her relationship, but I feel we should do something. There's no way she's happy with him. She's lost her spark since they started dating; as you just saw, he only argues with her. He's probably in there right now telling her not to hang out with me anymore."

88

"They're opposites," I piped up. "They'll break up naturally. No need to get involved and rush it. That would only hurt Bianca's feelings."

"You're right," Avery sighed. She continued to stare at the stars. "Thanks for coming out here in the cold. Without you, I would've left. Sorry for being a drama queen. I can't stand Zach," Avery thanked me, her eyes still tethered to the sky. The moon was as bright as the sun in my eyes. I stared at the ground instead.

My palms were sweaty. It took all my effort not to mix up my words. Her soft voice soothed me. No matter what we talked about, Avery's tone remained serene. She was mesmerizing. In my nervous state, I couldn't remember much of what I said. Whatever it was that I had told Avery, I remember it had an effect on her. She listened to every word I uttered. By the time the conversation ended, Avery was in better spirits.

"Before we head inside, I wanna ask you something," Avery paused as if waiting for approval. I nodded. "I've got a big race coming up. It's to make up for the amount of track meets I missed when I was sick. Bianca will be waiting for me at the finish line. After what happened tonight, I'm not sure Zach will let her be friends with me anymore. Can you go with her? I'm worried she's gonna cancel at the last minute. All you have to do is have water ready for me and cheer me on for the beast that I am."

"I'll be there. Even if she cancels, I'll support you," I reassured. Maybe I was laying it on too thick. If it weren't freezing, I'd be sweating. Doting on her was sure to get myself locked in the friend-zone. In that moment, I hardly cared. This was already much further than I thought I'd make it. My fingers fidgeted with my phone while I spoke.

"Where is it gonna be?" I handed over my phone.

"I got this!" Avery declared as she swiped my phone from my hands. Her fingers tapped away at the screen. In a flash, she was done. She had added her cellphone number to my contacts. The map app was open when I handed my phone over. I thought she was going to pin the event location on the map. This was much better! Avery lowered my phone away from her face, flipped it around. A light flashed in her eyes. She had taken a contact picture. I laughed as she handed back my phone. It felt so unreal. She was a ton weirder than I imagined, and I loved it! Not only that, but I got her number! The thought screamed inside my head. It often repeated afterwards. *I got her number!*

"Done!"

A tiny picture displayed next to Avery's contact information. Her face was perfectly framed. She cut out her bulky winter jacket making the picture appear timeless. Avery made it to the door when something caught her eye. "The stars are gorgeous!" Avery cheered, pointing to the sky.

"Uh, yeah," I replied, staring at an empty sea of blue.

Everything had changed in one night. Lionheart was going to be on tv screens across the country. Avery gave me her number. Zach was a jerk, yet not as bad as I expected. It wasn't clear what the deal was with Avery terrified of Zach forcing Bianca not to hang out with her. One petty argument was not enough for Bianca to agree to throw away a friendship that's lasted since kindergarten. At least it was a good sign that Bianca would soon break up with that nuisance. For some reason, that thought made me smile. It's not that I wanted Bianca to be single. It was that Zach was not a great guy. He deserved to be put in his place, and she deserved to be with someone better.

16

SELF-CONTROL

My dreams were coming true! That night with Avery had changed me. She loved Lionheart! Her dad aired numerous clips of me totally kicking butt! There was a lot for me to think about. If I could track down that sound, I could take out that Gravemaker man and become even more celebrated. However, that would only make Lionheart more loved. How would I go about boosting *Andrew's* chances with Avery? I paced around my bedroom. Oliver meowed as if he were replying to me. Bianca knew I was Lionheart. At least stopping Gravemaker would help *her* think more fondly of me.

The only problem was that I had ignored the sound all night, and it was long gone. That, and the fact that Gravemaker is apparently far more dangerous than my encounter with him suggested. Energy flowed through me as I pushed thoughts of girls out of my mind. *Focus,* I instructed myself. *What direction was the sound coming from last night?* My ears twitched as I mindlessly walked in circles. When I closed my eyes, I could picture the trees lined up in the distance. *West!* Golden light enrobed me as my uniform and mask teleported on. A surge of psychic energy pooled within my mind.

If memory served, the noise will either lead me to him or an Armageddon facility like the last time. Searching across my list of Armageddon locations the only one west of me was outside of Hunterdon. No matter how hard I tried to teleport there, nothing happened. Aside from that weird sanctuary area,

I couldn't teleport somewhere I couldn't picture perfectly. If I could only teleport based on memory, then I should be able to teleport to a parking lot behind a gym in Hunterdon. Red spots indicated where people were looking. In an instant, I appeared crouched behind a car where no one would notice me.

The drastic change in lighting stung my eyes. Getting used to these powers meant dealing with all sorts of issues I never thought about before. The car I appeared behind didn't help my situation either. The surface was too shiny. It reflected light as if it had never been driven before. As my eyes adjusted, I noticed it was no ordinary car. The neon green paint job made that clear. It was a sports car with spotless black wheels. Whoever it belonged to took extraordinary care of it.

Fresh air filled my lungs. Teleporting from the warmth of the inside to the cold winter air sent a shock to my system. It felt like I was jerked awake by a bad dream. Goosebumps covered my skin. I was wide awake now. The sounds of birds, traffic, and people filled the air. All these sudden changes dazed me for a moment. After a few crisp, cold, deep breaths, I finally started to get my bearings.

The Armageddon facility was only a short sprint away. When I stood up to run, I was surprised to find people standing beside the car on the opposite side. Without thinking, I crouched down beside the back of the sleek car. Clutching onto the rear tire, I peeked around the corner to scope out the scene. It was okay for people to see me; I didn't want to scare them, that was all.

"You hit my car; you owe me five hundred bucks!" a male voice demanded.

"I-I don't have five hundred bucks," stuttered another voice.

Peering underneath the car, I spotted the legs of five people. Four pairs of feet on the left pointed towards the one facing them on the right. Each person was wearing different colored shoes. The guy on the right was wearing a pair of beige pants and polished black shoes. The rest were wearing sneakers of different shapes and designs. One of the people on the left moved closer towards the beige pants guy.

"Look at your car! Look at your clothes! You're telling me you can't afford five hundred bucks?"

"My parents are rich, not me!" the beige pants guy yelled. He sounded much younger than the others. The mention of parents made it seem like he was a student. His voice wasn't as deep as mine, though if he could drive, he had to be around my age.

"Leave me alone!" the kid yelled. He pushed someone back.

The angry man's feet stumbled backward. Suddenly, everyone's feet started scuffing back and forth across the pavement. I popped my head up to see what was happening. Of course, they were fighting. The four men on the left were beating up the kid on the right. The angry guy had the beige pants kid in a headlock while the others punched him. They were attempting to steal his keys and wallet.

This was a waste of my time. I was in the middle of a massive investigation into two huge conspiracies. There was the mystery of Mr. Poundz, the strange events at my school, and now this Gravemaker guy. If I stopped here and there to deal with petty crimes, I'd never make any progress. I was a superhero. I should be out saving the world from peril. This was so beneath me and what I can do.

A pain spurred in my chest. I was too good of a person. There was no way I could leave without intervening. With my powers, it would only take a second anyway. Doing good deeds could only lead to more positive publicity and love. Especially more love from Avery. Bianca too! She was the first to encourage me to use my powers for good. Maybe I'd spend the day fixing every little crime in New Jersey. That way, I could focus fully on my investigations afterward.

I sprang over the car and landed behind the man who had the beige pants kid in a headlock. They were much taller than I thought. Although their muscles were far larger than mine, my powers made me stronger than all of them combined. I launched forward, breaking the guy's hold on the beige pants kid. In one swift motion, I grabbed his upper arm, shoved my right shoulder under his armpit, placed my right foot behind him to help trip him, and flipped him over my shoulder using my hips. He collapsed on his back. The sudden shift of weight made the beige pants kid fall back.

Their full attention was now on me. The kid in the beige pants rushed into the green car. He gave me an odd look as he started the engine. The sound of screeching tires echoed in the air. It took him a mere second to peel out. Meanwhile, his attackers blamed me for his getaway.

"What's this? Are you some type of clown?" one of the guys teased. He grabbed at my mask.

"Don't touch that!" I warned.

The bully ignored me and pulled on my mask. My skin erupted in pain as the mask remained sealed to my face. It was excruciating. At any moment, I thought my skin would tear off my face. Suddenly, a burst of psychic energy released from the mask! The blast forced everyone back. The mask must have had built-in defenses to protect itself and me. I know I certainly didn't make it do that. It did it on its own. The light from the energy pulse temporarily blinded me. My vision cleared in time to discover that all four of them were charging at me instead of running away!

Smack! Someone punched me in the face. *Wham!* Another hit me in the stomach. They circled around to prevent me from escaping. Hits came from every angle. When I tried to fight back, they slammed my head into the pavement. My body hunched over in pain. At Tae Kwon Do, they taught us never to show emotion. This intimidation technique tricks the opponent into thinking that nothing they did was effective, and they'd soon give up. The pain was overwhelming. I struggled to hide it. *Bam!* Someone stomped on my back. Fear took over. Lionheart, the legendary hero, was being pummeled by a bunch of ordinary punks. My face grew hot with embarrassment. What kind of hero gets assaulted in a petty fight? The thought made my eyes water. Shame poured over me like a hot shower. My dreams were being crushed along with my body.

With each blow, I could feel Lionheart becoming the same nobody as Andrew. Anger boiled within. There was no way I could allow my alter ego to fade into the unknown, too.

Splitting pain coursed throughout my body. I tried to ignore it, push it down, conceal it. *This hero thing is nothing more than a stupid attempt at being popular,* I started to think. *I'm not cut out for this. All of this just to impress a girl with a boyfriend. Smack!* A sharp kick knocked the air out of my lungs. Anger surged within me like lightning. *"No!"* I yelled in my mind. *"I'm not a loser, and neither is Lionheart. I can take a beating, and I can give one, too! I'm not done yet!"*

With that in mind, I shot up from my crouched position. I swung my right foot back and raised my fists to guard my face. This time, I was expressionless. I had no reaction when they hit me. Fear filled their eyes. Their hits became weaker as their confidence dropped.

"What's going on?" one whispered.

Although it hurt, I leaped out of the ring of people. One man turned to punch me. I swung my leg around in a crescent kick, striking him in the head. Without putting my leg down, I struck him in the stomach with a round kick. He stumbled and fell. My anger woke my psychic powers. I reached my hand out and used my mind to lift the three men into the air. The higher I raised my hand, the higher they floated.

The men screamed and hollered in pain. In my anger, I was not only lifting them. I was crushing them. It never occurred to me how powerful my psychic powers were. Mere thoughts could tear them apart. If they were going to make it out alive, I had to relax and control my emotions. Cuts and bruises formed as my psychic powers tore at their cells. The anger was hurting them. Their screams pierced my ears. A chilling sensation of fear stopped me cold. It was unlike anything I'd felt before. I was afraid of myself. I was scared of what I could do.

The feeling of fear outweighed my anger. It snapped me out of my fit of anger. They were released from my telekinetic grasp. The sudden drop wasn't nearly as painful as what I had already done. Instead of attacking me again, they bolted.

My chest stung when I breathed. The rage got to me. I could've shredded them, separating all their bodies' molecular bonds. Luckily, a few cuts and bruises were all they suffered. A shiver ran down my spine. The cold feeling rested in my bones. It wasn't my intention to hurt them like that. The anger took over my thoughts. When using psychic powers, thoughts became actions. Losing control of my thoughts meant losing control of my actions. There was no way I would ever allow that to happen again. My psychic powers would only be used when I was calm and fully in control of my emotions. I made that promise to myself.

Cuts and bruises decorated my own body. Scabs started to form already. It appeared I healed faster than an ordinary human, though nothing spectacular. I still had to be careful.

After that traumatic experience, Gravemaker wasn't so scary. Although he should have been, considering he had tremendous powers and I had just gotten beaten up by regular dudes. At least that Armageddon facility was nearby, and I'd soon have answers. Hopefully, I'd find a way to stop him or disable his super suit. That would be too convenient, but you never know. I winced as my bleeding feet carried me off.

17

ZEN-KT

The Armageddon facility of interest was a lab complex. There was a shortcut off the road and through a nearby forest. Once clear of the small forest, a wide-open field was revealed. There were no roads, trees, or anything except for one towering building. The land sloped downward toward the building, placing me on top of a steep hill. That must have been why I had never seen the facility before. Hills on all sides surrounded the tower. It looked unnatural as if it were built in the center of a crater that had a blanket of tall grass grown over it.

Grass stains coated the bottom of my uniform pants by the time I reached the entrance. The stains were noticeable on my white uniform. If I was going to be a famous hero, I would have to ditch the ugly martial arts uniform and Venetian mask combo at some point. The mask was too powerful to get rid of, though the growing stains on the uniform were reason to reconsider my outfit. My reflection greeted me in the sleek black windows of the building. The grey and black scheme of the tower was uninviting yet futuristic.

Teleporting inside was quite easy. All I had to do was peak through a window and poof! I was inside. The lab was occupied, though it was not full of staff. It was a real skeleton crew at this time of the day. Part of me felt as though it were a trap. I had no problem getting in and no problem staying out of sight. The most trouble was going to be what to do next. I didn't expect to get this far so quickly.

Lab benches were set up with glassware throughout the second floor. I skipped over the lobby, which had a deserted reception area and a sleeping security guard. The potted plants looked nice, though. They really liked the vegetation at this place. Art of plants hung on the walls, and vines cascaded down some walls, flowers, cacti, ferns, mini tree-looking things, plants were everywhere. A lab environment was not good for the plants. This was clear by the sheer amount of drooping, soggy, stems around the room.

On to the next floor, there was nothing to gain from searching drawers of round bottom flasks and tables with titration setups. The next floor held numerous instruments. Gas chromatography, H-NMR, FT-IR, and endless more apparatuses I had never heard of. All of the floors were for conducting experiments and testing. What I was after was information. After the testing was done, where was it entered, and where was it stored?

The elevator dinged once I reached the next floor. I hid behind a nearby plant the second the doors opened. In my snooping, I had forgotten I wasn't alone. The sound of the elevator made people look toward it. I hid too fast to be spotted. If they had spotted me, they were awfully silent about a Black Belt with a mask on waltzing around their workplace. I breathed a sigh of relief. This particular floor was divided into cubicles and offices. If I could access one of their computers, I could search their databases.

My back pressed up against the side of the cubicle. It was difficult to check if the cubicles were empty without being spotted. Even if it was empty they had no privacy. I could get caught easily if I got too comfy browsing data on their computer. The offices had doors, doors that I presumed could lock. I had to use a computer in one of the offices. All the offices were occupied. Most of them had their blinds drawn. The only office open was the corner office.

A satisfying click rattled when I locked myself in an office. Whoever it belonged to must have been important. The room was much larger than the others. Papers were scattered across the desk. A large presentational whiteboard was covered in writing toward the front of the room. I ignored it all and sat down in a rigid seat. Two potted plants kept me company at each side of the desk.

Please enter password, the computer prompted. Nothing I tried worked. The username and password had to be written down somewhere. That's how it worked in the movies. I opened drawers and emptied filing cabinets. There weren't any documents that contained login information. But if I could use my psychic powers to unlock a door and fuse broken objects back together, I could use them to unlock a computer.

I concentrated on the monitor. An exotic pink flower wallpaper stared back at me. My breathing slowed as I focused my psychic energy on the computer. The monitor flickered. I relaxed my mind. The monitor went black. "Uh, oh," I blurted out to myself. Forget being tranquil. I pressed the power button on the monitor and desktop. Nothing happened. I unplugged the computer from the outlet and plugged it back in. Nothing happened. I unplugged and then re-plugged everything. The computer did not respond. My psychic powers broke it.

There were three or more floors left to check. I was already losing hope. Even if I gained access to a computer, I didn't know what I was looking for. The only thing I could think of was to find some type of data entry software or database and search keywords like Onarm, sound, sonic, psychic, and blue gas. The thought of sneaking around trying to find an unlocked computer was exhausting. I melted into the stiff office chair.

The whiteboard was slanted, making it easier to read while slipping out of the office chair. At the top of the board, a title was written: Chemistry: Matter and Reactions. It was the same title as my Chemistry textbook from last year! There was no way that it was the same. I shot out of the chair and zoomed over to the whiteboard. I reread the title over and over. The first connection to my high school. It felt too good to be true.

Focus, I instructed myself. There was more written on the whiteboard than just a title. My phone wasn't on me as Lionheart. It was too risky to teleport my normal clothes, which contained my phone, back on me. I needed to copy everything by hand and slip it into my uniform top. The rest of the whiteboard didn't make any sense. I'd worry about that in the safety of my home later on. My palms grew sweaty as I tore apart the office for scrap paper and a pen.

At the top of the page, I wrote the same title. The rest of the lines were diagrams. They appeared to be chemical structures, though they were written as plain lines, not the ball and stick models I was used to from school. Arrows were often drawn next to the structures. In time, I noticed a pattern. Arrows were pointing to different parts within the structure, followed by a larger arrow pointing to the next structure. The structure that followed always contained the changes indicated by the small arrows in the previous diagram.

What did it mean? Did the compound morph over time? No, that wasn't it. Some of the large arrows had chemicals listed above them or small sketches of entirely different structures. They were steps in a chemical reaction. The whiteboard displayed a pathway to turn one substance into a desired product. A triangle was drawn above the arrow for the last step. That made no sense. At the bottom of the board, the final product was circled and labeled as Zen-KT.

Ink covered the side of my hand. It felt like I was doing homework on my days off from school. I checked the paper several times over. Each diagram was copied exactly as it was displayed. Not a single arrow or pair of dots were missing. I folded up the paper and shoved it inside my uniform top.

Bang! A loud noise echoed outside. People rushed around the office. *Bang! Bang! Bang!* The office erupted in screams. Fear brewed within me. Those were gunshots. The sound was unmistakable.

A cloud of smoke exploded toward the right side of the building. I peeked out the window to locate the source. Cop cars were parked randomly on the grass. Their lights flashed red and blue across the side of the dull facility. With the office distracted, I dashed to the nearest staircase without getting noticed. Instead of rushing down the steps, I jumped down the center. My cat-like abilities allowed me to land safely without risk of injury or damage to the floor. The impact of my landing hardly made a sound.

Loud gunshots rang in my ears. The fight took place directly in front of the entrance. My anxiety drained me of all psychic energy. I felt hollow. The only way to escape was if I got involved. When I reached down to my belt, I was shocked to find a long sword in each hand. Both swords were identical. They had a black leather handle with a golden lion pattern. The blades were extraordinarily sharp. They were katanas! Since my Tae Kwon Do academy taught mixed martial arts, I was trained in a few Aikido moves. However, those lessons were extremely rare. It didn't help that we practiced using wooden swords. My body tensed as I held a pair of weapons I was inexperienced with.

Dozens of policemen fired at a group of people wearing black and red. Their uniforms included a black long-sleeved shirt with red stripes down the arms and a Q logo on the left shoulder. Their pants were also black, with many thick red stripes running up and down each leg. They fired back at the police with some type of black and red automatic gun. Their weapons fired more rapidly than the police. I didn't recognize what type of gun they were using. It was new technology.

The police ducked behind their car doors. Each door was riddled with bullet holes. I crept around the cars. Crouched like a lion stalking prey, I continued onward. To my right were the police; the ones who spotted me weren't sure whether to aim at me. Directly in front of me stood three men with that strange attire. They were too focused on the police to notice me. The smell of charcoal filled the air. It was coming from their bizarre guns. Their weapons would rapidly fire an excessive round of bullets before smoke blasted out of a vent on the side of the gun. When this occurred, the gun was unusable. There was a cool-down period before the weapon could be fired again.

There were four men and two women with the unusual guns and uniforms. Three guns discharged smoke at the same time. That was my chance to make a move. I rushed in and kicked the first guy in the stomach. He fell backward, knocking into the man on his left. They fell to the ground. I zipped toward the others. They shot at me as I zoomed closer. The bullets whizzed to my left and right, none came close to striking me. The first man tried to aim his gun at my chest while I crescent-kicked it out of his hands. I used the momentum of my kick to follow through and sweep his legs. A cloud of dust puffed around him when he hit the ground.

Bullets flew from my right. I raised my sword in a natural reaction. To my surprise, I blocked the barrage of bullets. It must have been my cat-like reflexes. There was no way I could intentionally move like that. Every block was a natural response to danger, like the knee-jerk reaction of touching something hot. In time, the guns ceased firing and burped out exhaust. I bolted forward as fast as I could. Once I was within range, I used the handle of my right sword to knock the gun out of a woman's hands. She lurched forward to tackle me. I stepped to the side and stuck my foot out to trip her. She landed face-first in the dirt. Her eyes burned with rage. The corners of her mouth drew back in a snarl. I sliced her gun in half before she could scramble to retrieve it.

The others opened fire on me. I dashed between them. They stopped firing to keep from shooting each other by mistake. They were close enough to hit me. I spun low to the ground to sweep one man's legs. He accidentally fired his gun when he fell. The bullet struck the other woman's gun, causing it to expel smoke. The smoke provided cover. My mask activated the breathing shield as I forced my eyes to absorb light. The attackers coughed out the black fog. I crept behind the woman with her gun still spewing smoke and hit her in the back with the handle of my sword. She toppled to the ground. Her gun was trapped beneath her, blocking the smoke from leaking out.

My eyes returned to normal as the smoke cleared. The psychic breathing shield withdrew into my mask. A man jumped out of what was left of the cloud of smoke. He tried to hit me with his gun. It was one of the first two gunmen. They both had retrieved their guns and rejoined the fray. I blocked his strike with my sword and swung the left blade downward, cutting the gun in half. The front part of his gun fell onto the grass. It sputtered out a puff of smoke. I sliced off another piece of his gun, leaving the man holding nothing but a trigger. I put one foot behind his legs and pushed him backward. The man collapsed from the forceful shove-trip combo. He crawled backward like a crab before running away.

Pop! Pop! Pop! A gun fired behind me. I turned around, slashing my sword across from my shoulder to my hip, blocking the bullets. It was the second man who I had taken down. Bullets flew above my head as I approached. At the last second, I ducked low and swung my swords down in an X-shape, cutting his gun apart in two places. His face turned pale. He booked it as the pieces of his gun fell to the ground. A cop car cut in front of him. The men who tried to flee were seated in the back of the police car.

Pop! Crack! A bullet struck me directly between my eyes. The impact caused me to stumble backward. Although my mask was indestructible, the shot still hurt. Police surrounded the man with their guns drawn. He paid them no mind. "Why are you protecting Armageddon?" the armed stranger spat. He shot me again in the forehead. His shots were too fast to block. Nothing was protecting the rest of me. He might have been aiming there on purpose.

"Drop it!" an officer commanded.

"They never paid my company a cent for our contribution to a project we spent years designing. All of my skills, my perfect aim, digitized into software. My business cannot take a hit like that. We need compensation for our work," the man explained.

"Shooting up the place was supposed to resolve that?" I interrogated.

The man looked me in the eye. It was a different look than when he aimed. "You look too young to get it. My deadly accurate aim, it can be anyone's now. We created an AI tool trained by yours truly. Imagine an army or police force that's as sharp a shot as me. I thought it was only right to share my gifts with the world. Only, not for free." The man had a slight southern accent. He appeared calm. Gently, he raised his hands into the air and dropped his gun.

Police immediately swarmed him. They handcuffed him while he made no effort to resist. "Look out, kid, this place lost my Quickdraw program. Came here to find the servers wiped. Someone took it. You're all in great danger, thanks to Armageddon. With that software out there, any average Joe can be a deadly shot!" the man screamed as he was carried away.

The man's story made little to no sense. I was in the middle of tracking down enough threads. I didn't need another. His rambling could be heard in the distance. A cold wind blew across the field. The police had rounded up all the criminals. My swords vanished now that the threat was gone. An officer approached me. Sweat poured down my face. Before he could speak, I teleported to the top of the building. My mind was at ease with all the chaos settled.

The police thought I was gone. They never thought to look up. Eventually, they gave up their search. The officers drove off except for one car that had doors that wouldn't shut from the damage it had accumulated. An officer tried to drive it anyway. The door fell off as he picked up speed.

I laughed and teleported home. Even with the power of teleportation, I was running late to Avery's marathon. It was funny; I had just been shot at, yet I was more nervous to see Bianca again. Hopefully, she would be there. I know Avery was worried she'd cancel at the last minute. That was the whole point of why I was invited.

Knowing this was a big chance to impress Avery, I tried to dress well. When I checked myself out in the mirror, I was speechless. There were cuts, scrapes, and bruises all over my body. The ugly swelling of the start of a black eye diminished my face. It was distracting. I was hideous. My stomach hurt. Bianca and Avery were gonna throw up at the sight of me.

18

COME HERE OFTEN?

There was nothing I could do. If I canceled on Avery, there might not have been anyone there for her at the finish line. It wasn't a big deal if I skipped it. She didn't really need someone there. Bianca was only going to support her friend for fun. I didn't want to go looking like a delinquent. However, Avery herself invited me. Ditching her first invite felt unquestionable to me. I had to go.

Red dust appeared and vanished. Teleporting places I had never been didn't work, yet teleporting to people did. I appeared a few feet behind Bianca. There was a limit to how far away from someone I could appear. Last time, I scared her by being too close. She was far enough away that my presence was not detected. The large crowd waiting at the finish line helped hide my sudden appearance.

"Hey!" I called out to Bianca. Her eyes went wide when she saw me. Zach was at her side. Long, thin cuts covered his arms in parallel lines. He didn't care enough to look my way. Bianca grabbed my arm and pulled me out of the crowd. Her fingernails hurt. They were razor-sharp and freshly painted sky blue.

"What happened?" Bianca whispered. She spoke in a hushed tone as she dragged me away. "Come on, I don't have much time to fix you up." She pulled me toward the parking lot. Once I knew where we were headed, I shook my arm free from her clawed grasp. Bianca led me to a rusty black car. Duct tape held one of the mirrors onto the car, part of the passenger door, and the back left taillight. She didn't need keys to open the car.

"Is this your car?" I asked flabbergasted. I'd never seen a car in such disarray. Bianca shook her head.

"Zach got in trouble with his dad again, so he took away his fancy sportscar. Don't tell anyone you can enter without keys. Not that anyone would want to steal this thing," Bianca explained as she searched for something. Fast food wrappers and bags from various stores covered the car's floor. It was like driving in a garbage truck, where the trash is held. After a few minutes, Bianca found what she was looking for underneath the passenger seat. It looked like a pallet of paint.

"Yes, my emergency makeup kit!" Bianca cheered. Her hands flew at break-neck speed. She rushed to dollop makeup onto a fluffy brush. "Hold still," Bianca commanded.

"Wait!"

"Stop moving!"

"Is that makeup?"

"It's concealer. I can cover up your cuts and bruises if you stop squirming," Bianca insisted. I listened. If she turned me into a clown, I could always wash it off. The brush felt odd. It was as if she were hardly touching me.

"Done," Bianca proclaimed triumphantly. She held up her phone with the camera on so I could see myself. In a matter of minutes, Bianca made all the cuts and bruises vanish from my face. It didn't look like I was caked in makeup, either. Everything looked natural.

"Woah, thank you! You're incredible!" I gushed. Bianca pulled her phone away to get me to stop admiring myself. She blushed at my genuine compliment. "You must get a lot of practice from helping Zach," I laughed. Bianca's blush vanished. She turned white and silent. Perhaps I had complimented her too much. The slightest frown appeared in the far corners of her lips before quickly turning upward when refocusing her gaze on me.

"Let's goooo!" Bianca ordered. She tried to pull me again. I moved my arm swiftly to break her grasp and followed her closely this time. Zach was not happy to have me back. He put his arm around Bianca the second she returned. There was an odd look in his eyes. It felt like he was mad that I did something wrong. I tried to think of something I could've done. Nothing occurred to me.

People cheered as some participants made it to the finish line. Avery was not in sight. "Andrew, your birthday is soon, right? We have a surprise for you?"

"You said you'd wait until Avery was here," Zach reminded her. He rolled his eyes.

"I can't wait that long. I got tickets to see that hilarious comedian, Roberto Caceres! It's in New Brunswick next Sunday! You, me, Zach, and Avery!" Bianca beamed. She didn't have much time to celebrate.

"I'm not going. That dude is a has-been," Zach scoffed. He removed his arm from Bianca. They began to argue. Apparently, Zach knew of Bianca's plans for my birthday and didn't have a problem with it until now. Of course, Zach acted like this was all new to him. "He's for little kids, Bianca. I don't know why you like him. He's lame. We'd be the only adults in the theater. The guy has never cursed in his life!" Zach complained.

"You don't have to curse to be fucking funny!" Bianca shouted. Her outburst caused people to look our way. Zach's face grew red with embarrassment. "We'll go without you then and have a great time."

Something had caught Zach's attention. He didn't acknowledge what Bianca said. His eyes were locked on a woman within the crowd. She had long, curly, black hair and a pale, white face. Her puffy winter coat made her look like a marshmallow. "Yo, some lady is staring at you," Zach growled. Bianca's head swerved from side to side, trying to spot the person Zach was talking about. When she did, she laughed to herself.

"That's the guidance counselor, Mrs. Rose," Bianca smiled and held up her hand to passively say hi. The woman responded in kind.

"That's embarrassing. I haven't even started thinking about college yet," I confessed. "I wonder why she's here."

"There's lots of people from school here," Bianca smiled. She was right. I spotted several classmates and a few of the gym teachers. Zach stared off into the distance. He took no part in any of this. It seemed he was not done fuming about the stand-up tickets. The rage building within him bottlenecked at his throat, keeping him from talking about anything else. "Look, there's Principal Perfetto," Bianca added.

Everything moved in slow motion. Only a few hours ago, I confirmed the school was connected to Armageddon. The man mere feet before me had a hand in what happened at school. A fake smile plastered my face. There was no way I could focus with such a threat present. I had to act now. If I let him get away, he could do more damage to the school. Whatever he had Mr. Poundz do, it failed. There was a real possibility he would try something again. With my little voice, would I be able to interrogate him properly? He'd laugh at me. *No,* I thought, *I don't need a booming voice, actions speak louder.*

Without saying a word to Bianca, I slipped into the crowd. People filled my vacancy as soon as I left. It was as if I were a drop in the ocean. Zach and Bianca didn't notice. I weaved through the crowd toward Principal Perfetto. He clapped and cheered as a student reached the finish line. While he was distracted, I used my psychic powers to lift his phone out of his pocket. The crowd's commotion made it hard for him to realize his phone was levitating behind him. I made the phone bump into his head.

"What?" Principal Perfetto turned to be face to face with his floating phone. As one might expect, he was bewildered. Before he could scream and make a scene, I tossed his phone far away. It skidded down a nearby alleyway. "Hey!" he yelled as he chased after his phone. In the distance, a few runners were making their way down the home stretch. None were women. Good, I hadn't missed Avery yet.

Principal Perfetto inspected the damage on his phone. There were a few scratches here and there, nothing major. Out of fear of him drawing attention, I made sure not to be too rough with his phone. My mask and uniform teleported on when I entered the alleyway. A nearby dumpster slid across the ground. I moved it with my telekinesis. The screeching sound made Principal Perfetto jump. He was cornered.

"You're that cat man, right? What do you want with me?" He sounded afraid. Although my goal was to interrogate him, he already trembled in fear. This might be easier than I thought. Not exactly the evil mastermind I had predicted.

"Lionheart," I corrected. It felt stupid to say aloud. A name change might be on the horizon. "Armageddon has a project titled after a textbook in your school. There was an Armageddon pen on your desk. A science teacher from your school was found dead after conducting a dangerous, expensive, secret experiment that went wrong. You secretly work for Armageddon? What are you planning? What is Zen-KT?" I interrogated. In my inexperience, I may have shown all my cards at once. My heart pounded so fast that I couldn't stop talking once I opened my mouth. Now that all that I had to say was out, I went silent.

"I- I- it wasn't me. Of course, I knew of- I mean, I don't work two jobs. I don't work for Armageddon. I don't know anything. It's my wife. I was just trying to save my wife. She's the one that works for Armageddon. Ask her. She knows more than me," Principal Perfetto stuttered.

Although I did not see that coming, it made slightly more sense than him working at Armageddon and the school. "Ok, where is she?" I asked in an unassuming tone. It was as if I forgot I was supposed to be intimidating. He stopped stuttering and stood up straight.

"Right behind you," Principal Perfetto stated in a monotone voice. Out of the corner of my eye, I could see that a woman had slipped past the dumpster. The noise of the crowd prevented me from hearing her footsteps with my powers. There was no time to turn and look at her. All I could see was the figure of a woman in my peripheral vision while lightning struck me in the back. The electricity caused my muscles to react without my input. With my muscles contracted and unmoving, I fell to the ground. My jaw clenched shut. I nearly bit my tongue from the involuntary response. The sound of electricity coursing through an open arc filled the fridged air.

19

INTERROGATION TECHNIQUES THEY DON'T TEACH YOU IN SCHOOL

A psychic barrier formed over my mouth and nose. My mask activated it automatically the instant Mrs. Perfetto attempted to pepper spray me. The shock of it all kept me from speaking. I felt like a fish flopping on the ground.

"What do we do with him? He's one of Gravemaker's guys. We can't let him go. Kill him to send a message? He's only gonna send more after us if we don't," Mrs. Perfetto brainstormed. It stung that they knew to call that sound guy Gravemaker but not to call me Lionheart. My feelings would've been more hurt about it if she hadn't suggested killing me. Luckily, Principal Perfetto was hesitant enough that they didn't have time to pull anything.

"I'm not one of Gravemaker's guys. I even fought him before. Why would he send people after you? Do you know who he is?" I questioned as I recovered. A tingling sensation ran through my fingertips. It felt like my hands had fallen asleep.

The two looked at me like I was an alien. They blinked at each other. "Oh, it's just a stupid kid," Mrs. Perfetto blushed once she saw my face. I reached up to make sure my mask was on. "The less you know, the safer you are," Mrs. Perfetto advised. She tapped her husband on the shoulder and nodded toward the dumpster. As they walked, I scrambled to my feet. The movement was too quick. I fell to my knees.

110

"Wait!" I shouted before they could squeeze past the dumpster. My frozen fingers struggled to pull out the scrap paper with the Zen-KT reaction on it. When Mrs. Perfetto saw it, she turned pale. She stormed over to me. Mrs. Perfetto took the paper from my hand and tore it up. Before she could turn around, I used my psychic powers to merge the shreds of paper back together. The expression on her face was priceless.

"Listen little shit, this isn't funny," Mrs. Perfetto scolded me as if I were a toddler. "This information is dangerous. You can't have this. Some people would kill you to get this," she added.

"You left it on a whiteboard in your office for anyone to see," I smirked. Mrs. Perfetto did not appreciate that response. After a few cursing fits, she recalled that the custodians no longer cleaned the whiteboards at night since they erased something important once, and she grew cross. "Tell me everything, or I'll post this paper online with your name on it," I threatened. She laughed. "I'm a stupid kid, remember? The internet is my forte." My persistence worried her. The gears in her head churned. Eventually, she concluded that I was indeed dumb enough to do something like that.

"Listen, that's an old chemical reaction created by Argone. The version you copied is the original formula that I revisited recently to see if it would be better to restart from the beginning rather than alter the current variant. Zen-KT is their creation, not mine. The man who held my position previously was fired for resurrecting that project. He worked tirelessly on it every day, draining the company of hundreds of hours of overtime pay while wasting their resources. Armageddon had a routine audit where they discovered his secret project, and he was let go. That's when I was hired. A month or two later, I began receiving threatening messages. They came as emails, letters, and engravings on the earth. Whoever it was, they knew everything about me and made it painfully clear that they'd hurt me and my family if I didn't continue working on the Zen-KT project," Mrs. Perfetto explained.

The details went over my head. It sounded like I stumbled upon a whole new mystery. I thought she would give me all the answers. This investigation into the school and Armageddon was supposed to be over. The last thing I needed was for this to merge into one massive undertaking. "So, Zen-

KT is the gas that gave me these powers. It nearly killed me. Does that mean Mr. Poundz made you do it?" I attempted to connect the dots myself. Mrs. Perfetto sighed. That wasn't it.

"No, Mr. Poundz used to work for Argone back in the day. When I told my husband about the threats, he agreed to help me. Instead of working on the project myself where we could have another audit and I could get fired, my husband hired Mr. Poundz as an unassuming science teacher to carry out the project in a lab that was off the radar and the books," Mrs. Perfetto elaborated. She combed at her pink scrunchy. After pawing at it, she removed it and redid her ponytail.

At that point, I could stand. "What about Gravemaker? Who is he?" I asked sternly.

"Are you not listening? He's the man who was fired, my predecessor, who held my position before me. There's no doubt about it. Gravemaker has vast knowledge of Armageddon's projects and has been stealing equipment from said projects to make himself more powerful. In addition, he's slowly hunting down various Armageddon locations, collecting everything required to recreate Zen-KT and administer it to himself safely," Mrs. Perfetto explained as if it were obvious. She started to get an attitude.

"What about the fire at the Poundz's," I questioned.

"What about it?"

Mrs. Perfetto's blunt response caught me off guard. She raised an eyebrow as if she expected an answer. This was supposed to be an interrogation, not a casual conversation. I took a breath to try and find some patience. They whispered to each other and attempted to turn to leave. Loose gravel pricked my feet as I walked toward them. Mrs. Perfetto spun around and aimed her taser at me. *Click!* Nothing happened. She frantically pressed the button repeatedly. It needed to recharge.

"Listen to me!" my voice echoed down the narrow alleyway. Gravel and pebbles floated all around. I levitated them with my psychic powers. The swarm of small stones gathered behind them. It was a bluff, though it looked like I was ready to pelt them with rocks with the slightest misstep. Suddenly, all the rocks fell to the ground. Mr. and Mrs. Perfetto looked at each other in confusion. I sighed as the last rocks struck the pavement, clattering like stone rain.

"Sorry, I'm not going to hurt you," I apologized.

112

"We know," Mr. Perfetto replied.

"I feel like I've been so in the dark about everything in my life right now. You two are the first people I've encountered who have answers. You're right that I should stay out of this, and I'm way over my head, but I'm a part of this now. I deserve to know what gave me these powers and why people are so hellbent on obtaining them. Maybe Gravemaker is too dangerous, yet I'm in the best position to stop him. If you're truly afraid of him or whoever has been threatening you, let me in, let me help you. I can protect you."

An awkward glance was shared between the couple. Intimidation did not work. I hoped that being honest would. They knew I was a kid, and they were parents. If anything would work, sympathy would. "Should we tell him?" Mr. Perfetto whispered. Mrs. Perfetto rolled her eyes and sighed.

"We have a theory," She began. Mr. Perfetto appeared pleased that his wife agreed to help me. "We think whoever has been threatening us and forcing us to create Zen-KT must have done the same to Gravemaker. That would explain why he resurrected the project and to this day is trying to recreate the formula."

I nodded. Mr. Perfetto nudged his wife to encourage her to continue. "Only he's doing more than acquire tools for creating Zen-KT. He's been stealing weaponry like that sonic suit. It could be related to the creation of Zen-KT, but we fear he may be trying to gather the resources needed to fight the one threatening us instead of giving into the demands."

"Do you have a guess as to who that could be?"

The two of them turned pale. "No," they stated suspiciously in unison.

"What *can* you tell me? How about the fire like I'd originally asked. The fire has to be connected to all of this. It was soon after Mr. Poundz was exposed."

"So, then it was Gravemaker," Mr. Perfetto stated plainly.

"Are you just guessing?"

"Look, I told you more than you should know," Mrs. Perfetto sighed. She rubbed her temples. "After everything that's come to light recently, we're trying to distance ourselves, not learn more. I'm not sure why he would burn the Poundz's residence. He may have had the formula for Zen-KT or spare canisters of the finished product. That would give him reason to be there, though the fire seems excessive."

"Stop it with the he this, he that, I want names! Who is he?" I demanded.

"John? Joe? Josh something?" Mrs. Perfetto pondered. "I never worked with him; I replaced him. He didn't exactly leave Armageddon on good terms. It's not like they have an employee of the month plaque in his honor in the hallway," she snapped. It felt like that was a lie. She just didn't want me to know too much. Principal Perfetto tugged on her sleeve. They turned to head back to the finish line. The crowd was silent. I had a feeling there were not many people left out there. Principal Perfetto whispered something about missing their son.

"One last thing, how do I stop him?" I asked confidently. Gravemaker had to have a weakness. He was dressed in experimental tech. There was no way it all worked flawlessly. Mrs. Perfetto appeared cross.

"An ordinary person with a taser defeated you. You can't stop him."

20

I QUIT

Everyone was gone. That was a lie. A few people stood around to chat. The majority of the crowd had dissipated. There were no signs of Zach, Bianca, or Avery. Tears welled in my eyes. I breathed deeply and blinked them away. It was a minor thing to get upset about, though I felt terrible. Avery invited me to support her. Bianca helped me hide my injuries using her makeup. In return, I bailed on them. No tears fell, though I felt like curling up into a ball and dying.

When I teleported home, my parents spotted me. An icy chill ran down my spine. *Noooo!* I teleported my mask off and prayed that they didn't realize my martial arts uniform was not my own. "Look at you, ready for Tae Kwon Do?" my Mom asked. Impeccable timing. It looked like I was dressed and ready to go to class. I made sure to keep my back away from them. The giant "Lionheart" lettering combined with the silhouette of a mountain lion on the back would've been hard to explain.

"Yep, of course I am," I replied as casually as I could.

My Mom tilted her head as if she were puzzled. "Are you ok? You never get ready for Tae Kwon Do until I tell you at least three or five times."

I rolled my eyes. Big mistake. "Don't roll your eyes at your mother," my Dad boomed. "You're actually a bit early. I have to go to the store; you want me to drive you?"

115

The idea of being dressed in a martial arts uniform while in a grocery store sounded like a nightmare. Unfortunately, they didn't know I could teleport. I had to respond the way I would have before all this Lionheart stuff happened. "That would be great, as long as I can wait in the car while you're in the store."

"Ah, alright, then we should head out now," my Dad gestured with his head toward the door.

"One second, I need to use the bathroom," I exclaimed. I raced to switch into the correct uniform. The uniform was similar enough to fool my parents, not the other martial artists. Odd how I could be embarrassed to be seen in one uniform while running around town in the other. Driving felt like torture when I could teleport. It was all worth it if it meant keeping my secret safe.

Instructors were cracking down on sparring because of the Winter Tournament that weekend. The special Sunday class I had attended was a mini tournament to practice for it. Fighting people for fun felt strange after fighting that sound guy. My powers made sparring awkward. Everything I did had to be watered down to ensure nobody got hurt. It didn't feel like sparring. It felt like bad acting.

"Mr. Corleone, that's the fastest I've ever seen you move!" Mr. Michaelson complimented. It was not common for an instructor to compliment a pupil. They didn't compliment students unless they honestly meant it. I took Mr. Michaelson's compliment as a warning to slow down. People had to hit me more often. It was the only way I could look natural. To them, I had to be the same old Andrew.

My eyes wandered off my opponent briefly to glance at Mr. Michaelson. His uniform was dark, night-black instead of our plain, white ones. Mr. Michaelson's black belt had his name and rank stitched in neon red, while ours used bright gold stitching for the writing. All those differences were earned by passing numerous tests throughout his martial arts career. They reflected his high rank.

"Ow!" my opponent blurted out. The shock was not hidden well on my face.

"Hey, lighten up, Mr. Corleone! You're hitting too hard," Mr. Michaelson commanded. We continued sparring while Mr. Michaelson kept a watchful eye over me. It was hard to pull my punches while trying to move quickly, but not too quickly. Sweat glazed my forehead as I did my best to keep everything under control.

These powers were complicated. It was nearly impossible to fight lightly. There had to be a way to get them under control. I cursed inside my head. Everything in my life had gotten so complicated. I didn't understand the mask, that room, the powers. Mrs. Perfetto gave me more information than I had to work with this entire time, yet I felt more lost now. Each time I uncovered something, two more mysteries sprung up. I wanted it to be over.

Thoughts swarmed my head. They distracted me from what I was doing. Who was forcing Mrs. Perfetto and, previously, Gravemaker to make Zen-KT? Why was Gravemaker still trying to make Zen-KT? Why was he arming *himself* with Armageddon technology? The rampant questions caused me to hit my opponent too hard. He didn't complain. This brought my attention back to martial arts.

It was possible that I had to quit Tae Kwon Do. If I couldn't figure out how to hold back properly, I'd be a danger to everyone. The ethical dilemma of competing in a tournament hadn't occurred to me until now. I'd never gotten a first-place trophy, and I had trained for this tournament for months! There was no way I could give up now. Although, it might not be fair if I competed. *Great,* I thought, *more problems to ponder.*

"Ah!" my opponent gasped. My life flashed before my eyes. *Not again.*

"Sorry!" I exclaimed. It didn't sound genuine. Instead, I sounded like a crazy person, blurting something out to avoid getting in trouble. Most people were oblivious. Mr. Michaelson was not. He looked me dead in the eye.

"Mr. Corleone, come see me in my office after class," Mr. Michaelson demanded. He ran his fingers through his short, brown hair and walked away to help another student. My heart raced. The last time I was asked to meet with a teacher after class, it didn't go too well. Nobody got called into Mr. Michaelson's office without a serious problem.

My hands trembled as I turned the knob to the office door. The white blinds were pulled down on each window. Stacks of papers and martial arts weapons littered the office floor. Every inch of the walls were smothered in tournament posters.

Mr. Michaelson sat behind a sizable metal desk in the center of the room. He ran his fingers through his hair continuously. His other hand repeatedly tapped the armrest of his cheap office chair. Without speaking, he shook a computer mouse to wake up the monitors aligned to his right. He seemed to be ignoring me. His focus was on one of the computer screens. The silence was killing me. A keyboard slid out from a drawer beneath the desk. After a few minutes of typing and clicking, Mr. Michaelson turned to me.

"Andrew, you're not in trouble, but I need to talk to you about something." His expression was fiercely stern. "You've been doing well. However, there are a few things I noticed you could improve." Mr. Michaelson reached out and tilted two of the monitors in my direction. My jaw almost dropped to the floor. The screens displayed videos of Lionheart.

Mr. Michaelson fast-forwarded the video to a part where Lionheart was fighting the thieves at Armageddon. He paused the video. "Right there!" Mr. Michaelson said, pointing at Lionheart kicking a guy in the stomach. "Do you see how this guy's foot is angled? He's kicking with the wrong part of the foot!" Mr. Michaelson declared. "You do the same thing. You see, he's kicking with the entire bottom of his foot. You're supposed to kick with the ball of your foot when executing a front kick," he explained. My blood felt cold. Mr. Michaelson sped up the video to show another scene. "Look at how he holds his escrima sticks incorrectly: the sticks should always form a ninety-degree angle with your arm." Mr. Michaelson never took his eyes off the monitors.

Sweat dripped down my hair. The smell of sweat mixed with my fear made me want to hurl. Mr. Michaelson shifted his attention toward me. "I'm trying to show you that not everyone is perfect. Not even this Lionheart guy that everyone's been raving about is perfect. There's always something you can improve. He makes a lot of the same mistakes as you. I think you could learn a lot from watching this," Mr. Michaelson advised. He continued to search through the video for more examples. His lips curled into a smile.

I watched myself fight the group of thugs with my bare hands. They toppled to the ground exactly how I remembered.

Mr. Michaelson paused the video. There were no mistakes in my form. "What was wrong with that?"

Mr. Michaelson sighed. "In that video, Lionheart punched with his right hand about eight times out of ten," he observed. "Watch, do you see what I mean?"

"He's probably right-handed, so what?" I asked. My tone sounded a little defensive.

"You're right-handed too, and you prefer to attack with your right just as he does. I'm trying to tell you that if you favor one side when fighting, you become predictable. Becoming predictable is a good way to lose!" Mr. Michaelson stared at me intensely. "If you switch up your fighting style, people won't know what to do when they fight you. They can't be prepared if you're unpredictable."

Mr. Michaelson's words stuck with me long after I had left. The conversation replayed in my mind the entire car ride home. He had to know I was Lionheart. It couldn't be a coincidence that he used clips of Lionheart to demonstrate what I needed to practice. He knew Lionheart, and I made the same mistakes. Not only that, but he knew that Lionheart had the same right-dominant fighting style.

All that protected my identity was a Venetian mask around my eyes. It struck me as odd that he didn't tell me he knew. Instead, he hinted at it. Part of me felt he supported my actions as Lionheart and was trying to help him become a better martial artist. There was no way I could be sure. I didn't want to reveal my secret to him by accident.

It wasn't clear if Mr. Michaelson knew; however, I trusted him to keep my secret. Mr. Michaelson was right: Lionheart looked and fought like someone from his academy. That would certainly attract reporters or investigators to his doors. My secret was at stake. If Mr. Michaelson could analyze my fighting and figure out Lionheart's identity, others could do it too. Especially if I were to fight in a big event all day like that Winter Tournament. Something had to be done. There were already moral concerns with the tournament and controlling my powers. In time, I made a difficult decision. To protect my identity, it was necessary to quit Tae Kwon Do.

21

STUBBORN AS SOUND

The questions that taunted me throughout Tae Kwon Do persisted into the night. Shortly after arriving home, a thundering headache wracked my brain. Visions streamed in my head as if a movie were playing in my eyes alone. An image of Gravemaker aiming his speaker palm at me flashed through my sight. It jumped back to the glass on the floor of Bianca's house reforming. Next, it played a second of the sun burning bright. Once again, I saw myself return to school looking burnt out. The visions jumped back and forth in time. Pain coursed through my veins. Finally, I saw Mr. Poundz trying to breathe in Zen-KT through that mask he created.

Teleporting my mask onto my face caused the visions to cease. The mask was supposed to aid in the use of my psychic powers. Apparently, that meant I could use it to stop future sight from taking over. I had no clue what triggered those visions. It did help me figure out how to beat Gravemaker, though. Mrs. Perfetto was wrong. If I couldn't fight him head on, I could prevent him from getting the necessary equipment to become more powerful. All I had to do was stay one step ahead of him. Thanks to that searing vision, I was. I knew what he was going to target next.

To successfully intake Zen-KT, one needed a safe, controlled way of breathing it in. Mr. Poundz knew this and created a makeshift oxygen mask of sorts. Of course, things still went terribly wrong for him. The important part was that

Gravemaker would need a mask or some device capable of controlling the flow of Zen-KT. At least I was hoping that's what the vision was trying to tell me. The severe pain it caused made me feel as though it were quite urgent that I prevent him from getting such a device.

Fortunately, I had a guess: Armageddon Optics. Way back when I had researched all the Armageddon locations in New Jersey, an article popped up about the optics division's latest success. What they had developed was no ordinary helmet. It was military-grade blast-resistant and fitted with an advanced electronic display. Until now, I had dismissed it as it had nothing to do with sound. It seems he had branched out since then.

The sound of tools at work echoed down the halls. Teleporting there was tricky. I had to appear three miles away at an ice cream place I had gone to one summer. My head was pounding by the time I found the place and teleported inside. Those psychic abilities took a toll on me. It already felt like I could pass out. I searched the expansive walls of the testing site. A large poster on the back wall caught my eye. Many dark blue colored paintings encircled the text in the center of the poster. The text read, "Be prepared for the worst-Armageddon." It was a play on their normal slogan, yet it felt like a threat in my scenario.

My ears twitched. The sound of a drill echoed down the vacant halls. I was too late to destroy that helmet before Gravemaker arrived. He was already in the process of stealing it. There goes my psychic powers. The energy flow out of my body was almost tangible when I lost my nerves. I stuck my hand out to try and use my psychic powers to move a painting on the wall. Nothing happened, *rats!*

Tiny plaques labeled each corridor. The helmet was close. As I neared a corner, the sounds grew louder. Whispers filled the air. It was all meaningless jabber. "Wow, it's heavier than it looks!" someone whispered. Gravemaker wasn't alone this time. The voice was coming from the next room. I peeked my head around the corner. A man and a woman were lowering the helmet off a red pedestal to the left. Three more men stood around them. They didn't see me as I crouched against a display case for a VerdeSole Electronics partnership project

121

near the arched entrance to the room. None of them were Gravemaker.

"Freeze!" I yelled as I sprang out to startle the robbers. They flinched and dropped the helmet. An alarm rang out the instant it hit the floor. There were sensors in that room. I had somewhat foiled their plans. The alarm would trigger the police. However, my enhanced hearing left me sensitive to the loud noise. My hands involuntarily clasped my ears.

"Book it!" one man ordered. They ran toward the back of the room, where a series of ropes dangled from a giant hole in the ceiling. "Freak!" screamed the woman. She grabbed the helmet and dashed for their exit. They climbed up the ropes and onto the roof. The three men who weren't tampering with the helmet's sealed pedestal display stayed behind. One man shouted back to his fellow fleeing felons, "Go! We'll keep him busy!"

The man dashed forward and punched me in the stomach. It was hard to react with the screeching alarm piercing my ears. I flew back and crashed against the back wall. My heart pounded like a drum in my chest. The same man came at me again, that time with a kick aimed at my face. In a split second, I dodged to the left. His foot crashed through the sheetrock of the wall.

"Ergh!" he grunted angrily. The man paused to wave his accomplices forward. While his attention focused on them, I launched forward to side kick him in the back. The man flew forward, landing flat on his stomach. The other men turned white. Their eyes widened with fright. They ignored their orders and quickly shimmied up the ropes.

The first man rose from the ground. His face was twisted with anger. He charged at me like a raging bull. I stepped back and lifted my right leg, allowing him to run straight into my heel. He collapsed to the ground, practically using my leg to kick himself. Meanwhile, the other men were escaping. A pair of legs were making their way up the ropes. I grabbed one foot and yanked the man down. His landing shook the room. He crawled on his back to get away from me. Squeaks emitted from his leather jacket, rubbing against the floor. His hands flew up to protect his face. To his surprise, I walked past him. My focus was on those who were fleeing.

Moonlight poured through the hole in the ceiling. Ropes and pulleys were set up to hoist the felons. I climbed onto their makeshift platform and leaped outside. The nighttime air froze my lungs. Nobody was on the roof. I tried to listen to them. Leaky air conditioning units were the only sounds I heard besides the ringing alarm. A long ladder leaned against the edge of the roof. The ladder led to a van down below. A black pickup truck was parked next to the van.

The engines of both vehicles revved to life. A cloud of exhaust blasted into the air. The white van sped down the street, followed closely by the pickup truck. My ears perked up. There were sirens not too far away. In fact, it sounded as if they were getting closer. Three police cars sped down the road. They turned right at the next intersection. The red and blue light reflected off the nearby buildings. It was the same direction the van went. I pounced down from the roof. The police cars were already gone. It didn't matter. I saw where they were going. A chilling breeze swept past my feet.

There weren't many cars on the road late at night. It didn't take long to catch up to the white van. *Screech!* The van dramatically picked up speed. Soon, I found myself sprinting. I was almost within reach of the van. *Boom!* The black pickup truck came out of nowhere. It made a wild turn and slammed into me. I careened to the left. A small tree snapped as I was flung through it. Police cars roared by. Blood-stained footprints were left on the concrete once I stood.

There wasn't much pain to shake off. I bolted down the street. My bloody feet made a wet, slapping sound as I ran. After a few blocks, I caught up to them once again. That time, it was the pickup truck that was nearly outside my grasp. The crooks in the back of the pickup truck pointed guns at me. Their mouths moved; however, I couldn't hear anything over the sound of rapid gunfire. I weaved left and right to dodge their bullets. Doing that created a large gap between me and the van. They were protecting the van. The robber's shots grew closer.

Their cars were faster than me. I ended up dashing behind the police. My poor feet could barely keep up. I forced myself to run faster. My heartbeat boomed like thunder. I shot past the cop cars, leaped over the pickup truck, and landed on top of the white van. The two men stopped shooting at me.

They didn't want to shoot their van with their own people. *Pop!* The men shot the tire of a police car. They were shooting at the police! They knew it would force me to target them instead of the van.

I launched off the van and onto the front of the pickup truck. While in the air, I motioned towards my belt to summon a weapon. A pair of strong, metal nunchucks appeared in my right hand. They were black with a gold lion insignia on each side. I landed on the truck with a loud thump. The force of my impact made the car swerve. I glared at the driver before sliding onto the bed of the pickup.

The truck made a fast turn, forcing one of the men to drop their gun. The other gunman held onto a handle attached to the roof. He aimed for my head. The car went over a bump, and his shot missed. I struck the gun out of his hands with my nunchucks before he could fire. I let go of my nunchucks while they rotated. The chain wrapped around my hand before I caught them on the other side in a reverse grip to complete a wrist roll. *Crack!* I followed through with the momentum of the roll to hit the man in the temple. He collapsed to the floor of the truck.

I rolled the nunchucks vertically to return to a normal grip. The momentum continued as I struck the other man in the head. He fell stretched out on his stomach. His hands started reaching towards the back of the truck. The gun he had dropped earlier rattled close to the pickup truck's edge. I swiped at the gun, knocking it into the street. The man jerked his head toward me in surprise. He snarled and stood up to fight. The truck went over another bump. The man fell back down. The bumpy ride didn't faze me. I stood up straight no matter how hard the truck bounced.

It was my cat-like abilities. Although I didn't have a tail, I was gifted the miraculous balance of a cat. I bent down to peer over the end of the truck. The wheels spun rapidly underneath. I didn't have any projectiles or anything sharp to pop the tires. When I thought about slashing the tires, my nunchucks morphed. A long scythe-like blade emerged from the bottom end of the nunchucks. The razor-sharp edge intimidated me. I couldn't use them like normal nunchucks, or I would stab myself by accident. It takes years to master bladed nunchucks. I knelt at the back end of the truck and peeked over. I swung the nunchuck downward at the wheels below with one quick strike. *Pop!* The blade cut through the tires!

The truck swerved out of control. The rough turns made the blade fly close to my face. *"Please go away!"* I thought to myself. To my surprise, the blades retracted into the nunchucks. It was perplexing that I couldn't control what weapon I summoned, yet I could easily control the features of the weapon I was given. Finally, the truck stopped. One of the police cars pulled over to arrest the driver. It was time to move onto the van.

Police officers gave me wicked stares as I ran alongside their cruisers. The van turned a corner. I cut across the sidewalk, circled my nunchucks around my head, and then down to strike the front tire! The blade activated for a split second to pop the tire. With one of the wheels giving out at such a high speed, the van careened out of control! My nunchucks teleported away. I cleared my mind of anything other than the van. It continued barreling down the road. I pointed my arm toward the van as if telling it to stop. The van didn't yield. I closed my eyes and breathed out slowly. Suddenly, my eyes shot open as I stuck out my hand again. The van rose several feet into the air! Psychic energy flowed between me and the van. It became a part of me. Closing my hand into a fist caused all the tires to pop simultaneously.

Cops surrounded the driver of the floating van before he knew what had happened. Before I could gently lower the van to the pavement, a massive blast shot it out of the air! *Oooom!* The van tumbled onto its side. Sparks flew as the heavy van scrapped against the pavement. A small frisbee-shaped disk landed in the center of the circle of cop cars. My eyes narrowed into cat-like slits. *Vooom!* The metallic disk erupted in a tremendous soundwave. All the cop cars were blown away along with me.

Burning, crashing metal fell from the sky. My heart stopped. There was no sound. Gravemaker was here. A bumper banged against the pavement without any noise. Policemen shouted, trying to locate each other. Their mouths moved but produced no words. It was nearly impossible for them to coordinate and tend to their wounded. A sickly combination of gas, smoke, and blood filled my nostrils. My mask activated the breathing shield. There was too much ash to see clearly.

It was all a distraction. Gravemaker assumed I'd help out the policemen. He was wrong. I was only after him. If he got away, he'd do worse than this. Backlit by the flames, Gravemaker was a silhouette amongst the chaos. He collected his prize from the destroyed van. From somewhere within his armor, he attached a cord to the helmet. The eyes on the helmet flickered. As he tinkered with the inner mechanisms of the advanced headwear, I crept closer, undetected.

Details of Gravemaker's suit became more defined as I approached. He had repaired the damage from our last encounter. Not only that, but it also looked reinforced with more Onarm than before. A bright green flash within the helmet must have indicated something was finished since Gravemaker raised the helmet above his head and slowly slid it into place immediately afterward. *Click!* It locked into his suit. The action was done leisurely, drawn out as if it were ceremonial.

OOOM! Only two seconds had passed since the helmet connected with Gravemaker's suit. He wasted no time to whip around and blast me with the speaker in his left palm. The blast stirred up the surrounding ash and fire. There was no way I could let him escape. His actions this time around were indicative that he was capable of murder. The people he paid to help him, in the van, he didn't care for their safety.

Blood-soaked feet carried me back into the fray. Gravemaker's new helmet appeared skull-like except black and lacking details. Piercing red lights illuminated both eyeholes. The helmet was almost skintight, like a cross between a ski-mask and a motorcycle helmet. The helmet's menacing, red LED eyes were permanently fixed in an angry, glaring expression. He shot something out onto the road between my feet. It made me stop in my tracks. A small disk lay beneath me. "Tell that hotshot this is all for him. You can't stop me," a voice spat angrily in the distance. The voice wasn't talking to me yet- *Eeeeeee!* Before I could react, the disk beside me emitted a terrible screech.

Eeeeeeeeee! The high-pitched shriek of the little metal disc was incapacitating. I fell to the ground and gripped my ears. It felt like my head was going to explode. A drop of blood fell from my nose. All of my strength had to be focused on opening my eyes. That mechanism certainly *was* designed to counter *me* like that voice had said. Once open, I spotted the disk by my side. That was all I could muster. With my eyes squeezed shut, the painful, ringing sound destroying me from within, I raised my right hand and executed a hammer fist upon that cursed gadget. It shattered to pieces. The sound stopped. I gasped for air. It felt like I couldn't breathe while that thing was going off. When I opened my eyes, mangled police cars and ash-covered policemen were all that I found.

22

USER NOT FOUND

There was nobody I could turn to for help. Gravemaker was much more ruthless than I had initially thought. He would only get more powerful if I kept failing to stop him. It felt overwhelming. What a terrible hero I turned out to be. I didn't know where to go from there. He had what he wanted. What else did he need? It was a longshot, but maybe Bianca had some ideas? There was nothing else I could come up with.

Bianca! I ditched the marathon and never apologized. I'd been too busy running around as Lionheart. My phone was only on me when I teleported my regular clothes back on. It was late at night, though she had to be up. We were teenagers with no school the next day. Of course she'd be up. I had to make things right with her and Avery. My text didn't send. An error message popped up on my screen. Failed to deliver.

Our internet plan was not the greatest. The Wi-Fi was always dipping in and out. I paced my bedroom floor, waiting anxiously for my text to send. After waiting a few minutes, I rebooted my router and tried again. The same message appeared. I tried one last time using my cellular data. The error appeared under that text as well. At that point, I realized it was no error. Bianca had blocked my number.

No, there was no way. We were getting to be such great friends. One tiny mistake was not enough for her to cut ties with me. I really had to apologize. It appeared I screwed up more severely than I thought. My heartbeat thumped inside a hollow body as I frantically tried to contact her through social media. None of her accounts showed up. Bianca had blocked me from everything.

Lionheart was dead. At least it felt like he was. Bianca had blocked me across every platform imaginable. We had only become friends recently, yet it stung like I had lost a lifelong friend. She was a big reason why I was trying to stop Gravemaker and find out what was happening at school. It was her encouragement that drove me. She insisted I could be a hero. With Gravemaker escaping and winning, I was already feeling terrible. Social media was petty and not the mark of true friendship, I knew this, but it did nothing to ease the ache.

There was no apologizing. Bianca made it painfully clear she wanted nothing to do with me. If I saw her again, I would crumble away into dust. Without her, it was hard to motivate myself to go out as Lionheart. In fact, it was difficult to motivate myself to do anything. I couldn't muster the strength to get out of bed. Hours passed me by as I stayed in my room, repeatedly checking my phone. Nothing had changed. I was still blocked.

It felt like life had been drained from me. There was no energy within my bones. I stared at the blank profiles that had once been Bianca's social media accounts. The emptiness I felt inside was no longer a feeling. It was me. I was nothing, a nobody, invisible, I didn't exist. Why did she do it? What did I do wrong? I couldn't ask her anything. I felt so isolated. There was no window into her life anymore. I would never know what she'd be up to or if she was ok.

An aching pain took root in my chest. It hurt so badly that I thought it was from Gravemaker. When I inspected myself in the mirror, there was nothing there. My bruises and cuts were nearly fully healed, thanks to my powers. Something was wrong. My chest felt so hollow. It was as if I could implode at any second. The pain was centered around my chest. Pressing it didn't make it hurt more. How odd. It couldn't be from Bianca blocking me. That wouldn't make sense. Was physical pain even possible from emotional pain?

Moving on was impossible. All I did was mope from my bed to the living room couch and back. Gravemaker was out there wreaking havoc, and I couldn't be bothered.

Lionheart stuff felt like a distraction. How could I focus on Lionheart's tasks when the biggest issue I was facing was losing touch with Bianca? She consumed my every thought like an obsession. Why did I care so much about some random friend I had just made? No matter how much I tried to focus on television, videogames, anything other than her, my mind circled back to Bianca.

In time, I remembered that she had bought us tickets to see that one comedian she liked. His name was Roberto Caceres, I think. For the first time that day, I felt angry. The emotion took me by surprise. We had fun plans for the future, and she tossed them away. No, Bianca tossed me away. She threw me out as if I were trash. She didn't explain it. She didn't say goodbye. I didn't get to talk it out or make it up to her.

Fortunately, Avery didn't block me. I texted her to see if she knew what I did wrong. She told me it had to be a glitch. The sun began to set, and the 'glitch' was not fixed. It was a conscious decision to block someone's number, email, and social media accounts. My banishment was no mistake. Bianca was so sweet. If she could turn on me and hurt me like that, then I couldn't trust anyone. A gaping void consumed me. All I felt was a soul-sucking chasm inside me. It was loneliness. Nobody else knew I was Lionheart. She was special to me. Why was I nothing to her?

About three days passed when I could rarely find the energy to get out of bed. Everything in life felt wrong. No matter what I did, the thought of my new best friend hating me whispered in the back of my mind. Simple tasks felt difficult. Whenever I heard the familiar ringing of Gravemaker's sound cannons in the far distance, I did nothing. I had given up. Lionheart was a piece of myself that felt heavily connected to Bianca. He couldn't exist without her.

An incoming call made my phone vibrate on the wooden coffee table. It was Avery checking in on me. I was unable to speak to a girl I was trying to impress. My current state was devoid of all emotion. In my desperation for some sort of solace, I answered her call. She explained to me that it was Zach's actions, not Bianca's. Apparently, he had access to her social media accounts and frequently checked them from his own devices.

Avery insisted it had to be Zach. That was hard to believe, considering it wasn't only social media, it was everything! Even if it was Zach, why didn't Bianca undo it? They were her accounts.

"Do you want to come over? I think talking in person will help you feel better," Avery suggested. There was a long pause before I answered. This was not a good look for me. It felt like I had turned into a husk of a person. Acting like a crybaby was surely not the key to winning Avery's heart. I was happy that she was trying to be there for me. I'd ditched her 5K and barely interacted with her previously, yet she was trying to make me feel better. Reluctantly, I agreed. Hanging out with her while I was a wreck was sure to doom any chances of a romantic relationship with her in the future. It hardly mattered to me anymore. All I wanted was for the aching to go away.

23

A VERY WEIRD PERSON

It was supposed to get colder throughout the week. The forecast predicted the temperature would drop lower each day, leading to heavy snow. I checked the address on my phone one last time before teleporting. Although I had never been to Avery's house, I had passed it on the way to school. Imagining her street allowed me to teleport onto the middle of the road. Ahead was a house that was somewhat reminiscent of The White House.

Two Corinthian pillars bordered the concrete slab in front of a towering entrance. Well-trimmed plants were scattered across her lawn with frost on top of them. A fuzzy, red welcome mat greeted me as I searched for the doorbell. From Avery's kind and humble behavior, I would've never guessed she came from a wealthy family. It must've been awesome to grow up in such a mansion. The architecture was somewhat simple, though the vast front lawn more than made up for it.

At last, I found and rang an ornate doorbell. Not a second passed before the door flew open. Avery greeted me with a shimmering smile that spread from cheek to cheek. She was wearing black yoga pants and a plain white T-shirt. "Awe, you look half asleep, wake up!" she greeted. Devil horns of hair formed by bedhead lead me to believe that she woke up recently. She was teeming with excitement. Avery ushered me forward with her hands.

Blinding light engulfed me upon entering Avery's house. It was hard to keep my eyes from turning into cat-like slits to dim the light. Everything was too white. The walls, the furniture, the picture frames, the flowers, the vases, all white. There was a certain air of tidiness that emanated from all objects being a pristine, clean white. Without color, the home felt too stern. Was her house always like this? I couldn't imagine being a little kid in such an uptight environment. The only color came from the green leaves of some potted plants. It didn't fit Avery's personality at all.

My lack of energy was the opposite of Avery's. It felt like she had been downing energy drinks all morning while I was ready for bed. I didn't do anything that day, yet I was exhausted. Avery's infectious energy was all that kept me awake. She stared me down. Warmth flowed through my face. I think she was waiting for me to speak. There was nothing to say. I'd told her everything over the phone in one big rambling mess. Coming here was probably a mistake.

A small frown formed on Avery's face. She breathed in and out slowly as if feeling melancholy all of a sudden. Avery didn't speak until she led me to her room. Although the floorboards were made of dark brown wood, the polished reflection gave off a bright white gleam. The instant my foot stepped upon the white carpet of her bedroom floor, a voice boomed down the hall.

"Hey, Ave, remember to leave your door open." It was her father, Mr. Amor.

"Dad, we're just-" Avery was cut off.

"Leave. The. Door. Open."

"Ok, ok," Avery rolled her eyes. She swung her bedroom door open wide for the world to see. Her walls were cluttered with posters, shelves with trophies, books, knickknacks, a few stuffed animals, and fake decorative vines. Everything was so white it made my eyes burn. Avery plopped onto a massive beanbag chair shaped like a cartoon frog. The eyes of the frog made a headrest, while the body and face were the base of the beanbag chair. At last, some color!

Avery ushered me to take a seat at the foot of her fluffy white bed. With Mr. Amor around, I felt more comfortable staying far away from her bed. I claimed a hollow eggshell-looking chair that dangled from a chain connected to the ceiling. A yellow pillow inside the little shell-chair further made me assume it was supposed to look like an egg. It may not have been intentional, though. Although there was still a lot of white, her room was much more fun and colorful than the drab, soullessness of the hallway.

"I'm sorry about Zach," Avery began once she realized I wasn't going to speak first. "This kind of thing has happened before. Bryce used to be part of our clique. Zach got jealous because he went to one of her swim meets. He was there for his sister, Amanda, but Zach wasn't ok with it. Same with Chelsea Green. She used to be friends with us, but Zach didn't like how much time Bianca spent with her." Avery gazed at the swirling chain above me.

I remembered Bryce. He was on the varsity football team. He was huge, the muscular kind of huge. He looked like he was in the grade above us. His sense of humor was amazing. It always got him into trouble during class. If he wasn't a class clown, everyone would've been intimidated by his bold appearance.

Chelsea, on the other hand, I didn't know much about her. Most guys at school would pick her as the hottest girl in my grade. I know this since there was a ranked chart passed between guys in the locker room freshman year. The kid who started it got in a lot of trouble. Other than that, I didn't know a single thing about Chelsea.

"You ok?" Avery questioned. It dawned on me that I had gotten sidetracked thinking about Bryce and Chelsea instead of responding. They weren't important right now. Avery was trying to be there for me, and I ignored her.

A fake smile plastered my face. "I'm ok," I stated in a robotic, automatic response. Avery threw up an eyebrow as if to say, you sure? It felt like I was a million miles away.

"Does Bianca really love Zach so much that she's ok with losing all these friends?" I pondered aloud. There was a sting in my voice. From my tone, it sounded like I was blaming Bianca. Maybe I was. I didn't know what happened. I didn't know what to think. She was proving herself to be the most caring person I'd ever met, and then she turned around and hurt me more than anything Gravemaker ever threw at me. How could she let Zach get away with this?

"You need to open your eyes," Avery warned. Her tone was soft. With any other inflection, I would've thought she was rude. Instead, it appeared she was genuinely offering advice. Her eyes sat straight, beaming through me. My lack of a reply once again encouraged her to continue. "That's not love," she added solemnly. An awkward silence grew between us. That was all she was going to add.

"Bianca bought tickets for us to see some comedian. We had plans together, and she threw it all away for him," I complained. It was hard to get the words out. I switched between staring at the floor or the cute ice cream sundae socks she had on. Anything to avoid directly looking at Avery. I wanted to hide how truly upset I was. It was kind of too late for that.

A small laugh escaped Avery. "Oh, Andrew, you know she doesn't hate you, right?" It was like she could read my mind. Bianca didn't like me, though. Even if someone forced me, I'd never shut a friend out like that. She gave up on me, let Zach exile me without hesitation. Of course, I didn't know how it went down. All I knew was that I swore I would never have done that if it were me. I was confident that she must not like me much for this to happen.

"We're still going to see Roberto," Avery giggled. The surprise was apparent in my eyes. My reaction must have looked odd since Avery giggled more.

"We are?" I couldn't believe it. How did she know? She had to have been guessing. I'd assumed all our plans for the future were gone.

"You're blocked, I'm not," Avery frowned for a second, "at least not yet."

"Bianca told you?"

"She sent me our tickets and told me to be dressed to the tens since we'll be going out on the town afterwards. Zach won't be joining us. He doesn't like the 'lame shit she's into,' and he doesn't know we're still going. It's going to be a good time. Do you have a fake?" Avery asked.

"A fake what?"

My question seemed reasonable, but Avery erupted in laughter. Her face turned pink from giggling so hard. "I guess that's a no," Avery teased. That did not boost my confidence at all. She slid off her beanbag chair, still red in the face, before

135

collecting herself and standing. She patted my head like a dog. "Come on, good boy, I want to show you something." Dazed and confused, I followed.

The walls were plastered with pictures of Avery and her family. Potted plants decorated each hallway. Avery led me into a tiny room to the right of the stairs. We gathered around a large, multi-monitor computer setup. The advanced set up felt like I was in an evil lair.

"Check this out!" Avery exclaimed. Fingers flew across the keyboard. A video popped up. "My dad's news channel made this. It's gone viral within the last twenty-four hours. I hope you haven't seen it yet. I wanna see your reaction." Avery flooded the room with her energy. Her excitement was tangible. She pulled a rolling chair out of her way and leaned over the keyboard. With a click of the mouse, the video began. It was titled "New Jersey's Own Hero."

The video was a compilation of security footage and civilian cellphone recordings. It was all about Lionheart. Despite not being professionally recorded, the video was high quality. There were shots of me bolting down roads, carrying weapons, and fighting criminals. My favorite part was the amazing song playing in the background. It was difficult to mask my joy. The video made me look like a real hero. Every shot showed off my powers. It was impressive. Electricity buzzed within me. People saw me as a hero.

I felt terrible about myself for several days. Seeing this tribute-like video made me want to try to be a hero again. I'd ignored the ear-ringing sound of Gravemaker many times over the last few days. My chest hurt thinking of how complacent I had been. Maybe it was time to stop feeling sorry for myself and finish what I started. After all, I didn't need Bianca to be Lionheart. It reminded me of her since this mess started the day she saved me. Truthfully, it was more so the video combined with hearing that we were still on for that Sunday that reignited my flame. I'd see Bianca again.

When the video was over, Avery refreshed the page. The number of views increased by ten thousand. The video already had over seven million views, rising by the second. It brought tears to my eyes. All I wanted was to be seen, to be heard and loved. Millions saw the viral video. They loved me.

"That's not all! This guy is a hot topic on every news site." Avery opened countless tabs, each containing a different article about Lionheart. "Everyone wants to find out who he is, what he is, or what he's doing!" She played multiple video clips of Lionheart in action. Avery shut down the computer and turned to face me. "The best part, my dad is going to be interviewed on live TV! I mean, not on his local news channel, obviously. We're talking national, baby! It airs tonight, at eight. You wanna stay and watch it with me?" Avery asked. Her pleading eyes reminded me of a kitten.

"I'm in," I laughed. It was amusing how excited she was over something so simple. It's not like she's never seen her dad on television before. If I could bottle up her enthusiasm, I would.

"You're a big fan of your dad's work. Are you gonna follow in his footsteps?" I questioned. Finally, I was starting to lighten up. Bianca gnawed at the back of my mind. The weird pain in my chest was still there, only diluted for the moment.

"Hell no, I'm following nobody's footsteps! If I'm ever on a screen, it will be the big screen. Look at this face, look at this body, I'm A-list Hollywood material," Avery boasted. She outlined her face with her hands when she said face and struck a pose when she said body. An evil smirk crept onto her face. I was speechless, and she was proud of it. All she did was be her chaotic, weird self, and I was hopelessly captivated.

"Then what do you want to be?" I followed up.

The smile quickly faded from Avery's face. She curled her lips downward into a frown. "Not sure," Avery hesitated. Her ice cream sundae socks fought each other while she thought. "Something in the field of biology. I want to save the bees and the turtles. I don't know what type of job that would be. Maybe a doctor, so I can save people instead? Actually, I got it! A mad scientist so I can turn myself into the next Lionheart except better!"

That comment almost made me slip up. I wanted to know what she meant by better. At the last second, I held my tongue. She could tell I was about to speak. I had to come up with something to say fast before I looked odd. "Speaking of biology. Our biology teacher, Mr. Poundz, after he passed away, his house caught fire. Thanks to your dad's work, you have your ear up to the ground. Do you know anything about that?"

Man, that was a fantastic response. Avery's eyes lit up with joy. She loved talking about her dad. Lionheart was no hero compared to him. I thought it was adorable how much she looked up to her father. It was impressive she still wanted to do her own thing and not follow after him. She was his number one fan. How cute.

"Arson," Avery cheered. She was elated that she knew the answer. Out of context, it would be uncool to be so happy about arson. "The origin of the fire was the desk of his home office. Desks don't spontaneously combust. The pattern looks like that of a flamethrower sweeping the room. My dad thinks someone he crossed wanted to eliminate information. That gas he concocted is what created Lionheart, after all. They can't let his work fall into the wrong hands. It might be connected to the fire at Armageddon R&D a few weeks ago."

Too much information was spilled at once. Avery was overjoyed to be of service. She could not wait to spill her guts about all the gossip and hearsay the journalists at her dad's work had gathered. I'd be soaking it in like a sponge if it weren't directly connected to me and my life. Sweat accumulated on my brow. "There was another fire? That gas made Lionheart?" I asked in a shaky voice that poorly hid my panic.

A sly grin illuminated Avery's face. "That's where Mr. Poundz worked several years ago, apparently. Someone broke in and torched the place maybe a week ago? As for Lionheart, stay tuned! You're sticking around to watch my dad's interview, right? He'll explain it all, including Lionheart's origin and identity!"

An enormous flat screen tv sat in front of us. We were sitting on a spotless white couch in her living room, waiting for the interview to start. The International News Channel played their intro. The couch vibrated as Avery bounced up and down with excitement. She grabbed a handful of popcorn from a cheap plastic bowl. If it were anyone else, I would seriously judge them for getting this pumped for a news segment. The warm glow of the television was the only source of light. With my eyes, the room was lit the same as in broad daylight.

Finally, the intro ended. The camera cut to an anchorwoman. Her white dress contrasted with her brown skin. She had a pin with their channel logo on it. The interview was held remotely with Avery's father, Mr. Amor, sitting in his own station's studio. The young anchorwoman introduced the audience to her guest, Mr. Amor. He smiled and waved at the camera. A rose was tucked in the left jacket pocket of his suit. His short, grey hair made him appear wise.

"How did you make this viral video?" asked the anchorwoman. A graphic appeared beneath the anchorwoman displaying her name, Mrs. Snyder.

Mr. Amor's smile illuminated his studio. "We received many videos of this man from our viewers. Each video was unedited and taken straight from the phones of individuals or security cameras of local business. My ex-coworker even saw him in person and that's when I knew I had a viral sensation on our hands! We compiled the footage and threw in some royalty-free music to accompany it."

Mrs. Snyder gave him a curious smile and asked, "Can you describe what your friend saw?"

"Certainly," Mr. Amor responded enthusiastically. "My friend now works for a nearby Police Department and claimed to have seen some guy in a martial arts uniform run alongside his cruiser. He must've been running at least sixty miles per hour! He says the guy sped up and ran faster than his car to catch the truck they were pursuing."

"That sounds unbelievable! However, I saw the video, so I know this man can run!" The woman faced the camera, directing her attention toward the viewers. "Mr. Amor claims to have a real treat for us tonight." She turned back to talk to Avery's father. "Care to share your findings about Lionheart?"

My fingers gripped the couch so hard I thought I would rip the fabric off. As if things couldn't get bad enough, the low hum of Gravemaker's sonic blasters buzzed in my ears. It was far away, and I didn't want to leave Avery's side. I allowed myself to ignore it one last time. Hanging out with Avery, the most angelic creature on earth, was stressful. Greasy, sweat caked my forehead. Bianca blocking me from everything still tugged at the recesses of my mind. I made a mental note to hang out with my guy friends sometime soon. Things were different with them, they didn't make me nervous, and we never talked about anything deep. It was stress-free fun.

Mr. Amor adjusted himself in his chair. He cleared his throat before speaking. "He's been spotted at several locations throughout New Jersey. He's stayed within a certain radius, which leads me to believe that he lives close by Maplewell, if not in it. What he's been doing is helping. This man has saved children from a fire, fought robbers, challenged Gravemaker, and disarmed criminals during shoot-outs."

A layer of oil coated my hand after wiping my forehead. My mouth was glued shut. I could barely breathe. He narrowed my location down to our neighborhood already. Mrs. Snyder's forehead scrunched up. She looked annoyed. "By disarm, you mean attack?" she questioned in an accusing tone.

"No, we've done our research, and the writing on his black belt is in Korean. Analysts have deduced that he uses the Korean art of Tae Kwon Do to fight, and Tae Kwon Do is a form of self-defense. He's not attacking." I was terrified and impressed by the research Mr. Amor and his journalistic team conducted. He had a clear picture of the Korean writing on my belt. That couldn't have been easy to get.

My attention was swiftly tugged away from the T.V. Avery inched closer to me on the couch. My heart nearly gave out. Under any other circumstances, I would have been all for it. The interview, coupled with Gravemaker ringing in my ears, made me beyond uncomfortable. I scooted away. She glanced over at me. When she saw that I was beet red, her lips curled into a smirk. Avery moved much closer to me, practically on top of me. I tried to focus back on the interview. The screen was blurry. It was out of focus because I wasn't paying attention. My mind was on Avery. Pain shot through my arm. Our elbows had collided as we reached for popcorn. Avery didn't seem hurt. She grabbed a handful of popcorn and tossed some at me as punishment.

"He mentioned me! No way!" Avery blurted out. Her eyes were glued to the screen. Meanwhile, my eyes were cat-like slits. I had focused them to see Avery's face. The room was midnight-dark, though her face glowed in the light of the T.V. She was breathtaking. It amazed me that we were hanging out together, alone, one on one. Some of the quirky things she did made me wonder if my feelings for her were reciprocated.

The thought fled my mind. There were too many things stressing me out at that moment. I didn't want to add more stress by overanalyzing her, reading into all her actions.

Mrs. Snyder peered down at her golden watch. She turned behind Mr. Amor and nodded. "It seems we're running out of time. Thank you to the viewers who submitted questions for Mr. Amor." Avery hastily lowered the volume.

I held in a laugh. Before Avery muted the television, Mr. Amor stated Lionheart must be in his late twenties. It made me feel respected. Although it was difficult to focus, my identity was safe.

"That's bullshit, they didn't let him get to his big reveal!" Avery complained. She folded her arms and pouted like a child. Her actions were purposely exaggerated and not a natural reaction. "He was gonna tell the world how Lionheart is an Armageddon employee. His high-tech weapons that appear out of thin air, teleportation, and telekinesis are most likely gadgets and gizmos from Armageddon. Afterall, he and Gravemaker appeared around the same time, and they obviously have beef with each other and a connection to Armageddon, considering that's what most of their actions revolve around."

All the neurons in my brain sputtered out. No words came to mind. We sat in silence as the television played the next segment. "Wonder how one became a hero and the other a killer," Avery pondered aloud. She yawned as she spoke. At the end of her sentence, she leaned against my shoulder as if I were a pillow. Part of her thigh was already overlapping mine, and now she was using my bony shoulder as the world's worst headrest. The smell of strawberries, vanilla, and a hint of cinnamon flooded my nose. It was her. She was so close to me. My cat-like senses were on high alert.

If all the anxiety of that night hadn't zapped me dry of energy, I would've been blasting off to the moon. I hadn't blown it. There was a chance. For once, I didn't think I was reading into things too much. Avery seemed to like me. She was at least comfortable around me. The ache in my chest resided for a moment. It didn't last long. My heart felt so full. Unfortunately, hanging out with Avery was impossible without thinking about Bianca. Once Bianca came screaming back into my head, the unyielding pain in my solar plexus returned.

24

FINAL STAND

Terrible news was announced overnight. School was going to reopen on Monday. The building was inspected and tested. No traces of the gas were found. After ignoring the sounds of Gravemaker last night and the last few days, I was far behind in my little cat-and-mouse game. Avery's information was valuable. Someone was after Mr. Poundz. They had torched the R&D lab he used to work in as well as his home. Gravemaker was after Zen-KT. It had to be him. Maybe he got the information he needed to recreate the formula and then set fire to cover his tracks. It would be hard to tell what he stole if everything left behind was burnt to ashes. I had to finish this stupid investigation. Saying I was impatient would be an understatement.

Red dust sparkled around me as I appeared in the breakroom of The Greenhouse, an Armageddon lab that once was a part of Argone. It was odd breaking in so easily. The Lionheart outfit made me feel even more out of place. This location was boarded up because of the fire. Large panes of glass made up the walls of the establishment. When driving past this place on the way to the mall, it never looked like anything other than a greenhouse. All that glass allowed me to teleport directly inside based on memory alone. Signage around the breakroom made it clear that this branch was sold to a green company, VerdeSole Electronics, to better use the many greenhouses that made up the small complex.

An eerie sound sent a shiver down my spine. It was a creaky door to a biology lab. My eyes were narrow like a cat, allowing me to see the shadows and darkness. They gradually returned to normal. I needed my never-ending daylight vision to search the cluttered room.

Most of the mess had been cleaned up. Ashes and scorch marks decorated the lab in seemingly random areas. The room was crammed full of supplies. Shelves were rigorously cleaned and cleared of most Armageddon products. A few beakers, test tubes, and droppers had Argone logos on them, but anything other than simple equipment was taken away. Mr. Poundz's computer was either confiscated or burned to a crisp, along with anything that had to do with those gas containers he used. I was busy scanning the shelves of chemicals when I stepped on something. Soot covered my feet. I was standing on a small pile of ashes. There were no remnants of whatever had been burned.

Upon closer inspection, there were burn marks clustered in one corner of the lab. Glass beakers had been melted into goop, clumps of metal pooled into solid sludge, and the ceiling and countertop were blackened and peeling. A trail of burn marks on the tile floor lead out of the room. I bent my knees to search the floor. Buried in ash was a wrench-like device with an Argone logo. The tool looked outlandish. It was an electronic device with buttons, yet it appeared to be a plastic wrench.

Out of curiosity, I pressed one of the buttons on the peculiar device. Electricity bridged the gap between the two points on the wrench like a taser. The unexpected ark of electricity scared me. I pointed the device away from me to avoid getting zapped. Getting tasered once in life was more than enough. Two beams of electricity shot out of the tips of the wrench. One beam struck an innocent grasshopper that found its way inside, the other struck a broken piece of glass on the floor.

When the electricity stopped, the grasshopper had been turned to glass. My heart skipped a beat. The wrench was the most powerful device I'd ever seen. Suddenly, the grasshopper skipped around the floor. It was alive! I slid the terrifying device between my hip and black belt for safekeeping. The grasshopper was entirely transparent. I scooped it up to carry it outside. It was the least I could do for ruining its life. My grasshopper friend and I noticed burn marks on the tile floors leading to the nearest exit. At last, the grasshopper was free. It felt like a glass statue, though it behaved as if nothing were wrong. I named him "Glasshopper."

There was more that had to be done besides saving grasshoppers. I wrapped my fingers around the wrench and headed back to the lab. That odd tool and the scorch marks were the only clues that I had found. Looking back at the room from a different angle the scorch marks lined up. Everything was burned on the same side. When I had previously entered the room on the opposite side, all I could see were the black marks on the floor, ceiling, and walls. Standing at the other entrance, I could see that everything facing this entrance was burned. Whatever did this, it came from this direction facing into the lab.

Ash clung to the bottom of my feet. There was an eyesore near where I found the wrench-like device. The lab table next to the pile of ash was not burned on the side now facing me. The bottom of the lab table covered up a burn mark that seemed to stretch before and after the table. The lab bench was placed on top of the burn mark. It was not in this spot when the mark was made.

I pushed on the bottom of the lab table where the cabinet storage area made the table into one solid rectangle. Surprisingly, the lab bench was difficult to move. When I opened the cabinets, I found heavy instruments, most of them burned, crammed inside haphazardly. Equipment like that was not meant to be shoved in storage. The burn marks further made me conclude that these hefty instruments were only in there to make the bench harder to move.

Normally, I would not have been able to move such a weighty obstacle. My powers made the task possible with a little effort. Screeching filled the room as the lab table scratched the floor on its way to the wall. The horrid noise made my ears twitch. A slight nervous shiver rushed down my back. Underneath the lab bench was molten metal and a pitch-black pit. No doubt the fire was some manmade flamethrower that was used to bore a hole into this secret room.

Water splashed against my feet as I landed in the pitch-black room below. Using my cat-like powers, I could see clearly with only the scarce light from the hole above me. Ripples covered the walls and floor. Almost everything was melted or smashed. There was no telling what anything in the room used to be. Metal, glass, ash, nothing of substance. My lips twisted in a disappointed frown. The walls were made of cinderblocks, some broken in a strange ring-like pattern. Glass was shattered into a million tiny fragments, similar to Mr. Poundz's house. The ring-marks and the obliterated glass were key evidence that it was Gravemaker. The only exit was a door that revealed a cinderblock wall when opened. This place had long been abandoned, except when he decided to torch it.

A faint beeping caught me off guard. There was something of value in this room. Gravemaker destroyed everything, but one corner was less touched. A burned monitor screen had a fist-sized hole in the display. The computer it was connected to had fallen when the desk was smashed, though it was still intact even underneath all the rubble. A faint beep echoed inside the computer case. I broke it open to find it was powered with a hefty rechargeable power bank. The power bank had an LED battery life indicator that beeped quietly until it faded. The red LED indicator turned off.

There were no outlets in the odd hidden room. I lugged the computer into the lab above and removed the power bank. On the ashen floor of the lab, I connected the least broken monitor I could find and a frayed power cable to the computer. Light flickered in the cracked screen. At first, I thought all was lost. Before my heart could sink, the monitor glowed to life! A video began playing without me touching anything.

"They want me to keep going, so I am," Mr. Poundz declared live and well. He appeared much younger; the video must have been from many years ago. Unfortunately, Mr. Poundz was probably still dead. His spotless white lab coat had an Argone logo embroidered below his left shoulder. He worked here back when it was still Argone, not Armageddon. That dated the video more than his youthful appearance. He gestured to lab rats beside him. "None of these mice have survived treatment with Zen-KT," Mr. Poundz explained.

The mention of Zen-KT piqued my interest. This is what I've been looking for! Real answers. My eyes widened, and my ears perked up. Suddenly, I found myself immersed in this blurry, low-resolution video. "When delivered in a gaseous state, the Zen-KT does not kill the subject immediately; however, this is only a slight delay. The result is always death," Mr. Poundz sighed and raised the cage of mice to the camera. They were all dead.

"The cells of the deceased test subjects prove that the Zen-KT works. The desired alterations in the DNA have been achieved, only it kills the subject within hours," Mr. Poundz placed the cage back down and strode leisurely to a pull-string light. A soft click sounded when pulling the string, and the dark background of Mr. Poundz's location sprung to life with horrid, flickering tile lights. Endless cages of animals suddenly surrounded him. They were all dead.

"The smell is unbearable," Mr. Poundz continued as if that were the only issue with his surroundings. "I asked if I could stop trials and reformulate the Zen-KT to work for the specified animal, but I was told not to waste my time adjusting it for rats. Instead, they want me to move on to other animals with brains that are more complex and similar to humans'. I do not see the point unless they give me an ape or gorilla." Mr. Poundz pointed to a dead pitbull in a cage. "It seems cruel at this point. They said these animals were going to be put down anyway, but-"

I stopped paying attention. The animals around him were nearly blue. Some were piled on top of the others as if they were nothing. It hurt to see such a disregard for life and a man who was once my teacher shrug it off and talk causally. Tainted blood trickled from endless rows of cages. The dark room was basically a tomb. The cinderblock walls were barely visible, with cages stacked high along every square inch of the room. Cinderblock walls, exactly like the room I was just in. Vomit threatened to climb up my throat. Why waste all this time when it's clear the formula didn't work? My hands shook. The answer was in front of me. It's because it did work. Far in the background of the video, partially obstructed by Mr. Poundz himself, was a fluffy orange kitten pawing at the blue corpse of its mother. Oliver.

Suddenly, the video cut as if it didn't want me to know the rest. The screen went black. "You see?" a voice questioned. The slithery tone of voice was unfamiliar. "It's not a pipedream. It can be done if formulated correctly. I don't have a death wish. No need to worry about me. It will work if I can adjust it to work with my DNA specifically, like he said. You keep trying to stop me, and yet if you really wanted to, you knew where to find me. Think about-" the video ended there.

Fire sparked within me. The pain in my chest flared up. I couldn't do anything right. Every time I searched for answers, I got more puzzles to solve, nothing coherent. I was done. Seeing the animals laid out like that and poor little Oliver all alone in some lab-grave. They experimented on him so young. He was around that age when my Dad first found him. How much pain did they inflict on him to give him those powers? It was enough torture that he never trusted us to speak or use his abilities until I was in danger from the same experiment.

That video mentioned someone trying to stop the narrator from recreating the gas. It had to be Gravemaker. He left that message for me! Little did he know that Oliver was in that video. Instead of threatening me, I was enraged. If he had known the fire it would ignite in me, he would never have left this little clue behind. There would be no more teleporting here and there, finding scraps. I was done trying to make sense of breadcrumbs. I couldn't connect all the dots myself. With all I had gone through, I'd ignored Gravemaker for far too long. He probably had everything he needed already. Meanwhile, I was moping about doing nothing. At this rate, I would never be one step ahead of him. In fact, I'd have to learn a lot more to catch up to him. I had no idea what his goals or motivations were besides acquiring and using Zen-KT.

Instead of tracking down answers, I was going to take the fight to him exactly like he wanted. I knocked a small piece of his armor off the first time we fought. The rest of the time, he ran away. That was good enough for me to think I could best him. He said I knew where to find him. That was not exactly true. I didn't know where he was, but I didn't need to. I could teleport to places I've been, places I can see, and people I know. That might be enough to teleport directly to him on a whim.

Teleporting to someone usually required me to know their physical appearance. Last time I tried, it didn't work. All I knew was what his armor and new helmet looked like. That was more than I had memorized previously. Why was it still not working? Maybe I was too worked up. Deep breaths lowered my heart rate. The image of Gravemaker reappeared in

147

my head. His movements replayed in slow motion. An uneasy feeling took hold of me. My stomach felt weak. I had encountered him enough that I could teleport to him. I felt it. Out of desperation, I followed through and teleported to Gravemaker. If I teleported to him and punched him in the face before he could react, how could he beat me? It was time to end this.

Nothing on earth could have prepared me for what I found. Macabre was the only word that came to mind. A strong metallic scent filled the air. It was sour, pungent, rotten. Blood. There was blood and twisted metal all around me. Numerous police cars were utterly obliterated. A red car had turned into a puddle of molten metal. Shattered glass covered the road. Smoke and dusty debris clouded the atmosphere. Gravemaker was nowhere to be seen. He had to have done this. He was near. I teleported to him.

The trail of destruction carved a pathway to an old shed on the edge of a bay. A dead K9 unit lay outside the door to the shed. Bullet holes riddled the door. A circular explosion-like opening made the door pointless. They shot at him, and he used those speakers full force. In the distance, I heard the wails of a baby. A hostage? There were no remaining officers to make a hostage necessary. It was coming from inside the shed. The grizzly scene made it impossible to use my psychic powers again. I had no choice but to save the child. I was trapped there.

25

GRAVEMAKER

Technically, it was not too late to run. Teleporting home was out of the question, with my heart beating faster by the second. Running was still an option.

A fishy, marine smell emanated from within the rickety shed. In its prime, it would've housed large boats for cleaning and maintenance. Despite the cat-like powers, the fish smell was not pleasant. The scent of blood, decaying wood, and soot mixed into a toxic cocktail. Most of my energy went into keeping myself from coughing. Bile rose up my throat. I stood still to calm myself. It sank back down. I crept forward on legs made of gelatin. Blinded by the rage of seeing Oliver in such a poor condition in that video, I inched forward.

Gravemaker fiddled with a mountain of electronics inside the shed. Long, black tubes were connected to pressurized gas containers of Zen-KT. The system of tubes appeared to be able to connect to each side of his helmet, around where his cheeks would be. He refrained from connecting them. His full attention was on the monitor before him. As long as he didn't turn around, I had a shot at sneaking up on him.

To avoid being spotted prematurely, it was necessary to see where there were shadows to hide in. My eyes adjusted to cat-like slits. Darkness enveloped the room. Too dark. It was jet black aside from the gentle glow of the monitor. Several errors popped onto the screen. He tried to initiate the gas flow, but the software wouldn't let him. His suit had five hours of power left, not enough to administer the Zen-KT. I hid behind towering support columns. Each wooden pillar was large enough to hide my whole body. Slowly, I made my way from column to column. Like a cat stalking prey, I didn't make a sound.

He was completely distracted. All his focus was devoted to overwriting the minimum power requirement. I got low to the ground and stayed out of sight. There was no going back now. The safety of the pillars was behind me. If he turned around now, there was nowhere for me to hide. I'd pounce before that happened. As I snuck closer, the sound of the child grew louder. At last, I was within striking distance. My hand reached toward my belt to summon a weapon. Suddenly, the sound of the wailing baby ceased! The monitor went dark. In the time it took for my eyes to return to normal and see the room well-lit, Gravemaker was gone.

Ice flowed through my veins. It was an auditory illusion. There was never a baby in danger. I fell for a trap. A really stupid trap, too. Ever since I had arrived, there wasn't a single sound except for that ear-piercing infant. How could I not realize there were no other sounds? The flashing lights of the cop cars should've indicated that I couldn't hear sirens. Granted, those cars were blasted apart like a bomb went off, but no seagulls, waves, nothing? I should've known.

"You teleported here, interesting," a voice called out. I spun rapidly to locate the source. His helmet disguised his voice. It sounded electronic, pitch-shifted, masked. "So that means Zen-KT does work," Gravemaker inferred. Although his voice was hidden, his attitude wasn't. He sounded cocky, confident, pleased with himself.

Pillars surrounded me on my left and right. There was no one there. My ears twitched. Gravemaker had muted all sound. I couldn't locate him. It was as if his voice were playing directly in my ears. He could be anywhere. Each pillar was equally dangerous. "Kenneth Pounds died from it, so I had my doubts," Gravemaker added. Part of me preferred it when he used to be silent. If I weren't drenched in nervous sweat with my heart beating like a thunderstorm, I would have loved Gravemaker finally spilling all his secrets.

"Of course, he was a has-been that didn't acquire any of the proper equipment and he didn't listen and tweak the formula to account for the specific user's DNA," Gravemaker boasted. For someone yet to carry out the experiment, he had a lot of faith that it would work seamlessly. As he spoke, I turned from pillar to pillar. It wasn't possible to face all the pillars at once. The only way to do that was to stand at the shed's entrance or the far back. Standing toward the entrance was better than being trapped further inside. I kept turning as I gradually headed to the entrance.

"Which begs the question, how did you do it?" Gravemaker tested. There was malice in his tone at the end of his sentence. It was as if he were jealous of me. Before I could fully process what he said, Gravemaker struck me in the back of the head with an armored fist. My trembling knees gave out. Gravemaker kicked me in the stomach. His foot flew like a rocket. It was being propelled by miniature sonic blasts from the speakers on his calves. I tumbled backward. That suit made him too fast to dodge.

Wham! Gravemaker used his suit to blast himself forward and back. A rocket-punch to the face, back, stomach, ribs. He zipped across the room. The speakers worked in short bursts to assist in quick movements without losing control or balance. It only worked in linear motions. Once he extended his limbs fully, the speakers ceased to prevent any harm to him. All I had to do was knock him off track from his zigzagged lunges.

Crack! Blood spattered out of my mouth. I kept coughing up more. Did that cracking sound come from within me? A swift punch to the solar plexus left me winded. *Crunch!* The odd wrench-device I had picked up from R&D crumbled to pieces. There goes my evidence. Gravemaker stood still and raised his right palm at me. *Oooom!* Sound reverberated through my soul. My body flew like a ragdoll across the floor and into the side of the shed. All his abilities came from that suit. Mine were a part of me. I had to win. I was better than him. I had years of martial arts experience. I'd never won a sparring tournament, though I could beat this nobody who didn't have enough training.

Wub, wub, wub! Several sonic blasts exploded the floorboards to my left, right, and then beneath me. I reached for

151

my belt to summon a weapon while the blast had sent me airborne. A pair of escrima sticks appeared in my hands. I landed perfectly on my feet only to be blasted by another sonic cannon. The escrima sticks slipped from my sweaty hands. They clanged on the floor before teleporting away. Years of martial arts training were useless when the opponent had high-tech armor.

This was a mistake. I had to get out of there. No openings presented themselves. He was playing with me, torturing me before killing me. Any moment, he could go in for the kill. I hadn't dodged anything he threw at me. I had to pay close attention to his movements if I was going to survive. His left shoulder armor piece was slightly burned. Was that a weakness I could exploit? My only way out was to dodge one time and run. Hopefully, the kill shot didn't come before that.

Out of nowhere, I found myself standing. Gravemaker usually didn't let that happen for long. He was hidden again. My uniform was stained with dirt and blood. I held my aching side. Were my ribs broken? There wasn't any time to inspect my wounds. Gravemaker was still here. "Curious, even with Zen-KT you should be dead by now," Gravemaker commented from the shadows. He was right. That gas gave me my psychic abilities, not my super strength. It pained me that he was learning more about me from this fight than I him. I spat blood as my forehead dripped more crimson onto the floorboards.

"What are you?" Gravemaker boomed in disgust. He wasn't looking at me when a grappling hook shot from his left gauntlet. Perfect aim without looking? *He* stole the Quickdraw software. The silver-tipped blades grabbed the front of my uniform along with some skin. Instantly, the lengthy cable retracted back into his gauntlet. The rapid withdrawal yanked me off my feet! I was sent careening toward Gravemaker! A split second before I crashed into him, he turned and caught me midair by the throat and slammed me into the ground. His grip on my esophagus didn't let up.

My hands involuntarily zipped to pry Gravemaker's fingers off me. It was futile. The more I struggled, the harder he pushed down on my throat. He had me pinned with one hand. *"Oliver, teleport me home!"* I pleaded telepathically. Nothing happened. My vision grew fuzzy. Black spots dotted my sight. This was it, the kill move. Shadows circled me as my eyes changed to cat-like slits out of fear. *"Oliver, teleport me home!"* I screamed telepathically. The speaker on his right elbow assisted in crushing my throat, forcing his hand forward.

Gravemaker spotted my unusual eyes. "Snake eyes?" he whispered to himself. His helmet amplified his voice enough that I still heard him. "Maybe reptile DNA is the secret to stabilizing the formula," he proposed. It felt like he was studying a specimen with how he looked at me. He was wrong, yet learning too much, nonetheless. My vision flashed on and off. Darkness curled around the edges of my sight. With my last breaths, I choked out one final plea, "don't, ugh, remove, my mask." There was no energy left in my hands. My fingers that were once tugging to pry his hand off me were now resting on his fingers.

Curiosity got the best of him. Gravemaker reached toward my mask with his free hand. His leather-covered fingers wrapped around the edges of the mask. A searing pain erupted as he tried to peel the mask from my face. Once again, before he could rip my skin off, the mask let loose a thunderous blast of psychic energy! The pre-programmed self-defense feature of the mask was more powerful this time. It was almost as if it could sense that Gravemaker could handle a stronger reaction.

The tremendous blast of energy sent Gravemaker flying! His helmet was partially cracked. The red light from his eye lenses gleamed through the cracks. His body tumbled out of sight. There was no time to run. My injuries prevented me from moving quickly. The only way out was to teleport. Gravemaker would recover from the controlled explosion at any second. All I had were a few short seconds to breathe and calm myself enough to teleport away.

With Gravemaker out of my sight, it was slightly easier to push him out of my mind. This was life or death. If I couldn't ease my heartrate in mere seconds, he'd finish me off before I could escape.

Where should I go? Teleporting home was out of the question. My parents would die of shock if they saw me this beat up. Whoever I teleported to had to care about me enough to help me immediately. They also had to keep their cool and not faint like my Mom probably would. The only person on my mind for the last few days was Bianca. No one else knew I was Lionheart. If she saw me like this, she'd help no questions asked. Avery claimed Bianca didn't hate me, though I was blocked from everything. Teleporting to someone who wanted nothing to do with me like that felt like a massive breach of privacy.

Blood trickled down my face. I had no choice. The sound of Gravemaker's suit rebooting echoed throughout the shed. No time to change my mind. I had to teleport to the easiest location. The ringing in my ears helped me tune out the sound of Gravemaker standing again. I closed my eyes and breathed deeply. Warmth embraced me as I reappeared somewhere else. Bianca's house.

"What the hell!" Zach bellowed.

26

OUT OF THE FRYING PAN

The floor of the De La Cruz's kitchen pooled with my blood. I didn't try to move. My body remained flat on the floor as I waited for assistance. Help never came. In my state, I was too tired to panic. Instead, I stared at the cream-colored ceiling, wondering when Bianca would see me.

"Wait, Andrew?" Zach gasped. The squeak of a chair scooting back abruptly caused me to wince in pain. Sharp sounds hurt. "Now, I get why she wanted to hang out with you. This explains a lot, actually," he remarked. The tone in his voice was unnerving. He sounded too amused for someone watching a broken kid bleed on the floor.

"Where... Bianca," I hardly managed to speak. There was no time for a conversation with Zach. Someone needed to help me before I passed out. Zach came into view. He towered above me as I lay on the tile floor. His oversized varsity jacket made him look huge. There was a slight smile etched into the tiny corners of his mouth. It was almost undetectable. How sick, was he enjoying this?

"Congratulations, Andy, there's finally something cool about you," Zach smirked. His smile was in full force. When I didn't respond, his sadistic grin faded. A strange expression took over his bruised mug. It was concern. "Dude, are you ok?" he asked in a worried tone that I'd never heard from him before. Even heartless people had their limits, I guess. He knelt by my side. My vision flickered for a moment.

155

"You were choked," Zach deduced while inspecting my neck. His eyes widened. "You look like-," he stopped himself, then finished his sentence with a different ending than he had planned, "shit." He inspected my injuries. The crumbled pieces of the wrench-looking gadget fell from my uniform. Zach staggered backward at the sight of them. He shook his head to recollect himself.

"Where's Bianca, Gravemaker," I managed to whisper. Zach didn't like it when I said her name. Each time it escaped my lips, his eyes lit up with rage. Only this time, he kept it bottled inside. He positioned me with my back upright against the lower cabinets.

"Gravemaker? Did you kill him?" Zach asked with more energy than anything he said previously. It was like he was interviewing a superstar and didn't care about my situation; he just wanted a good scoop. I looked up and down my cut-up, bruised body.

"Does it look like I won?" I scoffed. Zach shook his head. The sound of someone coming down the stairs took his attention off of me. It was Bianca. She rounded the corner wearing a magnificent maroon, red dress. It hugged her figure tight. She was breathtaking. Zach raced over to her before she could spot me. He positioned himself in a way that made her face away from me to look at him.

"You're not going out in that," Zach scolded like a father. He crossed his arms like one, too. Why was he trying to hide me? I needed her help, not his. Bianca fought back a bit. She insisted he had no right to a say in her dress. Truthfully, he was kind of right. Bianca was always cold, and that dress had open parts that exposed each side of her stomach and part of her upper back. She'd freeze to death in that. I thought that would make for a funny comment, but Bianca stormed off before I could speak up. Damn, she didn't know I was here. Maybe she did hate me. That might be why Zach was hiding me. Either that, or she'd freak out seeing me randomly slumped on her floor.

Dagger-like eyes pierced at me. Zach wiped the sweat off his palms onto his ripped jeans. He crouched down to be level with my face. "I'll make you a deal," Zach started. His voice was hushed. "With your powers, it looks like your cuts are already healing; you may want to get your head looked at.

Not only cause you're insane to come here, but you might have a concussion. Your secret is safe with me as long as you lay low, don't talk to Bianca, and don't hang out with her. She doesn't like you. After the rumors subside, I'll see what I can do."

My heart hurt. I looked at the mess of splinters, blood, and dust I had tracked along the clean kitchen floor. Zach followed my gaze. He applied pressure on my ribs. I yelped in pain. His fingers dug into my sides. "Never talk to her again, and I'll help you out and keep your secret," he repeated. His eyes locked with mine as a searing pain erupted from my ribs. "Deal?" he spat.

"I will never do anything to get between you and Bianca," I whispered. My vision was getting dark and faded. Waves crashed within my stomach. It felt as if I were sick. Technically, I did not make the promise that Zach wanted, though his beaming smile made me feel like I had made a deal with the devil. I tricked him by promising something other than what he wanted, yet it still felt wrong. I must have made a mistake if my rewording of his deal was enough for him to be satisfied. For the life of me, I couldn't figure it out. I outsmarted him, and yet I was left feeling vulnerable and guilty.

Teleporting to Bianca was a mistake. Not only did Zach learn I was Lionheart, but I also made a promise that would certainly lead to trouble the next time I saw or spoke to Bianca. It had been days since I had so much as gotten a text from her. With all my accounts blocked, I assumed things would cool off by the time I saw Bianca again. Zach smirked as he helped me. He enjoyed seeing me in pain. After that deal, he pried out of me. There was no doubt that he made Bianca block me. If rivers of blood weren't seeping from my wounds, I would've retaliated for all the pain that caused me. In my sate, all I could do was watch while he wrapped me up. My normal clothes teleported onto me as he helped me walk to the neighbor's house. They ended up helping me much more than he did. He ditched me as soon as he could.

All I wanted was to see Bianca. I wanted to know if we were still friends. That exchange left me more confused than ever. Avery said we're on good terms and it was all Zach's doing. Zach pretended to care; however, he also tried to hurt me by giving me an ultimatum. Once my superhuman healing kicked in I teleported home. An ambulance was on its way. The kind neighbor called for one when they finally stopped the bleeding. They were probably more confused than I was. Although I wasn't completely in the dark. There was one takeaway I could glean. Stopping Gravemaker would require planning.

27

THE FINAL BATTLE

Out of all my injuries, my ears took the longest to heal. A high-pitched ringing tortured me as I rested my bones. After all the cuts and bruises I endured, the aching feeling in my chest persisted. Absolutely ridiculous. Avery assured me we were still on for today. It will be awkward, considering I hadn't seen Bianca for days. Are we all really going to hang out together while she has me blocked? Despite what I've been told, I couldn't shake the feeling that I'd never see her again.

A sharp ache panged my chest. Why did my chest hurt? It had to be related to Bianca since it started when she blocked me. Maybe it would last until I was no longer blocked. That would be superficial of me. No, it would disappear once I was sure we were back on good terms.

Luckily, I'd have my answer soon enough. Avery texted me that Bianca was coming to my place later that day. She needed a ride to New Brunswick for the comedy show. After seeing her in that red dress, I knew Avery was right about dressing up. My heart fluttered. I'd been so focused on Bianca that I forgot that meant Avery would be dressed up, too. *I have to stop thinking about tonight,* I told myself. *I need my psychic powers for what I'm about to do.*

The low-pitched sound of Gravemaker's sonic cannons in the distance let me know it was time. That was my cue to teleport to Gravemaker. It would be different this time around. When we last fought, I underestimated him. This time, he'll underestimate me. That will be his undoing. After the embarrassing annihilation of a smackdown he gave me, I was certain he would dismiss me as a threat. I was counting on that.

Underestimating your opponent will increase your chances of losing. How will I flip the script? His suit was running out of power. The monitor in his makeshift setup warned him he had five hours left. Next time he dawned his suit, he would have five hours to acquire a new power source. That was five hours before he used it to fight me. He must have used it a bit after that fight, as well. He would run out of power soon. Technology like that didn't take AAA batteries. There were few options for him to recharge.

Teleporting around all the Armageddon facilities I had visited these past few days did not take long. The R&D Greenhouse, where Gravemaker left me a video recording, turned up dry. Most branches didn't have anything remotely related to what I was looking for. It wasn't until I reached where his helmet came from that I found a museum-like display boasting their breakthrough creation of a power cell made through a partnership with a green company, VerdeSole Electronics. The model on display was a replica, and yet it was missing. Very telling. Gravemaker needed that power cell; if Armageddon didn't have it, VerdeSole Electronics did.

Red dust scattered as I appeared at the scene of the crime. A small, heavily armed building stood before me. At least it should have been heavily armed. The unassuming white complex before me used to be a bank. Now, it is used as a vault for VerdeSole Electronics. There were no weapons stashed in this vault, no money either. The guards had been warned that Gravemaker had stolen the replica and would most likely be after the real thing. If he had stopped to read, he would've known the display was a fake. A careless mistake like that fueled my confidence. This was going to work; I could beat him.

As I had suspected, Gravemaker was already inside. A thick metal vault protected the power cell. His sonic cannons were useless on the vault door. *Clink!* Motorized sounds of microcontrollers and moving parts rattled within Gravemaker's gauntlet. The grappling hook he had shot me with sunk into the interior of the gauntlet. Taking its place was a red gun-like attachment. A fierce red laser beamed out from the attachment. He was full of surprises, and so was I.

"That's new," I taunted from a safe distance away. Gravemaker whipped around to face me. The red glow of his eyes was more threatening than I remembered. Fearful memories of getting beaten to a pulp flashed through my mind. I subconsciously tapped my ears to ensure my earplugs remained in place. When I caught myself, I stopped so as to not show my hand. I knew what I was doing this time. *Keep my head up, eyes open, don't let him think you're afraid,* I reminded myself. *Oooom! Oooom!* Two blasts of sound from each palm rocketed toward me. My pupils shifted to cat-like slits, focusing on my opponent. I dodged the concentrated sonic waves by leaping into the air.

"You said it yourself; a normal person would be dead by now from those things. *You realized that and still don't take it up a notch? You're practically taking it easy on me!*" I teased. Gravemaker listened to me and used the large speaker on his chest. *Wub, wub, wub, OOOM!* The massive blast was impossible to dodge. Being confined to a small room did not help. My back was embedded into the concrete wall of the building.

"Brat," Gravemaker scoffed. He turned to the vault door. Without skipping a beat, he fired the laser at the lock again. It was clear he was rushing. There couldn't have been much power left in that suit. I reached toward my belt to summon a weapon. An escrima stick appeared in each hand. Instead of using them properly, I threw them at him.

"Pay attention to me," I complained like a child. The escrima sticks bounced off his helmet and his burned shoulder pad. A slight wince was noticeable when the escrima connected with his shoulder. Perfect, he was angry at me now. Once more, the laser stopped. This time, he used the speakers to boost his dash over to me. I dodged at the last second and left a foot out for him to trip over. He crashed to the floor and bounced until he slammed into the wall. My plan was working. He was too worried about losing power to use more sonic blasts.

"Forget you," Gravemaker roared. He sprung all the sonic disks out from the confines of his gauntlets. They scattered all over the lobby-like room. Papers and pens flew as each disk exploded with a sonic blast or emitted a high-pitched frequency. The sound-based ones were more dangerous to me. They completely immobilized me. At least, they used to. The small, red earplugs I brought helped with the larger blasts but didn't do much for these high-intensity frequencies.

Gravemaker wasted no time getting back to the vault. He was already firing his laser at the locks while I struggled to move in the concrete hellscape of reverberating sound he created. With my hands at my ears, I zipped from disk to disk. The reflective chrome surface was satisfying to smash. Each disk crumbled easily.

"So, you don't find it odd that no guards are here?" I questioned. There was an unmistakable giddiness in my voice. I slammed my fist down on a counter to destroy the last disk. Gravemaker didn't take his glowing eyes off the vault. He couldn't afford not to. I'd already taunted him into using more power than he wanted to. The laser steadily ate away at the vault. "I warned them you were coming. I didn't want anyone to get hurt."

"How sweet, I'm muting you," Gravemaker huffed. Within a second, all sound disappeared. My petty hecklings were silenced. Instead of attacking him, I waited. It only took a minute of constant fire to break through the vault door. Multiple high-powered sonic blasts from the speaker in his chest sent the gigantic metal vault door crashing to the ground. Despite the impact making no noise, I could sense the tremendous weight of it through the vibrations in the floor.

An empty vault greeted Gravemaker. He scanned the entirety of the vault. His fierce red eyes flew all over before calling it quits. "You did this! You hid the power cell! Where?" Gravemaker demanded. His suit let him zip over to me. He punched me in the stomach, chest, and face. My lips traced the words, but nothing came out. Sound was muted, only his words could cut through his wavelength-blocking technology. Once he realized, he frantically disabled the feature to allow me to speak. His palms were trained on me, awaiting an answer.

"I knew you needed it, so I teleported in and took it before you could get it," I lied. There was no way for me to teleport inside a locked vault I had never been to before. In reality, the employees relocated it after I warned them of Gravemaker's incoming onslaught. Telling him I moved it was just my way of shoving it in his face more. I wanted him to think I beat him on my own.

A devastating shrieking noise erupted from Gravemaker's suit. The shrill sound rattled my brain. No earplugs could protect against something like that. "Where is it?" Gravemaker demanded. He shot multiple blasts from each palm. His chest charged up for a finishing blow.

Suddenly, sparks fluttered to the floor. Each palm hummed and sputtered out. The red lights in the eyes of his helmet flickered before shutting down. He could barely move with the suit unpowered. Grunts and muffled sounds could be heard from within the suit. He was trapped inside. His legs could hardly shuffle forward. There was too much armor and speaker technology for his body to move properly. It needed to be powered to assist in moving unencumbered.

Now that the fight was over, my heart rate settled. An obnoxious grin lit up my face. I placed my hands together as if I were praying, then separated them in a quick motion. Gravemaker's helmet split in half in sync with my hand motions. If my psychic powers didn't rely so heavily on my state of mind and heart, everything would be so much easier.

"Not much of a supervillain, huh?" I taunted. Gravemaker was powerless to counter. He stood, practically frozen in place by his mechanized suit. It was disappointing that I didn't recognize him. Part of me expected it to be someone I knew. It made no sense, but I thought maybe it was Mr. Poundz if he faked his death or maybe one of the Perfetto's. Brown eyes stared into mine. His black hair was sleek with sweat from wearing that bulky suit.

"You never did a villain monologue? That video you left me does *not* count. What were your big aspirations? Your evil plan?" I asked in a giddy, gloating tone. A massive weight had been lifted. Finally, the madness was over. I couldn't help but go a little too far in my victory harassment.

The stranger stared at me with dead, serious eyes. They were cold. It was as if he didn't see me as a person. He was looking at a thing. "George Bartholomew Rock," Gravemaker stated plainly. His face was devoid of any emotion.

"Ok? Nice to meet you, I guess," I joked.

Gravemaker shook his head. Red and blue lights illuminated his pale skin. The police had arrived with perfect timing. Of course, I had coordinated it all. The timing was all thanks to me. "Not my name, and that video wasn't for you. That's all I can offer to help. Those psychic powers are wasted on you. You hardly use them and barely scratch the surface when you do," he spat. Several policemen surrounded him.

"Well, I beat you without them, pretty emasculating for you, huh," I teased. Gravemaker looked concerned. The expression was odd on his unfamiliar face. His concern was not for him. Behaving like a child made him look disappointed in me. Who was he? He had some nerve to act like I was a dumb kid with a lot to learn after beating him. How could this murderer frown upon *me* and *my* actions?

"George Bartholomew Rock," Gravemaker repeated as if I needed to remember it. "If I had the powers granted to you by Zen-KT, I could stop him. In your hands, we're doomed." The officer's handcuffed him and tugged at him. His gauntlets fell to the floor as another officer tinkered with his suit.

"No, we're done here. No more cryptic clues, no investigations. I caught you, and that's that," I replied cheerfully. My happiness only made Gravemaker whiter in the face. He looked terrified. It wasn't me he was scared of. His eyes were trained on the ground.

"Good luck, snake eyes," Gravemaker's last words before being locked away. It was a moment I'd never forget. My first big win after so many failures. The greatest feeling flowed through me. At last. It took forever to get there.

A crowd of people swarmed me. Thanks to the viral video Avery's father made, everyone in New Jersey knew about Lionheart. They all recognized me. Before the video of me was released, people were confused and frightened by my strange uniform and intimidating powers. These people treated me like a celebrity. The pain in my chest subsided for a moment. Attention, adoration, were all I wanted. Everything I did was for Bianca, or Avery, or both. I hoped they saw me in the same light that these people did.

They chanted my name while cameras flashed. Real professional photographers were taking pictures of me. I was shocked that people would walk out during their shift at work just to catch a glimpse of Lionheart in person. A blue sedan slowed to a stop behind me. With all the excitement, I forgot I was standing in the middle of a parking lot. Never in my life did I think I'd have fans.

Everyone knew that Lionheart was a hero. I had taken down a major threat and didn't throw a single punch. My grin spread from ear to ear.

In the middle of that glorious moment, I couldn't help but wonder what it would be like if Andrew Corleone was famous instead of my Lionheart identity. It would have been incredible if the kids at school loved me like that. I was quiet and shy, too under the radar for most of my classmates to know I existed. Lionheart was loud, powerful, and loved. All I had to do was take off my mask, and everyone would treat Andrew the same as Lionheart.

For the first time in a while, I felt good about myself. Bianca made me feel so worthless. Although I'd apparently see her soon, she still didn't respect me enough to unblock me. My fingers lingered on my mask. A simple thought was all it would take to teleport my mask off and change my life forever. The rough edges of the mask grazed against my fingertips. Deep down, I knew I had to keep Lionheart a secret. If Gravemaker were the vendetta type, he'd come after those I loved. The crowd frowned as I lowered my hands, my mask remaining on my face. Red dust scattered around. I teleported home.

That fight took longer than I had anticipated. Bianca would be at my place any minute. There was much to do. How come I was always late if I could teleport? Tonight's outfit sat on my bed. It was the suit I had worn to my cousin's wedding. A fun night out. If Bianca wasn't coming, I'd feel much better. Avery claimed she didn't hate me yet- *Ding!* The doorbell rang. A shiver ran up my spine, *Bianca!*

28

TAKE YOUR SEATS

Unfamiliar clothes adorned my body. The clothes in question were a pair of black pants, a white collared shirt, and a black suit jacket. I rarely attended formal events. It was odd that a standup comedy performance required such fancy attire. Assumedly it was needed for whatever the girls had planned for afterwards. It seemed like overkill to me.

When my eyes altered to see like an ordinary human, the sky appeared dark and gloomy. It was going to snow. Oliver didn't care. He was all curled up on my bed. The doorbell rang again. My fingers were locked inside a navy-blue tie. It took me a second to correct it and free myself. Ties always gave me a weird, stifling feeling. Like a dog collar.

Through the front door window, I could see Bianca waiting for me. It didn't feel real. I thought I'd never see her again. Even when Avery told me everything was fine, it didn't feel right. Seeing her in person again was awkward. After being blocked and shooed away from her house, I didn't know what to say.

Bianca watched me walk down the stairs. I felt faint. My legs grew weak. There was a slight wobble in my knees as they carried me to answer the door. Bianca was stunning. Her hair was straight, like a waterfall cascading over a black sleeveless dress. Small, sparkling dots were spread throughout her dress. The dots were made up of lustrous stones sewn into the fabric of her dress. Her makeup was done up like a

166

supermodel. I'd never seen her like that before. Her lips were a deadly, bright red rose.

"Woah," I blurted out by accident. "You," I blushed and couldn't finish my sentence. Bianca wasn't shy in the slightest.

"Thank you, you clean up nicely, Andrew! You should wear dress clothes more often," she gushed. A cloud of sweet lilac-scented perfume flooded my nose. She wasn't wearing too much perfume; my enhanced cat-like senses made the scent seem like it was everywhere. Warmth filled my cheeks.

"I can't wait for tonight!" Bianca beamed. She clutched her hand into a fist in anticipation. Her enthusiasm was infectious. Bianca and Avery displayed such extroverted behavior it was hard for my introverted self to keep up. They didn't seem to mind. From what I could tell, most of their friends were outgoing. I brought something new to the table. Our relationship would be a perfect yin and yang balance.

"It's pretty bad out. My mom could drive us if you want?" Bianca stared at the sky. With my superhuman eyes I couldn't see the weather. However, I could tell my eyes absorbed less light than usual. The forecast predicted there would be a thin blanket of snow on the ground before the end of our show. Icy roads were not going to be a fun challenge. My phone vibrated in my pocket. We had to get going.

"I'll be fine. It snowed during my first few driving lessons," I assured. My driving instructor claimed the icy weather would be good practice. If I could drive during a snowstorm in New Jersey, I could drive through anything. It was the other drivers who scared me the most. Besides, Mrs. De La Cruz had already left. The whole point was to avoid making her go back and forth, as well as having to stay up to drive us home at night. We weren't sure what time we'd be coming back either. Hopefully not too late. I can't let Lionheart get grounded. Bianca flashed me the digital tickets on her phone. We were ready and raring to go.

"Does Avery have a ride? Did we ever figure that out?" I questioned. Bianca could tell I was nervous by my shaky voice. It sounded anxious, like a little kid about to ride a rollercoaster. The last I heard was that Mr. Amor was too busy to drive Avery.

Bianca straightened out her dress. She flattened out any wrinkles that formed while she was waiting for me. "Yeah, she needs a ride home, though. She was out running errands with her mom in the area. She might already be at the theater," Bianca laughed. It was a little strange driving Bianca instead of Avery. We tried to all go together, though it didn't work with Avery's schedule. Bianca threw a thick winter coat over her dress and hopped in the car. It was my Mom's car. I could use it as long as I was responsible.

Butterflies fluttered in my stomach. Not only was I excited to see Avery, but I was also excited to see the show. Bianca had sung Roberto's praises numerous times. The whole night was going to be thrilling. I had gone to exciting places with friends before, but not without parents, and we never got dressed up. Bianca thought the suit was a bit much. Too late now. Through my eyes, I saw splendid rays of never-ending daylight stream through the window. Energy coursed within my soul. I felt as if I were on the verge of something grand.

I didn't know where I was going. Bianca had to look up directions to the theater. It was the longest distance I'd ever driven. Which is kind of sad. Snow began to fall halfway through the drive. I was so preoccupied stressing about Avery that it took twenty minutes to realize it was snowing. Bianca tried to help me relax. She distracted me by talking about Roberto. Apparently, his ratings were through the roof! The windshield wipers were a metronome when coupled with Bianca's voice. I calmed down a bit. The gears of my mind spun and spun; no words were formed. Bianca did all the talking. I was thinking too much to speak.

It struck me as odd that Bianca never mentioned Lionheart or that I haven't seen or heard from her for days. Technically, I didn't know if she would show up today since I was told everything second hand by Avery. We were currently hanging out while I was blocked from texting, calling, and every app imaginable. It was bizarre. Was she really going to sit there the whole drive and not mention it? That was not normal behavior. My chest started to hurt thinking about it. Her acting as if nothing had changed put me at ease a bit. It would've helped more if she at least addressed it.

"When will you unblo-"

A loud gasp interrupted me. Bianca was in awe of the dazzling snow. I breathed in deeply. Tonight was about fun, not getting answers or talking about our problems. I told myself to let it go. The uneasy feeling within me remained.

City lights gave the street an elegant glow. Monumental buildings were surrounded by smaller complexes, which made them appear larger. It didn't look better than any other city. It was that night that made it special. Tonight, that small city was our destination. We couldn't wait to be there. The moment we waited so long for was finally here. A light layer of snow gave the sidewalks a radiant sparkle.

Pale, yellow lights flicked in and out of the car as I drove past each streetlight. A big sign with flashing light bulbs greeted us after rounding a corner. It was the theater. Roberto Caceres's name was pridefully plastered on display. Posters for his show were hung throughout the city. Bianca giggled and took her face away from the cold car window. Her breath left a foggy mark on the glass.

A parking spot called my name on the first floor of a new parking deck. It was almost too good to be true. My seatbelt flew off immediately. I walked around the car to open Bianca's door like a gentleman. People did it in movies all the time. The gesture didn't mean anything; I thought it was what I was supposed to do when driving a girl around. She had already hopped out by the time I reached her side.

The stones on Bianca's dress sparkled in the pale streetlights. She was wearing a piece of the night sky. They weren't rhinestones. They had to be stars. She was breathtaking. "Hide those eyes," Bianca whispered in my ear. I realized my eyes were cat-like slits. I quickly changed them back. What I saw when I turned around made me freeze. A lump formed in my throat. My mind went blank. Avery stood at the top of the cement steps of the theater.

Like Bianca, Avery didn't do much to her hair. They were both so gorgeous. Although I was dressed up, too, I felt way out of my element. Avery wore a lacy white dress with ornate floral and vine patterns. My legs didn't budge. I was frozen in her deep blue eyes. She stared at me with a warm smile. She looked at me as if the rest of the world didn't matter. All the aching vanished.

Everything moved in slow motion. I didn't mind. I wanted every second to be ingrained in my memory. Avery's lips tightened as I stepped closer. She tried to hold back a smile, but she couldn't. It broke through her lips and shed a light stronger than the sun. Her teeth were whiter than her dress. She brushed some of her long, blonde hair out of her line of sight. Avery didn't take her eyes off me. Never in my wildest dreams would I have thought someone as astonishing as Avery would be so excited to see me. I was nothing special.

"Avery, you look fantastic as usual," Bianca complimented. She practically leaped up the steps to stand with Avery. "I love your dress!"

"Thank you, it has pockets," Avery cheered. She demonstrated by pulling out each pocket. They were hidden among the seams of her dress. The intricate floral pattern concealed them well. Bianca inspected the pockets closely. She felt around Avery's dress as they chatted about clothing for a moment. Avery moved her head slightly to her left to see past Bianca. Her eyes were locked on me as she talked to Bianca.

They hopped up and down as they whispered to each other. Avery's smile was hypnotic. Everything faded away except her gleaming smile. They were talking about how it was funny that they both had the same red dress, yet neither wore it, just in case. Their words were muffled as I was beside myself. A shy smile crept across my face as I walked towards them. My eyes drifted down at the cracks in the sidewalk. The muscles in my face wouldn't relax. My goofy smile was stuck. The two of them reflected the same smiles back at me. I hadn't put one foot on the stairs when a loud voice echoed down the street.

"ANDREW!" boomed the voice. My ears twitched; my smile shattered into pieces. The voice belonged to Zach. He made it clear he didn't want to come to this. If he was here, it was because I broke his ultimatum. His voice sounded like it was coming from a distance. I whipped around as fast as I could to spot him. What I saw was not Zach. It was his hatred manifested into fire.

At first, I couldn't see him well. My eyes were too sensitive to light. I changed my eyes to cat-like slits for the billionth time that day. He came further into focus as my pupils grew thinner. By the time Zach was in focus, it was too late; he

170

was already flying towards me faster than I could run. His entire body was engulfed in flames. My jaw dropped. The break-in at Mr. Poundz's old R&D job was him. That's where I found the wrench-like device that fused living things with abiotic features. There were scorch marks in the lab. It was him. He had combined himself with fire. There was no explanation as to how he could control his powers. When I saw him last, he was normal. He was somehow able to turn his fire form off and on. Glasshopper couldn't do that! It shouldn't be possible. He had become a living ghost of fire.

29

PUNCHLINE

A being made of fire. I couldn't believe my eyes. His features were unrecognizable, but that voice wasn't. Zach flew exceptionally fast above the street as if he still had to follow the roads below. Streams of fire shot out from his outstretched hands like a flamethrower. The beams missed me. The blasts of fire melted the asphalt of the street. Had he lost his mind?

I turned to the theater. "Get inside!" I commanded Bianca and Avery. They were both in shock. Their eyes were wide with horror. More streams of fire barely missed me. Avery watched as my mask and uniform teleported on.

"Y-you're," Avery was speechless. Her knees wobbled. She acted as though she were immobile. Her face froze from utter shock. Although she couldn't move, she certainly turned red. Bianca cursed herself for forgetting to turn off her phone. She was supposed to leave it off for some reason. *He can track her!* I finally realized. That day in Princeton when he somehow knew she was out having fun without him. He had access to her social media accounts to block me, he was certainly the type to track her phone's location.

"C'mon, get inside!" Bianca ordered. She tugged at Avery's arm. I saw Bianca drag Avery inside the theater out of the corner of my eye. Her mouth hung open as she was pulled inside. They were off the streets and safe inside the theater. I turned to face Zach. He shot two fireballs at once, one from each hand. They both hit the same silver car. The car exploded.

172

Melted piles of metal were left on both sides of the street. Nobody was in any of the parked cars. My chest tightened as I dashed into the middle of the street. I stood firmly in front of Zach. Although I was petrified, I made sure my face was emotionless.

Zach's face wasn't emotionless, it was furious. His body, face, arms, digits, hair, everything was fire. He floated above the ground, slowly bobbing up and down as if the wind affected him. It was hard to believe that it was Zach. He didn't have any legs. After his stomach, there was a thin trail of fire. There was nothing human about him. He was a ghost or a genie made of fire. White flames took the place of his eyes. Red and orange flames made up the rest of his form. His fingers were five thin, pulsating flames. His head was one giant flame with thinner flames blazing out of it like hair. This form was more demon-like than human.

We stared at each other, anticipating the other's movements. It was horrifying. Heat radiated from his body. If I stood any closer, he would've given me a sunburn. When I opened my mouth to speak, Zach raised his hands and hurled a fireball at me. He aimed too high. It sailed above my head, streaming toward another car. I reached for my belt to summon a weapon. A Bo Staff appeared in my right hand. I dove into the air and slammed the orb of fire with my staff. The fireball split into separate flames, which died out before they hit the ground.

My fingers were white from how hard I was gripping my Bo Staff. The snow froze my hands in place. Nothing prepared me for this. Gravemaker almost killed me, and now someone far more dangerous stood before me. I'd only beaten Gravemaker because all his powers came from a mechanized suit. If his suit hadn't run out of energy, I may not have been able to stop him. Zach's powers were permanent and limitless, to my knowledge. It would be a mistake to assume otherwise.

"Stop! What're you doing?" I yelled.

"Like you don't know?" Zach spat. His voice had changed. It crackled and popped like a campfire. The air wheezed and sizzled in his flaming windpipes. I didn't answer him. He cocked his head to the side. "Wow, you actually don't know. You ruined my life, and you don't even know! You don't even care!" Zach boomed. The heat grew more intense the angrier he got. My pupils were razor-thin to offset his fierce light.

Zach stretched out his hands, releasing a constant stream of fire. I did a figure-eight motion with my Bo Staff. To the naked eye, the staff spun like a propeller. I held onto it with my right hand only. The Bo Staff wasn't spinning fast enough to block Zach's fire. All my energy was directed into spinning my Bo Staff. My mind wasn't on anything else, not even Bianca. Footsteps clopped behind me. Innocent bystanders were running away. Zach stopped shooting fire once they fled. "Your little ultimatum deal? Hanging out with Bianca as friends is hardly ruining your life!" I shouted.

The flames of his eyes glowed white-hot. "So, you don't know! If that was it, I would've killed you when you were bleeding out on the floor." Fire sprang from his body like solar flares on the sun. They leaped and circled his flickering figure.

The wheels of my mind spun. Nothing clicked. My silence enraged him. Blue flames spat out here and there. Subconsciously, I retreated backward due to the heat. Zach did not like me creating distance between us. Sparks popped from him as if he were a natural fire. His anger soon turned most of his flames blue.

"Whatever is wrong, I'm sorry. We can-"

Zach's face distorted into twisting flames. "I wasn't finished," he growled. "Gravemaker is my father! I've tried to save him so many times. I tried to be one step ahead of him and get the gas canisters before him. I used the last of his money to hire people to swindle the helmet and that cursed armor before him, yet he just took it from them! I burned the Poundz's residence and his old lab to eliminate that dreadful Zen-whatever formula! He knew the armor was carcinogenic. He knew that gas would probably kill him! He knew all of the risks, but he never cared. He's hellbent on getting the abilities necessary to bring down George. Your very existence encouraged him!"

What did he say? Gravemaker was his father. Zach hired those goons to try and *stop* Gravemaker? I thought they were stealing *for* him, but they were trying to prevent him from getting those things. My brain struggled to stay afloat. The presence of danger was too harrowing to figure things out at

174

the same time. Gravemaker stole money in addition to technology. That money wasn't for his plans but to support his family. He lost his job after the audit. He needed an income to sustain the lavish lifestyle him and Zach were used to. Could that be it? Why call him a monster then? Was he just as cruel to his son as his foes? Gravemaker didn't seem like he'd make a good father. Zach was furious that he was locked away, though. How conflicting.

A twisting solar flare popped from Zach's shoulder. That was all I needed to jog my memory. Gravemaker's shoulder was burned! He fought Zach before. There were burn marks all over that greenhouse. Gravemaker told me that the video I found there wasn't for me. He even called me hotshot once. *No,* now that I think about it, he said hotshot as if it were a specific person, not a quip. The marks on Zach's throat in school, the bleeding from his chest at dinner. Those were identical to the injuries I sustained after fighting Gravemaker! He recognized those wounds when I was bleeding on Bianca's kitchen floor. Did Gravemaker really do that to his own son?

Flames shot from Zach's mouth as he screamed with all his might. There was a tremendous amount of pain in his wail. Even as a fire-being, I could feel it. If he wasn't hellbent on killing me, I'd feel sorry for him. "You took away my father as Lionheart and my Bianca as Andrew. There's no future where your self-righteous ass gets away with this! Bianca is coming home with me, and you're staying out of our lives!"

A trail of fire spun behind Zach as he flew toward the theater. My heart stopped. His fire-form was too hot. He'd burn it to the ground if he went into the theater. The whole audience was sheltered inside, including Bianca and Avery. He zoomed toward the entrance at top speed. "Stop!" I yelled as I leaped into the air. Zach continued toward the theater. I swung my staff from over my right shoulder, across my body, to my left hip. The Bo Staff swished straight through him. It didn't do anything. He was intangible.

"Oh, you're completely made out of fire," I commented almost comically. It was no laughing matter. The butterflies in my stomach turned to lead. A molten ball of metal sunk deep in my chest. Zach was different from Gravemaker. Worse than his terrifying powers, he knew me. His hatred seeped beneath

Lionheart, down into my very being. I felt lost. There was no way to hit him.

An evil smile crept across Zach's face. Flames spewed out from his wicked grin. His focus was no longer on the theater. A rudimentary plan popped into my head. It might be possible to distract Zach, lead him away from the theater until he cooled off. While he charged at me, I changed the way I held my Bo Staff. I gripped the staff incorrectly, holding it with two hands at one end like a baseball bat. It was reckless but powerful. I wound up like a baseball player and swung with all my might. The staff whiffed through him again! I wanted to scream. My mind went blank. He truly was living fire. Out of the corner of my eye, I saw the flashing sign of the theater. It didn't matter what he was. He had to be stopped.

A fierce, popping roar bellowed from Zach. It sounded like fireworks in a thunderstorm. His hands illuminated the street as he shot a fireball at me. It was at point-blank range. I had a mere second to dodge. My Bo Staff fell in the process. A loud clanging sound reverberated as it bounced on the pavement. As I expected, my staff teleported away before it could bounce a second time.

The pavement beneath Zach sizzled in proximity to his flames. Sweat beaded down my forehead as the temperature increased. The flames of his mouth turned blue as he prepared to speak. "My mother left us years ago because of his disregard for life, whether it was his or other's. She left me with that monster and never looked back. I hated him, but he was the only one supporting me. I wanted to prevent him from hurting himself, not send him to prison. You took him away from me, and now you're here trying to take away the only good thing left in my life!"

Flames shot out of his hands. The fire prevented me from moving left or right. I had to duck under the flames. Tae Kwon Do rarely taught ducking as it was not a reliable way to avoid attacks. My feet slipped on the icy street. I fell onto my back. Streams of fire flowed inches away from my face. Charcoal filled my nose. My uniform was stained with the smell of soot. When the flames passed, I sprang to my feet.

"I will not have nothing!" Zach boomed. His voice was ghastly. He flew at me with such blinding speed that I couldn't react. Glass shattered everywhere. It took a moment to process what had happened. He had shoved me through the window of the store behind me. My body tumbled through another window and wound up back on the street. Pain shot through my left side as I sprawled out on the pavement.

The building I crashed through was at an intersection. I didn't know what street it was, though I didn't see the flashing theater lights. He was slowly being drawn away from the theater. I pressed my hands against the blacktop to push myself up. Once I rose from the ground, I dusted myself off. Shards of glass fell from my uniform. There was a slight black burn mark where Zach had pushed me. He didn't touch me long enough to burn through the fabric.

"You can touch me, but I can't touch you! That's not fair!" I complained. Soot puffed up from my uniform. The street was quiet. There were no people, cars, Zach, nothing. My legs quivered slightly. "Zach!" I shouted. There was no response. With my cat-like eyes activated, the street was dark. It was cold, snowing, and dark. If Zach had returned to the theater, there was no telling what would happen. The knot in my stomach constricted my organs.

A noise echoed behind me. It sounded like howling wind. I turned to see if it was Zach. An empty alleyway faced me. The noise grew louder. I spun around in time to see Zach accelerating toward me. His wispy, fire fingers closed into a fist. I barely dodged his punch. The warm glow of fire whooshed by my face. Although his hit missed, the sheer heat stung on its own.

No snow surrounded us. Zach's heat kept it at bay. He followed through with his punch and crashed into the metal base of a building. The metal was left slightly dented instead of melted. Zach cried out in pain. I gasped. He was tangible when he tried to hit something. Hope sparked to life within me. If Zach could be hit, he could be stopped. There was a window of opportunity to strike whenever he attempted to hit me. It was going to be rough. He had many long-range attacks, while I had none.

Zach shouted and slammed a giant fireball into the ground! The fireball exploded into a wave of flames. Fire quickly swept across the street. I pounced into the air to avoid it. He predicted I would do that and flew upward. A burning punch landed hard in my stomach while I was defenseless in midair. I was sent rocketing downward, smashing hard on my right side onto a rooftop. My body skidded until it lost momentum.

Light blinded me. Zach's flames kept growing in intensity. His ghastly form went through the building and rose above me. That intangibility of his let him go through walls, too, great. He stared down at me as if he were a king. No words could escape my throat. Flames streamed at me before I could speak. Without thinking, I rolled to my feet and dashed forward. The flamethrower-like attack missed me by a foot as I leaped off the edge of the building. There was a river in the distance. Water beats fire. My physical hits certainly weren't doing anything. If I led him to the river, he'd be forced to power down. I could also jump in the river to boost my resistance to his attacks. A soaking-wet punch might hurt him.

The theater had to be far behind me. Rooftop after rooftop passed me by as I hopped across buildings. The crackling, screeching sound of fire chased me as I ran. Blasts of heat warmed my body in random intervals. Fireballs, jet streams of fire, sparks, bright flashes of light followed me close. For a moment, I thought I was doing well. That ended when Zach zoomed in front of me. He flew faster than I could run.

Zach blocked my path. He condescendingly crossed his arms. No rooftops were left to land on, only the street far below. If I had to play defense, I would need a weapon. I reached for my belt to summon a weapon. Zach must have been paying attention because he knew what that motion meant. A fireball knocked a pair of nunchucks out of my grasp when they appeared. They tumbled off the side of the building. A flash of light indicated they teleported away before hitting the street.

The white flames of Zach's eyes grew larger for a moment. "I'm wasting my time with you. I'm done letting you get between us," Zach scoffed. He turned to head back the way we came. His jet-speed flight and the ability to travel through solid matter made him hard to catch up to. Behind me, I heard the sound of the river. I was so close. That's what happened. He saw the river and got scared off.

A strange idea came to me. I bolted up the side of the tallest building nearby. Cat-like stealth prevented the windows from shattering. Each footstep grew lighter as I started to lose traction. I sprang off the side of the building before I could fall. The wind whistled in my ears as I flew across the sky. My cat-like flexibility allowed me to twist my body around and land feet-first on the side of an adjacent building. I had to start running before I hit the wall, or else there would have been a pause, and I'd fall to the ground. The lightning-fast pace let me run on the wall temporarily. A few steps later, I felt myself falling again. I leapt repeatedly until I was as high up as Zach and closer to him, too.

I launched myself as hard as I could off the side of the last building. Zach was only a foot away. The arc of my jump was aimed right at Zach. My hands flew to my belt to summon a weapon. An escrima stick appeared in my right hand. I stretched my arm out ahead of me and swung the escrima stick improperly. *Whack!* I hit him! He careened down to the street. The surprise attack shocked him. He couldn't stop himself from falling. I tucked in my arms and legs like a needle to fall faster. Wind howled in my ears as I fell toward Zach. I prepared my arm for another strike. When I was about to land, I swung at him. My escrima went right through him! He had spotted me at the last second.

Zach paused to give me a furious look. He fumed with rage. His breathing was out of control like a little kid throwing a tantrum. He raised his hands above his head, creating a giant fireball between them. Once again, he smashed it onto the street in front of him, sending out an explosion of fire. My escrima stick teleported away as I jumped to avoid the incoming fire. "Aw, man," I sighed. It was a trap. I had fallen for the same trick twice. Zach raced forward and punched me in the chest while I was in the air. I flew backward again, landing on my feet like a cat. My feet scraped against the rough stone roof of a building as I came to a stop.

The flaming ghost snickered in front of me. He punched me in the stomach with his right fist, then the chest with his left. Quickly, while he was tangible, I gave him a left jab to the Solar Plexus and a hard punch to the cheek with my right. My knuckles were burned from making contact with him. A sizzling sound emitted each time a hit connected. It was my skin burning. Zach backed up in disgust. He could dish it out but couldn't take it. My foot swung at his head in a perfect round kick. It flew through him. He looked unimpressed. Instead of attacking, he turned to look at the street down below. Sweat drenched my uniform. Bright lights flashed below us. They were the flashing lights of the theater. I had failed.

30

FINAL ACT

Hundreds were gathered inside the theater. Our fight had circled right back to where we started. Zach's attention was no longer on me. He turned toward the theater. I couldn't let him enter. There was nothing I could do to stop him. Fighting Zach no longer distracted him. With the theater in sight, he wouldn't forget about it.

A quick blast of fire sent me crashing off the edge of the building. My reflexes allowed me to twist and land on my feet. Pain erupted from my knee. The awkward landing injured it. Smoke filled my nostrils. A black burn mark stained the front of my uniform. Before I could stand, my face was smashed into the pavement. Searing, burning pain in my knee kept me down longer than it should've. When I rose, Zach was hovering outside the theater.

"Zach, you have to calm down. You can't go in there like that," I warned.

"Bianca is mine, not yours. Stop trying to separate us!" Zach boomed. His flames burned brighter. I had to partially shield my eyes with my hand. All the details of his body vanished. He was a bright, white light. A star in the sky. "She'll never be with you. Look at me. I am a flare for the world to see!" Zach exclaimed. His body erupted, sending laser beams of fire and light out at random. The blacktop beneath him melted. I took a few steps back. Although I was a decent distance away, it felt like he was right on top of me. He was hot enough to burn me from a distance.

That device must have scrambled Zach's brain. His behavior was similar to his old self, though more drastic. The ghost-like fire creature in front of me hardly acted human. It was only fitting that I called him something else, Flare, since he claimed to be one.

Flare raised his hands above his head. A giant fireball swirled between his white-hot fingertips. A gust whipped around it. Nearby objects fluttered while some zipped into the sphere as if they were sucked in. Not sucked in, *pulled*. That was no fireball. It was a miniature sun. Flare screamed as he prepared to hurl the grand sphere of twisting flames!

"Stop!" commanded a familiar voice. Flare stopped dead in his tracks. His mini sun smoldered into nothing. I turned to discover the source of the voice that compelled him. *Bianca!* A thunderstorm lit up my stomach. I faced the theater to see if Avery had left, too. The lights were dim. Barely visible was Avery's face peeking through the bottom of a window. It felt like someone was choking me. No matter how hard I tried, panic was setting in. Anxiety paralyzed me. I swallowed hard. Nothing came out. After a few deep breaths, I finally spoke.

"Bianca, get back!" I demanded. Fear weakened my voice. Bianca paid no attention to me. She walked closer to Flare. The clacking of her shoes echoed down the empty road. She held her head high as if she knew exactly what she was doing. Her eyes met the gaze of the burning beast. It was obvious she was going to try to talk him out of hurting me. Flare wasn't going to listen. Hatred fueled his flames.

The heat was intense. Bianca must have been sweating bullets. I took a step forward. "Don't you move, Andrew! I'll fry you. I swear I will. If you touch her-" Flare was interrupted.

"Zach!" Bianca called up to him. Her hair flowed behind her as the snowy wind blew. Flare aimed his right hand at me, ready to shoot fire from his palm. "Zach!" she repeated, softer that time.

"Don't you dare defend him!" Flare warned. His voice crackled as he spoke. The words he uttered popped and sparked whenever he emphasized anything.

Footsteps echoed down the street. Bianca cautiously approached Flare. It was astounding that she could withstand his heat. Despite being several feet behind her, the heat was too powerful for me to go any further. I could no longer see Bianca's eyes. They had to be holding back tears. Eventually, the heat became too much for her. She stood in silence for a moment. I tried to creep a little closer. Flare noticed and aimed his hand at me. Bianca was nothing but a silhouette against Flare's blinding light.

"Easy, Zach," Bianca whispered. Her voice was calm. It flowed like a gentle stream. "I know you're hurting Zach. Things have gone downhill. Missing your mom, your abusive father, the rumors about me, then having your dad get locked up, it's too much for one person. Anyone would be just as angry if they were in your position. You're not alone. I'm still here. Everything is going to get better; I promise."

The air cooled around me. Flare returned to his normal red flames. Bianca continued to talk him down. "It's ok to get help. If you think that you can heal your pain by taking it out on me again or Andrew, you're wrong. With your powers, you have the opportunity to change the world. Don't throw that away because you're mad at Andrew. I'm not asking you to be like him. I'm asking you to do what's right."

Flare gradually descended toward the ground. He hovered twenty feet above the pavement. His body language showed no signs of aggression. Only his tone was threatening. "You're acting like Andrew's a hero. Lionheart's never helped anyone. All he's ever done was try to bring down Gravemaker and even that wasn't him, his suit ran out of power! Lionheart's done nothing! What's his tragic backstory? Andrew has had an ordinary, cushy life. Nothing bad has ever happened to him. His father never choked him, left him bleeding, or killed people to reach his delusional goals. I should be the hero. I'm the one whose life has been a living hell living alone with that monster. How come I get blamed for everything? Why am I the one who has to stop? I was only trying to save my dad and me. You always scold me for everything," Zach hollered at the top of his lungs. He kept his distance, even though I knew he wanted to shoot fireballs at me. His eyes darted from me to Bianca. It was as if he couldn't decide whether to attack me or listen to Bianca.

"No one said you can't be a hero," Bianca reminded. She took a small step forward. "You said you were making so much progress in your therapy sessions lately. I'm sure you can do some self-reflection to find the true problem. Not everything has to escalate. There are other ways to deal with conflict." She held her hands together in front of her body. Her words sounded rehearsed, as if she had said this before. Bianca knew what she was doing.

"No, that's wrong!" Flare exclaimed. His light grew dimmer, his voice softer. "You guys always make me out to be the bad guy." I took a step forward, and once again, Flare stopped me. His head whipped around.

"Everyone always treats me like I'm this unreasonable beast who's controlling you. Why do you do that to me? All these years, taking up every sport just to try and make people like me, make my dad like me. No matter how many trophies I win, it's never good enough. You were supposed to be different. I was always good enough to you. You said you loved me! Why am I not good enough anymore? It's all Andrew's fault. You've been slipping away from me because of him, yet you won't listen to me!" Flare's flames increased and decreased in intensity unpredictably. His powers were linked to his emotions, too. Right now, he's unstable.

"That's not true!" Bianca objected. "If Andrew never existed, we would still have problems in our relationship. We had issues and arguments before he came along, remember?" Bianca cried. Her voice wavered like someone sobbing. From the sound alone, I knew tears were trickling down her face. My soul yearned to check on her, though I knew that would only enrage Flare.

"And I promised you I'd change! Why won't you give me another chance?" Flare pleaded. His flames grew weaker.

Bianca's shadow flickered on the pavement. Flare's blazing light made it stretch far behind her. My knees throbbed. A massive headache drilled away at my skull. I didn't dare take a step forward. Flare was already staring me down. Bianca was doing an excellent job of diffusing the situation. It was best if I stayed out of it. He stared at Bianca and slumped his head in sorrow.

"Zach, I'm sorry all this happened to you," Bianca apologized. "And I'm sorry for going behind your back to hang out with Andrew too, I really am. I should've listened. I should've been there for you more," Bianca admitted. She gazed up at Flare. The dancing flames of Flare's fire highlighted her beauty. His light illuminated the stones on her dress. She sparkled brighter than sunlight. Flare hung his head in shame.

My heart sang with joy. Flare listened to Bianca. If anyone could stop a raging animal with words, it would be her. His demeanor clearly showed that Zach was pushing Flare out of his system. The rage was no longer burning inside him. She soothed him. Some of his human features could be seen amongst the flames.

"I'm sorry," Bianca paused. Zach's heat kept her warm without a jacket. She was always so cold. "I was the only one who knew about Andrew's powers. I've tried my best to help him, and I'll try my best to help you. Zach, I am still your girlfriend. I'll always be here for you." Bianca sounded choked up as she proceeded to comfort Zach. "Everything will turn out fine. We'll get through this together," she promised softly. Her voice was gentle and sweet. It was as if she were talking to someone asleep. Zach delicately levitated closer to the ground, almost a foot above the street. His light dimmed. He no longer radiated burning rays of light.

Zach's hands shot forward and released a tidal wave of fire! I had no time to react. Bianca was at point-blank range. He was so calm; he was about to touch the ground! Out of the blue, he snapped and blasted a giant stream of fire down the street! I never saw it coming. *What happened? Did he? Oh God... he killed Bianca... he burned her to ash!"* I screamed inside my head. The flames were far past her when my eyes could capture what was happening. A horizontal tornado of fire passed by my right side. It twisted down the street as I stood helplessly on the sidewalk. There was nothing I could do but watch as the wave of flames crashed down the street. Flare kept the fire going long after it had struck Bianca.

My right hand reached out without thinking. "BIANCA!" I belted at the top of my lungs. My hand didn't touch the flames, yet it got singed. A knee-jerk reaction involuntarily retracted my hand from the heat. Suddenly, Flare stopped, the flames ceased, and Bianca was gone.

I didn't cry. Everything happened too fast. I saw what happened. It didn't feel real. An empty feeling numbed my brain. I couldn't comprehend it. One second, Bianca was there, and the next, nothing was left, not even bone.

Her death was fast. It was too quick for any cat-like reflexes to prevent. Somehow, I remember the moment in detail. My memory replays it as if it were in slow motion. The flames rolled toward Bianca like a wave at the beach. Her hair flowed and waved behind her in the wind. Flare's heat stopped any snow from blocking my view. I couldn't see her face. I only saw the flames roll up and swallow her like a crashing wave. In reality, it happened in an instant. In memory, it was a thousand terrifying pictures stitched together.

A few tears managed to leak from my eyes. I wasn't sad right away. It was strange. It didn't sink in. Bianca was gone, but it didn't feel like she was dead. There had to be another explanation. It was like she teleported. She was there, then flames, then gone. Instead of being sad, I was furious. Zach might have killed me. However, I never imagined he'd kill Bianca. Not even the cruelest kid would ever dream of hurting her. When we talked, she acted as if I was the only one who mattered. She always made me feel seen. Zach ruined it. He killed the person who saved my life: the most loving person I had ever met!

My body trembled. "You killed her," I whispered. Flare's heat increased rapidly. He was prepared to fight me again. The smell of molten asphalt assaulted my nose.

"I was so terrified to do that," Flare chuckled. Blue flames created a wide grin on his ghostly form. "I thought I'd feel terrible afterward. I always assumed I'd only be hurting myself, but now, seeing your face, I know I made the right choice. I feel so much lighter! Now nobody can have her, and I have nothing left to lose!" Flare proclaimed triumphantly.

A memory flashed in my mind. There was one time when Avery stated that their relationship was not love. At the time, I didn't understand. Seeing Flare celebrate Bianca's death made it click into place. His feelings toward her weren't love. It was obsession. Bianca died for no reason. There were no lessons to be learned. He killed her for nothing. You can't murder someone you love. If his jealousy led him to do this, then that's infatuation, not love. All this time, I was so focused

186

on Gravemaker that I was blind to the real problems in front of me.

Thinking back, Zach always treated her like an object. Bianca was always a *thing* that had to do as he said, a toy he needed control of. My stupid self had never been in a relationship before. I made excuses for him. I thought that's how possessive you act when you're in love. I had to take a step back. That's infatuation, obsession, fixation. Before getting closer to Avery, I'd have to learn what love really looked like. Why couldn't I see the signs until it was too late?

There were so many signs too. The fact he was always tracking her, his access to her social media accounts and messages. My jaw hung open as I remembered something crucial. The makeup. Bianca once covered my wounds using makeup. She did it so expertly that it was as if she had practiced it. At the time, I didn't question it since Zach was always scraped up. However, his wounds were always visible: the scratches, the bruises, he even bled at dinner! He never hid anything. The palette she used was for her skin tone. She's a swimmer. What wounds could she have to cover up? No, he wouldn't. All this time, I thought Zach was just the jealous type. I never thought he could- and yet now that he's killed her it- it makes sense. I should have stopped him then.

My pupils tightened until they were thinner than paper. Flare was in crystal-clear focus. My eyes were on fire. They had to be. I clenched my fists. Cuts from my fingernails digging into my palms formed while making tight fists. Flare felt my anger from my stare alone. I never liked him, and now, I hated him. Madness and fury enveloped me. There was nothing else inside.

A strong wind engulfed me. I could hardly hear between the frantic thoughts in my head and the howling wind. It looked like Flare was having a hard time floating in place. The air forced him back. He flew forward as hard as he could to keep himself from moving. My rage had awakened my psychic powers. I was not nervous or scared. The worst had already happened. All I felt was wrath.

A glass window shattered to my left. Cracks raced up the cement base of a nearby building. Anything that wasn't tethered to the ground started to slide. It wasn't intentional. My head wasn't in a good place. Psychic energy whirled around me. I tried to focus only on Flare. It didn't work. The flashing lights of the theater popped. Buildings shook as pieces crumbled away from them. Flare screamed in agony as my psychic powers tore at him. Shreds of fire were stripped from his body. I couldn't control fire. I was stripping him of oxygen. I was killing him.

31

ENCORE

Dust clouded the air. The melted street fragmented. My emotions were too wild. It was impossible to control my psychic powers. I had promised myself I'd never let them get out of control, yet I was unleashing my psychic fury on Flare. He howled in pain as wisps of fire left his body. The ground shook. Debris flew. Nothing could stop me. All the rage bottled inside me was gushing out.

It sounded like Zach had a terrible home life. The way he spoke to Bianca made me realize there was much I didn't know about him. Even before he became this Flare persona, I had trouble sympathizing with him. He was always the kid at school with the coolest car, the most expensive phone, the designer shades, the varsity jacket, the popular jock surrounded by friends, and the sweetest, most beautiful girlfriend. All of a sudden, he acted like he had nothing? I had nothing! He had everything.

A loud rattling sound distracted me. It was the window to the theater. Inside, Avery was peeking through the wobbling glass. The window was about to break. If the glass shards hurt her, I would never forgive myself. If I killed Flare, I would be a killer, the same as him. That last thought scared me. I *was* the same as him. He always acted out of jealousy. Did I not just recite all the ways I was envious of him? Wasn't being Lionheart my way of flaunting myself like his multitude of sports championships?

Closing my eyes helped me focus. Psychic energy coursed through my veins. Stopping the flow proved to be difficult. It felt like a dam within me had burst, and I had to repair it fast. Deep breaths and the darkness of my eyelids. Flare's light made my eyelids slightly more translucent, seeing red instead of black. In time, the wind stopped whistling around me. I opened my eyes once the sound of vibrating windows concluded.

All the enraged energy dissipated from my psychic powers. Heat flowed from my mind to my abs, fists, and feet. The anger no longer leaked out of me. I had regained control. Flare was released from my psychic grasp. He stared at me, his eyes fire, mine that of a lion. It took him one heartbeat to return to his maximum brightness. Steam seeped around us as his flames caused the snow to sublimate.

A thunderous roar exploded from my throat. It sounded precisely like a tiger. The sound waves pushed Flare back. His flames danced and tilted in the mighty gust. Aside from a little shove, it didn't do much.

"YOU!" I shouted. My voice wasn't as loud as my roar. Flare's mouth curved in an evil smirk.

"What are you so upset about? She was mine, remember?" Flare teased. "Besides, now you finally have a hardship to write about for your college application essays."

Part of me wanted to kill him again. That roar let out a lot of built-up animosity. All the psychic energy within me felt muted, locked away. There was no using it again even if I wanted to. It was for the best. I was tearing him apart using mere thoughts. If anything, his defeat should be slow. Give him time for that smirk to be wiped clean off his stupid candle-flame face.

We rushed at each other. He flew as fast as he could while I ran faster! Ignoring the pain in my knee wasn't an issue. My mind was too disturbed to feel anything as I bolted toward him. Flare aimed his right hand for a punch. I balled my right hand into a fist at the last second to keep him from seeing it coming. As we came within range of each other, I blocked his fist with an open hand and punched him. The punch struck him hard in the head. Flare crashed against the pavement. His body collapsed from the sheer power of my strike. It wasn't enough to keep him down, though.

"Weak," Flare taunted as if he didn't feel a thing. Meanwhile, my knuckles were burned a gross, charcoal black. I reached for my belt to summon a weapon. Flare launched at me while a katana appeared in my right hand! I swung the thin blade across from my left shoulder to my right hip! The sword sliced through Flare's body. He was intangible. I summoned another sword in my left hand and executed a similar strike. The blade went through him in the same fashion as the first attempt. Flare scooted back to get out of reach of my blades.

The fire which constructed his arm was dimmer in one line. I had cut him! I left two long, dim streaks. Gradually, those streaks became enveloped in flames. The dim lines disappeared as if they were never there. Flare scanned his arm and then looked at me. He half smiled. "You can't fight me, Andrew! None of your weapons work against me! They go through me like I'll go through you!" he challenged. His voice crackled. Flames spewed from his hands. Actually, they *were* his hands.

The pavement scuffed my feet as I dodged to the left. The fire didn't melt the asphalt. He was cooling off. I stepped forward with my right foot and sliced diagonally across Flare's body with my right sword. The right sword was now at my left hip. I repeated this move with my left side. With my swords at my hips, I slid to my left and sliced horizontally across his stomach with both swords at the same time. Each hand was now back on their respective side. Flare stumbled back. I spun my swords and caught them in a reverse grip. The blades pointed toward my pinky instead of my thumb, as I purposely held the swords incorrectly. I crossed my arms and stabbed each blade into his shoulders. Without hesitating, I uncrossed my arms, dragging the blades through the rest of his body in an X-shape.

"You can't cut fire dumbass!" Flare growled. He tossed a fireball at me from his right hand. I flipped my swords back into the proper position, with the blades pointing toward my thumbs. I used my left sword to block the incoming fireball as if holding an escrima stick. The impact of the fireball was enough to knock the sword from my hand. A loud clang echoed as it hit the ground before teleporting away.

Flare charged forward and shot fire behind him to boost himself. The longer I held the sword, the heavier it felt. I threw the sword in my right hand at him, blade first, like a spear. The sword sailed right through him and teleported away. I thought the sword would hit him or at least slow him down. It did nothing. I slid to the right at the last second. Flare barely missed me. A gust of warm air wrapped around me as he passed. My fighting style was risky. After what he did, it was impossible to think straight. Throwing the katana was reckless however, I was in no condition to be using such a weapon anyway.

As I ran toward Flare, I noticed his head was tilted slightly to his right. I followed his line of sight and realized he would attempt to dodge my charge. Flare tried to dodge to the right as I had predicted. I was ready and struck him with a haymaker punch in the middle of his chest. It wasn't a proper technique. If he hadn't tried to dodge, I would've missed. When the punch reached halfway through its motion Flare's body became intangible. The sudden absence of resistance sent me stumbling forward.

"I can control my powers!" Flare spat. He raised his elbow and struck me with it like a wrestler. The impact of his scalding elbow on my bony shoulder sent me to my knees. A shooting pain ran through my legs. The throbbing in my kneecaps wouldn't cease. It hurt too much to stand. My legs wouldn't budge. The pain grounded me. When my gaze met Flare, he released a chaotic fireball. I pressed my fists against the rocky street to take some weight off my stressed legs. It was enough of a break to let me spring into a fighting stance. The soles of my feet stung from all the movement.

"Ugh," I moaned as my muscles braced for impact. To my surprise, Flare didn't hit me. Instead, he grabbed the back part of the collar of my uniform like a bird swooping and catching prey. I was a kitten being held by the scruff of its neck. My body dangled in the frigid air as Flare carried me away. I attempted to free myself by summoning a weapon. When my hand began the motion, he let go! It wasn't intentional. His hands had burned through my uniform.

My back paralleled the street below as I free-fell down to earth. Flare came into view as I plummeted three feet away from him. He looked as though he were about to charge at me. My eyes widened with terror. It was hard to concentrate with the shooting pain throughout my body. The wind howled in my ear as I tried to acquire a weapon. It didn't matter which one. Whatever materialized in my hands, I would simply launch at him.

Two small, cold metal objects formed in my right hand. I threw one of them immediately. The first one was what I believed to be a kunai: a small throwing knife with a sharp, spear-shaped blade. There was no time to inspect what it looked like. It zipped through the air and straight into Flare's eye. He flinched. No time to waste. The second object flew from my hand less than a second later. It was a shuriken. The shuriken was small, black, and lightning-fast as it whizzed through Flare. Each projectile teleported away once they exited Flare's body. It wasn't clear if they hurt him. He may have simply been surprised by them.

The statue in the Lionheart sanctuary said the weapons I could summon were all weapons I knew how to use. However, I didn't know how to use a sword effectively, and I'd never thrown a kunai or a shuriken. The only time I had seen them was during Tae Kwon Do demonstrations. Somehow, I conjured the sleek, sharp weapons. They must be weapons I would master in the future.

Wind whistled in my ear. I tried to twist my body around to land on my feet like a cat. Flare wouldn't let me. He grabbed onto my arms and forced me downward. My head jerked forward as we accelerated down to the street.

Being locked face-to-face with Flare's demonic eyes caused me to seethe. "You're just like your father," I choked out in a raspy war-torn voice. His eyes grew white-hot with the realization that I was right; he too was a heartless killer. It was the wrong time to piss him off, yet I didn't care what happened to me. He growled, his body glowing brighter with rage.

A thundering boom echoed down the street. Flare forced my back into the sidewalk! Rubble erupted from the pavement like a volcano. A dreadful yell cried out from within me. The pain was too unbearable to hide. Flare didn't let go. He continued to push me forward and ground my back against the pavement. Cement crumbled apart as Flare pushed my body through the sidewalk like a snowplow. I tilted my head up to avoid smashing my neck and skull. My teeth ground together to keep myself from screaming.

Suddenly, a loud siren rang out. Hope fluttered to life. It was the siren of a firetruck! It didn't sound too far away. The alarm grew louder. Flare appeared to be unaware. He didn't see it. Each emergency vehicle had a distinct sound; maybe he didn't recognize it. The firetruck must have been about to turn the corner. If Flare saw it, he would have flown away. My only chance at ending the fight was to break free and get the truck to hose him down.

I looped my left arm from the inside, near my chest, around to the outside, grabbing Flare's upper arm. The palm of my hand burned as if I had grabbed something directly out of the oven. Fighting through the pain, I yanked as hard as I could. It wasn't enough to free myself. I punched him with my right hand at the same time. My actions had to be swift, or I risked irreparably scorching my hands. The third punch did the trick! His grasp on me was relinquished. Flare tumbled onto the street.

My chest hurt more than my hands. Debris dripped off me like water. Breathing was hard. Sitting up was harder. Flare had already recovered. He didn't try to push me through the ground anymore. Instead, he zipped over and executed a wild haymaker punch! The easy-to-block punch landed square in my jaw. Little energy was left within me. Flare was made of energy. He punched me repeatedly with his right hand. The blistering heat of his fists singed my skin with each punch.

Once I caught my breath, I was able to block again. Too many hits had landed for my liking. Although he had telegraphed each punch, I didn't have it in me to react in time. Until now. With strained muscles, I moved my left hand in front of my face, barely blocking Flare's punch. All my energy flowed into my right fist as I countered, unleashing a powerful cross directly in the center of Flare's pitiful, flaming face!

Blood trickled from my knuckles. The sore muscles of my arm stung from moving quickly. Flare skidded along the demolished sidewalk before regaining his composure and returning to the air. *Whammmp!* It felt like my ears were twitching. Any second, that firetruck would come around the corner. This was my only shot. If he spotted the truck, he'd flee.

Hatred burned in Flare's eyes. A sickening scream belted out of Flare as he zoomed toward me. His fist was cocked, ready to unload another reckless haymaker. I slid to my left at the last detectable moment. Flare was flying too fast to stop. Before he could attempt to correct himself, I accelerated his trajectory by running two steps and jump kicking him in the back with a flying sidekick! The firetruck came into sight. After that kick, his velocity was fixed. He shot straight through the side of the firetruck!

Gallons of water gushed out of the tear Flare had made. I couldn't see inside the tank, yet I knew Flare was somewhere in there. Clouds of steam blasted out. The sound of hissing vapor and bubbling water emanated from within. Soon, the street became a misty sauna shrouded in dense fog. Energy drained from my bones. It was hard to keep myself upright. With Flare extinguished, I let my guard down.

Light pierced through the cloud of fog. A fire-covered hand came groping through the steam. Flare emerged from the firetruck. Although he had enough energy to float, he appeared weak. He kept sinking. No matter how hard he tried, he only levitated a foot above the street. Flare's body looked like a campfire about to go out. Parts of his body lacked fire. Pieces and patches had visible traces of clothing or human skin. His right hand, hips, and chest glowed like embers. He was a crisscrossed mess of smolder, embers, and flames.

"You've tried so hard to stop me," Flare shouted. "But I-"

"If water doesn't put you out, this will!" I threatened. I kicked him forcefully with the ball of my foot in a right-leg front kick. We had talked enough. I saw past Flare's act. He pretended like the water didn't weaken him. The water dampened his powers. That's why he tried to resort to verbal intimidation. He was weak, and he knew it. His back banged loudly against the solid metal side of the firetruck and bounced off. Fear seeped into his eyes for the first time as he struggled to become intangible.

I stepped forward and punched Flare in the face with my right hand. His body ricocheted off the truck once more. Out of spite, I punched him three more times in the head, keeping his body ping-ponging from my fist to the truck. After the third punch, I allowed gravity to take Flare to the ground. He slid against the truck as he fell onto the pavement.

Steam rose from Flare's body. His fire smoldered until regular-old Zach remained. Somehow, his clothes and skin reappeared as if nothing had happened. Snow sizzled when it landed upon him. He still radiated heat. In time, snowflakes stuck to his varsity jacket. Zach coughed and attempted to sit up. I reached for my belt to summon a weapon. My Bo Staff appeared in my right hand. I gently poked the staff in the middle of his chest and pushed him against the ground. He was too weak to fight. The staff touched him lightly. Unconsciousness soon took him over. The exhaustion finally got to him. He had burnt himself out.

32

GOOD NIGHT, DRIVE SAFE

Thoughts of Bianca flooded my mind. She was gone. When Bianca died, I was too consumed with hatred toward Zach to feel anything else. Police arrived on the scene and arrested him. Alone in the dark street, sadness was finally able to seep in. It trickled into my veins like poison. An unwelcome energy caused me to bolt down the street like my life depended on it. Tears formed in my eyes, blurring my vision. My feet begged me to stop, which only made me push myself further. The energy was a self-defense mechanism. I was trying to run from my feelings, run from the pain. Flare wasn't chasing me, though I ran as if he were. Bianca's laugh rang in my head. It felt like I could reach out and touch her if I ran just a little further. It was all in my head.

Grand flashing lights appeared around a corner. The theater. The lights triggered a flashback of Bianca standing with her back to me as the flames slowly wrapped around her silhouette. My eyes were closed throughout the flashback. It was difficult to open them as if I didn't want to face reality. I forced my eyelids apart, and the first thing I saw was Avery. She was standing right where Bianca was standing when she was killed.

I wasn't paying attention to where I was running. My left foot plunged into a water-filled pothole. The water was formed by snow Flare had inadvertently melted. The sudden change in speed caused me to trip and somersault forward. My limbs flailed as I bounced and skidded down the street. New cuts and scrapes formed over my already bruised body. Gradually, I rolled to a stop in front of the theater. Out of the corner of my eye, I spotted Avery standing to my right. Another puddle reflected my ash-covered, bruised face. Soot, blood, dust, cat-like eyes, a venetian mask, what the hell was I? Avery was always so pure and effortlessly gorgeous. Some gross freak I hardly recognized stared back at me through the puddle.

Blood dripped from my lip as I stood. Avery and I stared at each other in silence. She watched me as I dusted myself off. It was difficult maintaining eye contact with her. My eyes darted from her dress to my uniform. She was clean and pretty. I was covered in soot and scrapes. It looked like I had been in a blender. My black belt was loose, my sleeves were shredded, the leg openings of my pants were torn, and burn marks decorated my uniform. Portions of my uniform turned black from fighting in the dirty streets with a soot-spawning ghost. Heat rushed to my cheeks. I was embarrassed. I was tired, frail, and bloody on the night I was supposed to impress her.

Tears trickled down her face. I wish I didn't look her in the eyes. They were filled with agony. She cried silently. It was as if she wasn't breathing. Not a single sound. There were no words to say. I certainly didn't have any. Avery stood there and stared at my broken spirit. Her teary eyes scanned me up and down.

Even when Avery's face was pink with tears, I couldn't believe how beautiful she was. Without Flare, there was no need for my cat-like eyes. They turned back to normal, seemingly turning the night into day. The bright sky didn't match my mood. Avery didn't have any powers. She saw the shadowy night, which mirrored our emotions more accurately. I wished Avery could see herself through my eyes. Her skin glistened in the light.

I wiped sweat and soot from my face using my torn sleeve. My legs wobbled as I tried to walk. I couldn't catch my breath. A sharp sting irritated my lungs when I breathed. The crisp, cold air didn't help. I teleported my mask off. With my back slouched and my feet pulsating with pain, I limped forward. The nice suit I was previously wearing teleported on to replace my uniform. The suit hid most of the bad burns. A bruised, bleeding, ash-covered man in a pristine suit. What a sight to see. Avery sniffled. She followed me to my Mom's car, keeping a few paces behind me.

Snow stuck to Avery's shoulders, blending in with her dress. She glanced back at the spot where Bianca had stood. After a long pause, she turned to look at me. We didn't say anything. Our thoughts were connected. We felt the same. Something cold grabbed my wrist. I spun around to see Avery holding me tight. Her hand was freezing and covered in goosebumps. Her eyes never left the ground. I wanted to go home, though her grasp kept me in the street. A chilling breeze swept around us. Avery slid her hand down from my wrist to hold my hand for a brief moment. Our eyes locked. Her hand left mine. We both wanted to get out of there. Her shoes clacked as she headed to the passenger side of the car. I had to drive her home as our night ended unexpectedly early.

There was much to talk about, yet neither of us spoke. Avery must have had many questions about Lionheart or Flare. We kept it to ourselves. Despite not feeling ready to drive, I started the engine and turned on the heat. The car shook as it came to life. I didn't drive right away. We went from standing in silence to sitting in silence. Avery peered out the window. Her warm breath created a layer of fog on the glass. She drew a cat face on it. The corners of her mouth bent upward for a fleeting second. She didn't dare erase her artwork. Several minutes passed before I began the drive home.

No words were spoken during the car ride. In fact, Avery fell asleep. I was envious of her ability to fall asleep so quickly. Throughout the fight with Flare, it felt like I'd never be able to sleep again. No matter how much my body wanted to rest, I pushed myself further. I kept glancing over at Avery to make sure she was ok. Her hair was everywhere! Her lips barely poked out through the mess of hair spread across her face. She leaned her head against the side of the car door as she slept.

"I'm so sorry, Avery," I whispered. She was still asleep. The sound of my voice caused her to stir. Her head rose gently. She brushed her hair out of her face and stretched her arms.

"Where are we?" Avery yawned. She looked out her window. The cat face she drew stared back at her. It must have been dark out because she couldn't tell where we were. Her eyes blinked, wiping away the drowsiness.

"Home," I answered. Avery followed my gaze. She recognized her house and nodded. The passenger side door clicked open. Avery stepped out of the car. Without turning around, she closed the door and walked away. Snow blew inside the car as I got out, too. I slammed the door shut with a clunk and walked Avery to her front door. It didn't look like anyone was there. With her father working for the local news, he might have left to see what was going on in New Brunswick. Avery almost slipped on hidden ice. She held onto me for support. I walked slowly and firmly to ensure I didn't fall myself in my weakened state. We hugged but did not say goodbye.

The tall red door to her house closed. Avery observed me through the window. The freezing air numbed my ears. Snow was already sticking to the ground. I grabbed some snow gathered on the windshield and applied it to my burned knuckles. The snow turned red with blood. I rolled up the sleeves of my suit jacket to keep it from getting ruined. Enough had been ruined for one night. When the snow melted, I shook the bloody water off and opened the car door. More snow swarmed in. I started up the car and headed home.

When I finally made it back to my house, the sound of the front door opening attracted my parents' attention. "Look who's home! How was it? I made dinner if you didn't eat with your friends." my Mom called from another room. The pitter-patter of her footsteps grew louder. I sunk my hands into the sleeves of my suit to hide my burned knuckles. My Mom turned the corner and freaked out upon seeing my ash-covered face. "What's wrong? What happened?" she cried. It was obvious I was upset. A few hot tears rolled down my cheek. My Mom wrapped her arms around me in a comforting embrace.

"A good person died tonight," I replied. My arms dangled over her shoulders. I didn't squeeze her back. There was no energy left within me. My mind was too blurred to think. I couldn't explain anything else that had happened. It

200

was impossible to utter the words I wanted to. A choking feeling stopped me when I tried to explain further. What I told my Mom was true. An extraordinarily good person died that night. I'd never be the same again. It changed me forever. That wasn't enough information for my Mom.

"Tell me everything! What happened? There's soot everywhere," she demanded. Her forehead wrinkled with concern. Without knowing any details, her eyes watered. I knew she would be upset at the mere sight of me. The air squeezed out of my lungs. There was no air to speak with. It felt like my chest was constricted.

"I heard Lionheart was in New Brunswick tonight. I didn't think anything of it. He's the only thing that's on the news these days. It was strange, though, a reporter said he was fighting a fireman?" my Mom questioned. Silence only made her speak more.

I shook my head. I couldn't breathe. Everything hurt. The last thing I wanted to do was start a conversation. All I wanted was to sleep. "No, not a fireman, a man made out of fire," I corrected. "That's what happened to me," I paused to think of a lie. "He flew right by me. It covered me in soot and a few minor burns, but I'm fine." My Mom gasped. She touched a scorch mark on my face. The wound stung. I cringed and pushed her hand away. "He was too powerful for Lionheart."

"Oh, no! He killed Lionheart?" my Mom interrupted. Suddenly, my Dad entered the hallway. He had overheard our conversation. My Dad patted me on the back. He looked me up and down as if he could figure out what happened by scanning me over.

"No, he killed someone before Lionheart could save them!" I blurted out. My Dad seemed confused, though I didn't want to say more. The words I had uttered already hurt too much. They were going to find out what had happened soon enough. I didn't want to be the one to tell them. It was too painful to think about. A tight feeling strained my chest. I had to go to bed.

"You alright? Who got hurt?" my Dad asked. His face was now pale with worry. My Mom cried and tried to hold me again. I backed away. "Give him some space, let him speak. What's wrong?" my Dad repeated.

"I'm not sure I can say," I started. My heart pounded. Pressure built inside my head, creating a thunderous headache. "My- I mean, it's Bianca," I choked out. They did not know her well. The name was only familiar since they knew I was going to drive her to the theater. Other than that, the details of our newfound friendship were not something I discussed with them.

"Is she ok? Do I need to call her parents? Wha-" I interrupted my Mom.

"She's gone," I stated vaguely. For some reason, I couldn't say that she died. It didn't feel like she was dead. I couldn't wrap my head around her being gone, either. That was enough to make my Mom break down. She clung onto my Dad as I trudged to the stairs. Each step creaked on the way up to my bedroom.

"Hey, get some sleep. You don't have to go to school tomorrow," my Dad offered. He smiled at me and turned to comfort my Mom. She was distraught despite not knowing all the details. I had spotted my backpack on the chair by the island counter. It was crammed with all the books and binders I needed for class the next day. Nothing felt real. My friend died, and school would continue as if nothing had happened. Although I should've taken the time off from school like my Dad suggested, I really wanted to see Avery again tomorrow.

It wasn't long before I forgot about school completely. Oliver waited for me on my bedroom floor. His ears perked up. He bent down, reached forward, and thrust his bottom into the air in a long stretch that elongated his back. "Oliver," I whispered. There was no energy left for my psychic powers. "Is there nothing you can do?" I cried as I bent down to one knee to talk to him. My knee quivered painfully as it hit the carpet. "Your psychic powers rearranged my DNA. You're more well-versed with these powers than me. You can heal her, right?" I sobbed. For the first time in a long time, I allowed myself to cry. "You can rearrange atoms and overlap atomic orbitals to make any compound you want! You could bring her back, can't you? Everything's made of atoms!"

Oliver's ears recoiled as if he were scared. He peered down at the cream-colored carpet floor. *Burning is a chemical change, Andrew. She was turned into soot, carbon dioxide, and water. Combustion reactions are not reversible. They can't be undone.*" His little cat eyes grew larger as he spoke. Recreating someone atom by atom would take a lot of time and resources. It was a long shot. I knew that, yet I couldn't accept that there was nothing I could do. Thinking it over, I felt ridiculous. There was no way to bring someone back like that. How could one even know where to place each atom? It was impossible.

It finally sunk in. Bianca wasn't gone. She was dead. There was nothing anyone could do to change that. I lowered my head to the floor. A warm, tingling feeling rushed through my body. My face felt hot and wet with tears. Most of the salty drops stayed in my eyes. I tried to hold them in, to hide weakness, but I couldn't. Out of nowhere, Oliver's soft fur brushed against my face. He rubbed his little cheek against me. His whiskers prodded my face. Cute, little mews leaked when he exhaled.

"I'm sorry."

After kneeling on the floor for a millennium, I crept into bed. I never changed out of my suit. If my formal outfit got wrinkled, I didn't care. The inside was already stained with soot and blood. It had to be cleaned before wearing it again anyway. The ceiling was all I saw for hours while lost in thought.

It seemed like my thoughts never ended. I failed to save the person who saved me. The one time I had to save a friend instead of a stranger, I couldn't do it. I let Bianca try to talk Zach out of it. Fire engulfed her while I stood safely to the side. There was nothing I could do at the time, but I could have prevented it. Avery told me how poorly Zach treated her. She insisted we should do or say something. I refused. When she saved me, people made up a rumor that she liked me. I wanted to distance myself from the gossip. If I had tried to break them up, it would have validated Zach's view of me. I thought it wasn't my place to interfere in their relationship.

There was so much that I missed. Zach was able to track her location at all times. He called her when he noticed she was out of her house without him knowing. She knew how to use makeup to cover up my wounds. I knew nothing about makeup, I'd assumed she was just skilled at it. Nothing indicated that she had wounds to hide. Zach always put down her interests like the comedian she liked. He told her she was overreacting when she was upset with him. Each time they argued, he made himself out to be the victim and she was crazy. He made her change the dress she wanted to wear. She cut most of her friends out of her life for him. Avery told me he had access to her social media accounts to block whoever he wanted and read all of her messages. At the race, she was the only one who knew the guidance counselor. Millions of signs something was wrong and nothing was done.

What could I have done? We should have interfered. Bianca was in trouble, and we did nothing. No, *I* did nothing. Avery always saw him as a threat. I excused his actions all this time since I thought I was biased against him for how he personally treated me. That and my envy of him and inexperience with relationships, girls, Lionheart, everything blinded me from seeing how awful he was for her. There was no way of telling if we could have gotten her out of that toxic relationship. However, doing something would've been better than nothing. Our inaction allowed Zach to escalate. He forced her to shut me out of her life. There were plenty of warnings, yet I didn't do a thing. It was all my fault.

Lionheart wasn't a hero. Zach was right. The statue claimed I was destined to be some hero who would save the future. Nothing I did was for others. All I wanted was to be seen. Every day, I followed the breadcrumb trail of clues that led to Gravemaker. I'd never truly helped anyone. I can count on one hand the number of people I saved. Although I wasn't heartless, I had an ego. Fighting petty crime and saving cats from trees were the types of things Bianca wanted me to do, and I never did. After my first fight with Gravemaker, doing anything else felt below me. My abilities were best used to stop powerful threats like him, not solve ordinary crimes or help prevent everyday accidents.

Everything I did, I did for myself. I craved fame. Once I had the opportunity to be popular, I took it. The statues were wrong. There was no apocalyptic threat. I used its words as an excuse to only fight Gravemaker, become well known, and make myself feel like I wasn't invisible. Even when all I did was focus on Gravemaker I still failed. There were countless times when I ignored the sound of his blasters in the distance. I disregarded the one task I assigned myself whenever it was inconvenient for me. Lionheart meant nothing to me. It was only a way to fight my insecurities.

My thoughts kept me up most of the night. I couldn't stop thinking. Hours of endless regrets flowed through my mind. They wandered through and stacked in an ever-growing pile. Sometimes, the pile toppled over, and I'd revisit old thoughts. I couldn't brush them away. They pulled on my heart. They fractured my mind. I was wrong when I said that the searing heat of a sunny day was the worst feeling in the world. Loss was worse. It made me regret everything. All the things I should've done and most of what I had done. If I could undo it all, I would have.

Ultimately, the thoughts died down. Thoughts are infinite. I couldn't lie there and think everything through, or I'd never leave my bed again. The throbbing in my head intensified throughout the night. There came a time when my thoughts couldn't keep me awake anymore. I felt dead-tired, yet I didn't fall asleep until my mind gave out like my body had. As my thoughts settled down, my eyelids grew heavy. It became difficult to hold them open. They sank down over my eyes. A few more thoughts ran through before I finally fell asleep.

Things were not peaceful even while asleep. Being asleep meant dreaming, and after the day I had my dreams were only nightmares.

33

BACK TO SCHOOL

Everyone rushed around me to get to class on time. The school was a hive of swarming bees. I moved like a slug. As I stumbled through school, I realized it was the vision of the future I had seen long ago. The same people walked around me. I entered through the exact door and was wearing identical clothes. The vision showed me making it to school, it never showed Bianca. A tall kid bumped into me. He continued walking as if I wasn't there. After all I had done as Lionheart, Andrew was still invisible.

A teacher ushered my friends along through the crowd of preoccupied students before I could talk to them. None of them were in my first class. I turned to the right and headed upstairs. The first day back was a redo of the same classes we had before the gas incident interrupted classes. We had an alternating schedule at my school. All students had two different schedules, one for A-days and one for B-days. The bell rang right as I made it to Biology.

The new Biology teacher introduced herself with a kind smile. "Hello, I'm Mrs. Williams," she greeted. She had on one of Mr. Poundz's old lab coats. It was too big on her. It looked like a dress. Mrs. Williams had curly black hair kept in a ponytail. "What's your name?"

"Andrew," I answered quietly.

"I'm sorry, what?" Mrs. Williams didn't hear me.

"Andrew," I repeated, slightly louder.

Mrs. Williams smiled and nodded. She grabbed a clipboard off the desk behind her. "Ok, sit at your assigned seat, Andrew. I have to take attendance." Mrs. Williams analyzed her seating chart. The pen wiggled in her hand as her eyes scurried up and down from the chart to the seats. I stared at Avery's seat. An empty chair stared back at me. Mrs. Williams made marks on her paper as she took attendance. Throughout attendance, I prayed that Avery would come to class. My heart sank thinking of her at home, locked in bed with grief. A knock at the door stole the class's attention. Avery was waiting outside. Mrs. Williams welcomed her in.

Relief flowed through my veins as Avery took her seat. Although I was awfully glad she was there, she shouldn't have been. She knew Bianca better than anyone. They had been friends since kindergarten. If someone was going to skip school that day, it should've been her. My stomach tied into a knot. We were devastated and still showed up. It was denial. Had to be denial. Part of me expected to see Bianca amongst the crowd in the halls. Last night didn't feel real. Now that we had made it to school, her absence felt more noticeable. We should have stayed home.

All day, Bianca was the talk of the school. Word of her passing spread fast, though the details were not always accurate. Biology was tough to get through. Pre-Calculus was far worse. No friends were in that class. Not even Avery. The desks were aligned in rows. My seat was in the back right corner, away from the door. The teacher, Mrs. H, didn't bother checking the homework. She was acutely stressed because we had missed so many school days. The school year would be extended to compensate for the lost time. The class groaned.

Mrs. H rushed through her lesson. It was impossible to focus. I thought it would be easier without Avery there to distract me. I was wrong. It wasn't her that was a distraction. It was my thoughts. That was something I couldn't get rid of. I jotted down some notes and worked out a few problems, though I zoned out for most of the class. When Mrs. H finished her lecture, she handed out a study guide packet. We had thirty minutes to do as much of it as we could. Using my dull pencil, I set up the first equation. Something in my head told me to stop. I scanned the room. Everyone was using the time to talk to their friends. Being the only one working made me feel alone. I stopped, too.

Mrs. H folded her arms. She looked cross. The class quieted down for a moment. Some students pretended to do their work. They wiggled their pencils above their papers to make it appear like they were writing. The phone rang before Mrs. H could scold us. She grabbed a bulky, black-corded phone off the wall and left the room. The door closed behind her, saving an inch, to allow the cord some room. The class immediately started talking.

There weren't that many equations. However, they each took an eternity to complete. No sleep, no food, I was running on fumes. My muscles had no power. My joints refused to budge. I felt the weight of the bones in my arm as I forced myself to write. When I tried to start, my ears perked up. Someone was talking about Zach. A chill ran down my spine. It was one of Zach's friends, Squeakers. They called him Squeakers because his sneakers squeaked when he walked. His real name was Dolan.

"Why isn't Zach in school?" Dolan questioned one of his friends. The image of Flare flashed into my head. It seemed like what happened to Zach wasn't shared with the public yet because they didn't know that the fire-covered man and Zach were one and the same. Everyone appeared to know about Bianca, though.

"How haven't you heard?" James from Biology class replied. His expression changed from excited to sad. A lump formed in my throat. I knew what he was going to say. "His girlfriend died, man. I don't think he's gonna be in school anytime soon," James explained.

"Aw, no," Dolan replied as if he were saddened by the news. "She was lava hot," he added. The other kids laughed. I was appalled. Their unbothered reaction hurt. Lead filled my stomach.

"Oh, yeah, she was a solid eight," commented Kofi, one of Dolan's friends. Nobody else spoke. They weren't upset by anything Kofi and Dolan had said. My mouth hung open. There were no words.

"No way! She was a nine!" James declared. He slammed his hands on his desk for emphasis.

Kofi and Dolan laughed. "No, ok, not a nine!" Dolan chuckled as if James were an idiot. "She was a seven or an eight." I gripped my pencil tight. They talked about Bianca as if she wasn't a real person. My teeth ached as my jaw clenched shut. I couldn't help but stare at them in disgust. When they stopped laughing, Kofi glanced to his right. He saw me glaring back at them. A slimy smile slithered across his face.

"Hey, Andrew," Kofi snickered. "What do you think about that Bianca De La- sol, De La suh, De La something chick?" It wasn't a serious question. He was trying to be funny. "What would you rate her?" His friends smiled as they waited for my answer.

"Rate her?" I replied angrily. If my emotions had been stable, my psychic powers would have unintentionally made the room spin. Luckily, my mind was scrambled, and I could not use my psychic powers. There was no energy within me.

James couldn't tell that I was mad. He thought I genuinely didn't understand the question. "Yeah, on a scale of one to ten, how hot do you think she was?" he clarified.

I frowned. "She's my friend!" I scolded. The whole class heard me. Most pretended to do their work, though I saw their eyes shift toward me. The quiet kid yelled. It was not an ordinary occurrence.

"She wasn't your friend!" James chuckled. I had only spent time with her outside of school during the break. Nobody knew I was friends with Bianca. Dolan gave me a stern look.

"She gave you mouth to mouth! That doesn't mean she liked you, creep!" Kofi sneered.

"We hung out a lot over the break! We're close friends!" I argued. I checked the door to see if Mrs. H heard me. She was still talking on the phone outside the classroom. It sounded as though she was shooting the breeze with whoever called her. At that point, everyone had stopped what they were doing and were paying full attention to our conversation.

"Yeah, right!" Kofi scoffed. "You expect me to believe that someone as hot as Bianca hung out with *you*?" Kofi and his friends laughed.

A girl in my class, Catalina, interjected. "Hey now! Andrew's not hideous! He kinda looks like Lionheart," she smiled flirtatiously. Her friends laughed at her. That was her twisted sense of humor. She wasn't interested in a relationship.

209

Most of her compliments were not real. Some poor souls believed her at times and ended up heartbroken. I saw past her facade. She brushed her straight brown hair behind her ear and gave me a wink. Catalina's light brown skin made her white smile pop. Her dark brown eyes locked onto mine.

"Hell, no!" Kofi scolded. Catalina shrugged her shoulders. Her friends sighed as if they didn't know what to do with her. They thought she was too funny to make her stop.

"Half the guys in school are copying Lionheart's basic-ass haircut," James observed. He motioned with his hand as if there were someone to point to as an example.

"Sure, but doesn't he," Catalina started. Dolan cut her off.

"Stop embarrassing yourself," Dolan warned. The class laughed. They thought it was funny that Catalina thought I looked like Lionheart. It was for the best that they didn't connect the dots. At the same time, it really hurt. My skin felt hot. There was too much attention on me, and not the type I wanted.

Mrs. H was still on the phone. With my enhanced hearing, I overheard a problem with our projector. Mrs. H was frustrated trying to get a spare lightbulb. Dolan poked at my shoulder. He was egging me on, trying to get me to defend myself. "I am friends with Bianca," I stated calmly. Arguments weren't my thing. I turned to James. "You're friends with Avery, right?" I asked rhetorically. "Ask her. I'm friends with her, too." That pushed Dolan over the edge. His face turned beet red.

"Too far!" Dolan yelled. "Avery's a straight-up nine. She'd never be friends with you either!"

"What am I?" Catalina asked with a sly smile on her face. She raised her hand as if she were asking a teacher. Everyone ignored her.

"Stop trying to be cool!" Kofi boomed. "I hate it when people spread rumors. She never talked to you." Bianca stared at me clear as day. It was her page on social media. Kofi had shoved his phone in my face. "She doesn't follow you on any platform guy!" An implosion forced the air out of my lungs. I couldn't breathe. How could I explain myself? They were Zach's friends. If I blamed him for her blocking me, they'd get nasty. However, all they knew was that she didn't follow me. They didn't know I was blocked. Forever blocked.

"You two were not frie-" Dolan got cut off.

"Yes, he was!" An angry voice from the back of the room stopped Dolan cold. Everyone's eyes went wide with shock. To my surprise, it was one of Zach's friends, Xavier. I had always assumed he was a jerk because he hung out with Zach. Xavier was a star athlete, too. He played on the school's baseball and football teams. Kofi was his closest friend. We never really talked because I had predicted he was a foul person like his friends. I was wrong. He stood up for me. I hardly knew him, yet there he was, helping me win an argument.

The knot in my stomach loosened. I had judged him based on his friends. Not all the athletic kids were full of themselves. Xavier had a good heart. I wondered how many other kids I had judged simply because of the impression Zach left on me.

Kofi stared at Xavier with a silent, angry glare. It must have been hard for Xavier to stand up against his friends. "I believe him," he whispered. Xavier was usually a megaphone-blaring type of person. It was unusual for him to speak so softly. "He was friends with her. He isn't speaking about her in past tense!" His voice shook the room.

"So?" Dolan scoffed, breaking the awkward silence. He kept his voice at a normal volume. An unsure look cast over his face. Arguing with Xavier was not something he was prepared for.

"When someone dies, it's difficult to talk about your loved one in the past tense," Xavier explained. He lowered his voice. My chest felt tight when he referred to Bianca as a loved one. That hollow feeling grew inside. Why wasn't he taking his friend's side of the argument? All this time, I had been judging him for being part of Zach's clique when it was clear he didn't assume anything about me. Without knowing me, he jumped to my defense. Sorrow filled my heart. He didn't say it, though I knew he spoke from experience.

The group of guys laughed. They didn't take Xavier seriously. Xavier studied Kofi with a stern expression that couldn't be found in the strictest of teachers. "Look at his face," Xavier stated calmly. He pointed to me. "See his eyes?

He's upset, he's tired, he lost a friend!" He didn't have to call me out like that. I did appreciate him, though.

"Everyone's eyes are tired," Dolan rebutted. The rest of his friends were silent. Their faces were red with embarrassment. Xavier had chewed them out. Dolan was the only one fighting.

"Dude, shut up," James whispered in Dolan's ear. He knew they were wrong. Unlike James, Dolan had to be told when to quit.

Xavier stood up to intimidate Dolan. He was easily the tallest kid in the class. His muscles bulged in his shirt. "You were rating the attractiveness of a dead girl! *You're* the creep!"

Catalina cheered at Xavier's victory. I think she did it to take the spotlight off Xavier and lessen his embarrassment. It seemed like she had expected everyone to join her and clap. For the first time ever, her face turned red. I didn't know she could be bashful. Nothing appeared to stop her before. She stopped pumping her fist. As usual, she made things awkward. Catalina was the only one with the moxie to do such a thing.

All I wanted to do was leave. It should've been a satisfying moment for me. Instead, I felt worse than I did this morning. There was too much tension in the room. Mrs. H entered as I exited. "May I go to the bathroom?" I asked quietly. She nodded. Miraculously, she didn't hear anything that had gone on in the classroom. Xavier was brave to stand up to his friends. They were inconsiderate, and he could've made fun of me to fit in with them, but he didn't. Once I left, I realized I never thanked him.

My ears twitched like a cat. Someone down the hall was crying. It was a girl's voice. A vision of Avery's tear-stained face outside the theater flashed in my mind. I sprinted towards the sound. Around the corner sat Chelsea. It took me by surprise a little. She sat by herself at one of the lunch tables. Her face was bright red.

Running down the hallway and stopping directly in front of her sure was one way to get her attention. My soul left my body. The embarrassment was strong enough that it felt like I was viewing the situation from the third person. Chelsea peered up at me with pink, watery eyes. Nothing fled my mouth as I strained to speak. Empty air moved up my throat and sank back down. I'd accidentally bolted up to someone and then stood mute like a freak.

"You're not the type to ditch class," Chelsea whimpered.

How did she know that about me? The unexpected feeling of being seen instantly vaporized the lump in my throat. "I didn't," I whispered. It wasn't loud enough. Chelsea had that look on her face that everyone does when my little voice doesn't make it to their ears. That vacant, distant stare. Technically, she didn't ask me a question, though her tone sounded like she wanted an explanation.

"You know what happened, right? Bianca died last night. I'm so sorry I started that rumor," Chelsea apologized. Tears formed in her eyes as she spoke. "There's no excuse for it. I was mad at her for blocking me. She stopped talking to me because Zach told her we hung out too much. We had been friends for five years, and she tossed me out like garbage. Zach had only been dating her for a few months. It hurt me so much. When she gave you mouth-to-mouth, I saw an opportunity to get back at her. I told everyone I saw her kiss you. I'm sorry, Andrew. What I did was horrible. Now, I can't apologize, and I'll never be able to make it up to her."

The pain in my chest grew worse. I knew exactly how Chelsea felt. Garbage, that's how I described the feeling when I was first blocked. Absolutely worthless. Without Bianca, I feared I would always feel that way now. She saved my life, and I did nothing to help her. Now she's gone. I accepted Chelsea's apology. Although she had been Bianca's friend longer, my heart didn't know that. All it knew was that Chelsea and I were in the same boat.

A lone tear rolled down Chelsea's face. I pulled out my phone to show her I understood what she was going through to the best of my ability. Bianca's social media accounts appeared as "User Not Found." Our text conversations were gone. There was no way to see her besides other people's posts. Zach had erased the evidence of our friendship along with Bianca herself.

"It's ok, I get it," I comforted as I showed Chelsea the blocked screen. She flinched at the sight of it as if it hurt her. Like me, she probably had spent too long looking at that blocked screen, wondering what went wrong. A light sob choked out of her. In a second, she recomposed herself, mostly. I made sure Chelsea knew it wasn't her fault. It wasn't her rumor that got me blocked. It was me. If it was the rumor, it would've been instant, not days after seeing my bond strengthen with Bianca.

"She must have loved you very much if Zach felt threatened by you so quickly," Chelsea tried to smile for me. The corners of her mouth could only wiggle. They couldn't remain upward. Love? That was a poor choice of words on her part since I don't- *no*, I'm thinking too much.

Veins like ivy riddled Chelsea's eyes from crying. A sunken feeling weighed me down. I had misjudged Chelsea, too. Guys always talked about her like she was some airheaded bimbo who wouldn't pay any geek like me the light of day simply because she's attractive. There was more to her than that. In this moment, she was vulnerable yet tender and sweet. Spreading rumors was not cool, though she was acting out of heartache and more than paying for it now. In fact, she apologized to me directly! She was wise enough to know right from wrong, what made her lash out, and was mature enough to own up to it. She was not the simpleton the guys who created that tier list made her out to be. If anything, I was for being so presumptuous and believing them.

People began to appear differently. They were less one-dimensional. Xavier and Chelsea were not who I thought they were. Although they were part of the popular crowd, they were no different from me. They shared similar struggles and torment. The pain in Xavier's eyes when he realized I wasn't talking about Bianca in the past tense haunted me. What did he go through? All the conflict within Chelsea, doing things out of spite, feeling guilty, remorseful, trying to make amends while mourning, felt like looking in a mirror. As a quiet man, I should've known there was more to a person on the inside.

All the background characters in my life were living complex lives of their own. The athletic kids weren't all jerks like Zach. The popular kids weren't all condescending. Their higher status was only an illusion perceived by me. All this time, my insecurities made me steer clear of people in those crowds like Xavier and Chelsea. It was never them. They turned out to have such caring hearts. Why did I assume they wouldn't be kind? I'd never talked to them before. How long had I felt like I was nobody while these practical strangers saw me and rushed to my aid today?

"I might not be a hero," I thought, *"but I can at least be a good person."* It was about time I stopped grouping people in my mind. Everyone in high school worried about how they were seen. They didn't waste time thinking about how they viewed others. I wanted to be better. Not better than others, better than myself. My anxiety and my insecurities had been blinding me like they had Zach. I saw the path that took him down and I wanted out. If I didn't improve myself, Lionheart would be dead forever.

34

WAVES

Throughout lunch, I checked my phone repeatedly as if I'd magically be unblocked or receive a message from Bianca. Life continued around me. My mind was stuck in the past. The empty feeling inside me was gone. The crevasse in my chest had torn wide open. All of me was empty. A hollow husk sat and ate lunch. Everything was numb. My friends were a great help, though sadness and I were starting to get along fine.

A pair of brown boots entered my field of view. I glanced up as they scuffed along the floor. The owner of the boots wore beige jeans and a white tank top with an unbuttoned, long-sleeved red and blue plaid shirt on top. Avery. I knew it was her from the boots alone. They barely left the floor as she walked. It was as if she had mustered just enough energy to walk. Her expression was emotionless. It hurt to see her so distraught. She ignored everyone as she trudged toward the guidance counselor's office. The door clicked behind her.

Metal knots twisted in my stomach. It felt like I was holding my breath.

We were going to drift apart. After what happened yesterday, I knew it wasn't meant to be. Zach had issues, and Bianca swore she would be there for him and help him. I had a lot of the same inner turmoil. Being with Avery would not make me feel whole. Zach was proof of how toxic it is to draw all your worth and happiness from one person. I couldn't do that to her. It would be the same as being Lionheart. I would be in it for the wrong reason, attention, love, trying to forge it into something that would fix myself. If I was ever going to be with Avery, I had to already be whole. I would have to focus on her, not repairing something within me. She is her own person, not a glue to piece me together.

A deep breath led to a small sigh. Part of me was already letting go of Avery. High school relationships didn't last long. There was no need to start a serious relationship at seventeen. The longer I thought about it, the more ridiculous it sounded. Avery and I were in no headspace to pursue a relationship. Despite this, I still had feelings for her. The desire never left. Butterflies still swarmed my stomach each time I laid eyes on her. She was an incredible person. It was clear I'd always like her. The motivation was all that died.

Bianca's funeral was on Sunday.

Lionheart didn't make any appearances. Nobody had seen him since the fight with Flare. People celebrated him as if he were a hero. All they knew was that he stopped a dangerous fire-guy the same day he brought down Gravemaker. Only some knew what a pyrrhic victory it was. That dumb sanctuary made me feel destined to be a screw-up. My whole life was depicted on those walls, even Bianca's death. I checked. It was impossible to tell what the symbols meant until the events happened. There it was, written in stone, a woman bravely facing a wave of flames. Confirmation that I was born to be a failure.

The wake was over. Everyone was leaving. Almost the whole town was there. Teachers and students flooded the halls as if it were our school. The full swim team, along with the coaches, were in attendance.

The main hexagon-shaped room was empty. Everyone had made their way to the parking lot. A dark purple carpet swallowed the floor. It covered everything except a small oasis around the pews. The altar and pews were comprised of the same light-colored wood. Sunlight beamed down from a skylight in the center of the roof. Tall windows on each wall drowned the room with light. The focused light made it as warm as summer. Rays of sunlight streamed down to the altar. On the steps of the sanctuary was a shrine for Bianca.

Colorful flowers of all kinds were arranged around a two-foot picture of Bianca. Sunflowers were prominently featured around the border of the frame. Smaller picture frames were cluttered around the steps. The smaller frames had more personal pictures of Bianca. Some were of her on vacation as a child or laughing with friends or family. I had never taken a picture with her. There was no proof that we were friends. Although that thought frustrated me, I knew she would always be in my memory.

The light warmed my skin as I neared the shrine. Wearing all-black attire attracted the heat like a magnet. I bent to one knee to come face to face with the large picture of Bianca. I ran my fingers through my hair. The hair gel in my bangs felt rough. It loosened as my hands grew sweaty. The flowers and pictures overflowed in each direction. She was so loved. I wished I had something to contribute.

"People say that muscles grow by being torn," I whispered solemnly. It was odd; something came over me, and I found myself speaking to the picture as if it were Bianca. The picture was all her family had. There was no body to bury and no ashes to place in an urn. Her ashes must have been spread so thin that when the fire extinguished, it looked like nothing was there. I quickly forced the terrible memory out of my head.

"The heart is also a muscle," I continued softly. "Therefore, it can grow by being torn too." I avoided eye contact with the eyes of Bianca's picture. "If I'm honest. It doesn't feel like my heart is torn. It's burned," I complained. Bianca's painted eyes glittered. "A chemical change, irreversible," I added without looking away.

There was a lot I wanted to tell her. It was only a picture, though I felt as if she were listening. My knees ached from kneeling too long. It was time to wrap up what I had to say. "Lionheart wasn't half as good a person as you were. I don't think I can be him until that changes. It will take some time, but I'll get there. I've realized I was headed down the wrong path, self-righteous, envious, and felt entitled to love. I saw where that leads, and now, I don't feel entitled to be with anyone. I want to focus on improving and fixing myself. The only way to be a hero is to be like you, a kindhearted person and a true friend."

Suddenly, a warm feeling coated my back. It felt as if someone was staring at me. I didn't turn around. Whoever was there didn't hear what I said. Speaking quietly enough that no one could hear me was my forte. No sound came from the observer. The mystery person took a few steps forward and knelt beside me. Out of the corner of my eye, all I saw was black. Like everyone else, they were wearing all black. I glimpsed to my right. The person kneeling beside me was Avery. She must have stuck around after the wake, too.

A tingling sensation fluttered throughout my arms, chest, and stomach. It felt like I was seeing her for the first time. The electric nervousness never truly settled. She dyed her hair black as if to accompany her outfit. Fractal patterns decorated the exterior layer of her black dress. The interior layer was only in a few areas to cover her up modestly since the material of interconnected patterns left tiny, needle-sized holes throughout the garment. The smell of black raspberry and lotus blossoms wafted over me. New hair, new perfume, an all-new Avery.

The stained-glass windows illuminated her face, red below her eyes and blackish toward her forehead. Seeing her in shimmering light took me back to when we sat at the pond. Though there was pain in her tear-sore eyes, she was breathtaking. We didn't speak all week. "I like your hair," I complimented in a hushed whisper as if it were a secret.

"Thank you. Everyone else says it's a real step down from my beautiful, natural blonde," Avery spoke with a fake self-aggrandizing tone. "I was reminded recently that life is too short not to do whatever I want. I've always wanted to try out different hair colors. If we can be gone in an instant, I'm living every single second being me, *really* me." Her eyes watered, though her voice never broke.

I stood. "Well, I'm glad there's something to take away from all this," I sighed as I headed toward the main hallway. It didn't sound genuine since I didn't believe it myself. We both knew Bianca's death was senseless. In our own separate ways, we tried to draw meaning from it. Copy pasting answers, lessons, anything that would fill in the black hole of why this happened. A look of understanding let me know she was

219

thinking the same thing. Trying to find positives in this mess was excruciating. We did our best.

As I reached the door, Avery called out to me. When I turned, she was standing, frozen, facing me. The stained-glass window cast red light on her face and dark blueish black on her body. Her ocean-blue eyes pierced through me. They caught me in a riptide.

"Please," Avery paused, "wait for me." She took a few steps closer. The heels on her shoes prevented her from moving quickly. I nervously wiped my palms on my pants. Colors flew through Avery like a kaleidoscope as she made her way down the aisle. "You said that your heart was burned," Avery frowned. *There's no way she actually heard me when I said that.* My puzzled expression made her smile. "That's what it feels like. My dad gave me the same speech; saying that if my heart is broken, then at least now it's open," Avery rolled her eyes as she poked me square in the chest. "Get it? Our hearts are open now, Lionheart," she added with a wink.

Somehow, I had forgotten all about Lionheart. Whenever I moved my hands to gesture, no psychic energy was emitted. All I had were my cat-like abilities. The psychic powers had vanished due to the horrible state of mind I was in.

"You didn't tell anyone about that, right? I mean, your dad has done a lot of digging. I'm already afraid he might get too close to the truth without you telling him. After Bianca, I can't have anyone find out about Lionheart, *ever*! Honestly, I don't know if I'm even going to be Lionheart again. That whole thing was such a nightmare. I can't be some super savior like she wanted. I am not a hero. I was so bad at it. I-" at last, Avery cut off my incoherent rambling. When a quiet person has to think while speaking, it is usually not eloquent.

"Andrew," Avery's voice sang sweetly. Her eyes glistened. There was a bright smile on her face. A wave of emotion swept through me. All week, I had wondered if I would ever see her smile like that again. "You talk too much," she smiled. That was the first time I had been accused of speaking too much. In this specific case, it was true. I had to laugh, something I hadn't done in a while. She stepped closer to me. We were shoulder-width apart.

"Don't be afraid to be yourself," Avery beamed. "Your problem is that you are trying to be some Lionheart character. You keep talking about him like he's not you. You have a good heart. Be Andrew when you're out there, not 'Lionheart'. I'm sure, when you're ready, you'll be an astounding hero."

I blushed. We headed toward the exit together. "Easy for you to say," I laughed. "You don't even know about the whole myth-statue-sanctuary place or my talking cat. My life is chaotic."

"Oh, no," Avery gasped. "I'm outta here! A talking cat is a deal breaker," she joked.

"Too late! You're stuck with me now!"

"Oh, what am I gonna do? Guess I'll suck it up and be friends with a legendary hero if I really have to," Avery teased. She skipped alongside me as best she could. A brick pathway led us toward the road. We were almost at the parking lot.

"Not a hero," I whispered. "*Just trying to be better.*"

35

FINE BY ME

I stood at the top of a snow-covered hill at a nearby park. Kids frequented the hill for sledding. The falling snow quickly buried the tracks left by their sleds. I gazed at the glistening snow-topped trees in the distance. My uniform kept me warm except for my bare feet. Oliver had repaired the uniform using his psychic powers. It took a lot out of him. He hasn't talked to me since Bianca passed. Most days, he sleeps without doing much of anything. Maybe that's normal for a cat.

My mask appeared in my hands. I didn't put it on. At this hour, in a storm like this, nobody was around to see me. The hard material felt cold. It seemed to conduct the heat away from my hands. I rubbed the smooth surface of the mask. The eyeholes peered up at me. It felt like it was staring me down. I had made up my mind. I'd use my powers to help others. Things were going to be different now. There was a reason for it. To honor Bianca, I was going to be better. Last time, I watched from the sidelines as my new best friend sank further into a toxic relationship. I would never stand aside again. If anything were wrong, no matter how small, I'd work to make it right. All she asked of me was to use my powers to help people. I never did. I never helped her, either. I owed her this.

There was a feeling inside me that I couldn't explain. I had non-selfish motivation. Bianca loved everyone and treated them as family. I intended to learn to be the same. Lionheart had been ennobled. No more would I be solely focused on

222

Gravemaker or whatever other menace comes next. Instead, I'd be a hero for the people as I should've been from the start. Following what Avery advised, I would be me, not a superhero, a good friend. Nothing could make me stray from the path I had chosen.

The empty feeling inside would be filled all on my own. Neither fame nor Avery could make me feel whole. The only thing that would work was accepting my mistakes and realizing I needed to work on, forgive, and care for myself. A bolt of lightning surged within me. Every cell of my body lit up with electricity. Energy built up inside, threatening to explode outward. The pain escalated until suddenly, the electricity flowed gently like a river. No, it wasn't electricity. It was psychic energy. After weeks of being dormant, my psychic powers had returned! Snow swirled around me. Lionheart was back!

There was once a time when I thought that if I took some time to help out the community instead of focusing on Gravemaker, I could stop all the crime and save everyone who needed a hero in two days flat. That way, I could return to focusing on Gravemaker uninterrupted with no "distractions," as I had put it. Day one of retrying to be a hero, I wore myself out within hours. My breath bellowed out like hot steam in the cold winter air. The woman I saved from a potential car crash thanked me and went on her day.

"Take the rest of the day off after such a close call!" I beamed. My triceps cramped up from exerting so much force throughout the day. The woman shook her head.

"Can't afford to. I've got mouths to feed, and I'm already gonna be late to my second job," she called back. The woman gave me a half smile. There was no air in my lungs to reply. Each intake of freezing air scratched my throat. *Second job?* I thought to myself, *restaurant owner and chef? Painter and sculptor?* I was not convincing myself. I knew it was neither of those glamorous options. It was whatever she could get out of necessity. Although I felt bad that there wasn't more I could do to help her. She was alive today because of Lionheart, which in turn meant her kids still had a mom because of Lionheart. Growing up in a comfy town where nothing really happened disillusioned me. Two jobs and no days off, even after a near-death experience. Wow, I really needed to see life from more perspectives. There were many things I didn't see until I went out into the world.

A slight pain in my knuckles brought my attention away from the woman. The burned skin had healed. Some of the thugs I fought that day fled at the sight of me. Summoning two katanas with paper-thin blades struck an unworldly fear in them. They didn't know that I never once used those swords to hurt anyone. Whenever they appeared, I used them as a cutting tool rather than a weapon. When I did use my other weapons to fight, I was careful. The people I fought today were left in custody with nothing worse than a few bruises.

"Thank you, Lionheart!" someone called from a car window. It was the driver who almost hit that woman. Stopping the car using brute strength left the front of her car dented as if ready for scrap. She was relieved I prevented her from accidentally hurting someone. A little smile snuck its way onto my face. Slowly, the metal of her sedan shifted and popped. In a minute or two, the blemishes on her car were repaired. "Wait, what's that noise? What are you doing to my car?" the stranger pulled over in front of me to inspect her car.

"I used my psychic powers to repair the damage," I explained as a headache brewed from overexertion. "It's going to need a paint job. I'm sorry, but I couldn't locate all the paint fragments. They're too small, and my powers are-"

"Amazing! That's no problem! Are you kidding? Compared to all the work it would need beforehand?" the driver cheered. Such an energetic response filled me with gratitude. This is what Lionheart was supposed to be. She turned sharply as if she were a soldier in the military. A hand stretched out for me to shake. "Thank you." When my hand made contact, it changed momentarily, as if it weren't my own. For a fraction of a second, it looked like Bianca's.

Over the next few months, I worked harder than ever. To be more selfless, I learned to let go of my self-interests and teleport away when I was needed. That made it hard to be a good friend, student, and son when I unexplainably vanished from time to time. My grades faltered a little. It was worth it if it meant growing as a person. The change in me was slow. The same pangs in my chest from jealousy and desire occurred. However, I knew I was getting better.

The police seemed to forget about what had happened at our school. Parents knew that Mr. Poundz couldn't have been acting alone. All eyes were on the principal and the school board. To my surprise, the Perfetto's left town. The trail went cold soon after. In the back of my mind, Gravemaker's warning to me replayed. He was scared of something, and he gave me a name. A name I didn't recall. Another hanging thread. With no big bad guy on the loose and no mysteries to unravel, I could dedicate more time to helping ordinary people, preventing normal accidents, and forming a stronger bond with the community.

Although it felt like things were looking up, inside everything was wrong. Avery and I never truly connected again. She frequently changed her hair and outfits as if she were undergoing a metamorphosis. Her darker, edgier looks earned her a lot of unwarranted hate from some. Meanwhile, my heart still pumped electricity instead of blood whenever I was around her. We weren't going to split apart. After talking at the wake, it was clear we wanted to be in each other's lives. However, I was hardly around.

If I'm honest with myself, I was afraid.

Perhaps I gave myself too much time. Months slipped by quickly. Pressure mounted on my shoulders as it was the last day of Junior year.

Nothing in life would be ok again. Screeching screams filled the air. It was no use. No matter how hard I tried, it was stuck. Wails of sheer terror erupted beside me. My psychic powers would have saved the day by now. Unfortunately, the shrill shrieks prevented me from being able to use them. There was little hope left of making it out. The constant yelling was all that motivated me to keep going. At last, my fingertips grazed the kite wedged between prickling pine tree branches. Sap stuck to my skin as I retrieved the kite and returned it to the hollering child.

"Thank you, Wionman," the little boy beamed. Tears stained his face, though he sniffled and smiled as if the tantrum was all in my head. He ran off before I could reply. It was for the best since I didn't know what to say. My nose picked up a familiar scent. Danger.

The potent smell of gunpowder filled the air. I teleported along the scent trail until I found the culprit. He aimed his gun at my head. The trigger clicked, but nothing happened. Panic took over the criminal as he repeatedly pressed the trigger of his gun. I closed my free hand. The gun crushed inward into a ball of metal. My psychic powers had disabled and destroyed his weapon. The man shrieked in fear. He turned to make a run for it. "You can run. I can teleport," I whispered. The look on the man's face when I reappeared in front of him was priceless. He dropped to the ground and surrendered.

Blue and red lights flashed across the alleyway. Police had arrived to arrest the would-be gun dealers. That was my cue to get back to class. I teleported into a vacant bathroom in school. It was a Friday, late June, and the last day of school. I had to skip most of my last class to stop some gun dealers. Afterward, I got a little sidetracked. There were only ten minutes left of History class.

A black T-shirt and dark grey shorts replaced my mask and uniform. The sound of my heartbeat faded from my head. Something didn't feel right. My mind wasn't put at ease. Armageddon wasn't what was bothering me. Gravemaker's final clue wasn't on my mind either. All my final exams were over. There shouldn't have been anything left to stress about. Mark had helped me with the work I missed while out as Lionheart. A fluttering feeling swam through my stomach. It was Avery. The last day of school meant I wouldn't see her for a long time. Everyone was always busy during the Summer. It might have been my last chance to talk to Avery in person for a while.

The door to my History class loomed ahead. It felt like I was approaching the final boss in a video game. A strange, muffled noise came from inside. Suddenly, everyone exploded out of the class. Every classroom door swung open recklessly as students dashed out. Students shouted and cheered as they rushed down the hall. Some ran carelessly toward the nearest exit while others walked and enjoyed their final moments of school talking to their friends. I shoved my way upstream to get my backpack from History class. Teachers stood by their classroom doors to wave goodbye to passing students.

My backpack was tucked underneath my chair just as I had left it. Instead of scolding me, my teacher, Mr. Wang, saluted me as if to say goodbye. Whenever I skipped his class to help as Lionheart, he always gave me a speech about how crucial his class was. He would ramble on and on, saying it was important to learn from the past. His disdain for technology, especially the all-consuming smartphone, fit his history teacher occupation well. Despite missing some classes here and there, I had gotten a high grade on his final exam. I'm sure that caught him by surprise.

The hallway was already empty. It had only been a minute, yet there was nobody there. I thought I blew it. Some days, I would talk to Avery on our way to the buses. "Hey, school's over, *she-devil!* What're you haunting the hallways for?" Kofi spat as he turned to bolt out the door. His gaze led to someone standing around a corner. My heart skipped a beat as I already knew who he was heckling.

"Call me that again. It's not too late to show the new principal the browser history on your laptop!"

I turned a corner, and there she was. She stood all by herself, a few feet from the exit. The sun lit up her straight blonde hair. The bottom third of her lustrous, long hair was dyed black. Remnants of her last hair color change. Last I checked, turquoise was up next. She gazed up at me and smiled without saying a word. I felt my cheeks blush. Avery picked up her worn, blue backpack from a nearby lunch table and gently swung it over her shoulder.

Everything slowed down. It was like my life was moving in slow motion. I heard my favorite song. The speakers in the school weren't playing music. Neither was Avery, yet I swear I heard it. It was all in my head. Every lyric and each instrument was there! It sounded so real that it felt like music *had* to be playing. I continued to listen to my favorite song as I approached. It fit my mood perfectly. I wished Avery could hear it, too, although I didn't waste time fiddling with my phone to play it.

The song's lyrics swam through my mind as I tried to think of what to say. Avery adjusted her black tank top while waiting. A pair of frayed black jean shorts and mini medieval sword earrings completed her outfit. She did a little dance as she walked up to me. We walked side by side as we headed toward the exit. "Were you out saving cats from trees?" Avery beamed. She found the name Lionheart hilarious. No matter how often I told her Tae Kwon Do was Korean, Avery insisted I should be called something ninja-themed.

"Nope, kites, actually," I stated with a smile. Avery always kept her eye on the media. It was more fun to tell her about Lionheart's exploits before she found out via her anchorman dad's journalists. She was never disappointed, though if it were too crazy, she wouldn't believe me until she heard it from her dad.

"Oh, you've cat to be kitten me!" Avery teased. She smiled at her own joke. It was not her best work, which only made it funnier to her. If anyone else had said it, I wouldn't have laughed. Her face was bright red with a grin from ear to ear. She was proud of her lame joke.

"Why do you- why do- just why?" I said in a fake, annoyed tone. She giggled at my reaction. Her eyes locked onto me as we walked together. It was her special talent to look someone in the eye while talking to them. How she could do it while walking was beyond me. "If you don't like the name, *you* can come up with a better one," I instructed.

"It should be something strong, cool, and not cat-related," Avery began. "Like, uh, what about Death Ninja?" she joked.

"I don't kill people, and I'm not a ninja."

Avery smiled. "Well, I'll come up with something and I'll pass it by you later. I'll have our lawyers talk something out. I'm sure the marketing department won't mind the rebranding," Avery laughed.

"You know, if you come up with a new name, you can't make fun of it anymore. It would be your fault for creating a lame name," I teased. Avery playfully slugged my side.

"But if I create it, it's not gonna be lame," Avery quipped. "I'm cool now, look," Avery beamed with pride as she raised the right side of her shorts. The flash of untanned skin made me nervous. Before I could question her actions, I saw what she was revealing. A tattoo of thick claw marks ripping downward branded her outer thigh. It was the tattoo of her favorite band's logo. There were no words or letters, only the symbol to make it more timeless. Those were her words.

"I thought you have to be eighteen to- your fake?" I interrogated. Avery nodded and laughed. "Your parents are going to kill you."

"Did I say I was a good influence?"

We continued to joke around on our way out. Her bubbly laughter gave me life. It reminded me of what I was there for. Avery came up with a few more bad puns. I followed up with an inside joke from science class that only Avery and I understood. It made her double over with laughter. Beams of sunshine reflected off her smile. There would never be a better moment. Avery stopped laughing to catch her breath. Her lips curled into a nervous smile.

"Avery," I paused to make sure she was looking at me. Her deep blue eyes glittered like the night sky. Electricity flowed through my veins. "Do you want to go out this weekend?"